THE CAIN CONSEQUENCE

By

Sal Cangemi

A HellBound Books LLC Publication

www.hellboundbooks.com

For Inna

An Undisclosed Federal Prison in What Was Once the USA

No one knew precisely how many lives were ruined the day Barclay Cain figured out how to manipulate reality. Cain had had twenty-three years to mull it all over and was still not the least bit sorry. No one ever truly died, he knew. Anyway, there were always casualties in any significant movement. Sacrifice is always a requirement. Twenty-three years. So much wasted time.

Cain tried to turn off the TV in the common room, but the inmate he had met here, a mountain of a man, gave him a sideways look that was clear—do not touch the remote. Cain squirmed as he watched himself (albeit over twenty years younger) on the screen. An interview from some '90s talk show when he was the preeminent paranormal authority of pop culture, dethroning Ed and Lorraine Warren (who were fakes, by the way). A photo of Veronica Sinclair was on the TV now, stunning as ever in a red sundress on the beach. He remembered it well. He had *taken* the picture.

"Boy, she was something," the man said.

She was something, all right, Cain thought. Veronica Sinclair was all that and more.

The colossal man raised the volume.

"So, Mr. Cain, tell me exactly how you communicate with the dead," the show's host said, giving the camera a sideways smirk.

"I don't speak with the dead—not exactly. We live in a multiverse. I can psychically investigate these other worlds. I can find another existence where the loved one has not expired. And this is whom I speak with."

"Wow, that is some claim. Well, folks, it's up to you to decide for yourself if you believe."

Ridiculous horror movie music occupied the piece. Cain shook his head as the past interview segment ended and went back to real-time. A current reporter looked into the camera, his award-winning smile patronizing.

"That was an interview with acclaimed occultist Barclay Cain. As you may remember, he was arrested twenty-three years ago for unlawfully altering space-time. His actions resulted in the Great Secession, creating 'the Lands.' This week, Barclay Cain's fourth and final appeal for release was denied. Back to you, Steve...."

The behemoth regarded Cain with skepticism. Sampson was known as the guy who could get things done. But Cain did not need cigarettes or porno.

Sampson smiled. It only made him look more menacing. Sampson. Cain did not know if the man had been born with the name or if this was a nickname. It didn't matter—the man had connections. He'd cleared the rec room so they could meet here today. This was no easy task as most inmates spent their free time in the recreation room, watching sports, playing games, or ticking off the hours staring at the walls.

"And people actually believed you with all this shit?" Sampson asked, pointing to the TV, which he promptly turned off.

"It's real."

"They say you're the one responsible for the Lands."

"That's what they charged me with. However, the prosecution could prove nothing one way or the other. As you can imagine, one cannot prove or disprove magic."

"But here you are."

Barclay Cain held out his thin arms like a scarecrow. "Here I am."

"You were married to that actress…"

"Veronica Sinclair."

"She was murdered, right?"

"She died of an opiate overdose. I suppose you could call that murder."

"Sorry to hear it," Sampson said, though he appeared nothing of the sort. "And you tried to bring her back. And it didn't work. But all these Goddamn Lands were created."

"I was accused as such. As is often the case, there is more to the story."

"Hey, I was already here when the Great Secession happened…so I could care less."

"I think you mean you *couldn't* care less."

"A Satanist and a wise-ass," Sampson said.

He looked to Cain like a bronze statue of a long-forgotten god. Cain thought perhaps Sampson was of Hawaiian or, possibly, Kiribatian descent. From some angles, the man looked to have been forged of gold.

"I'm an occultist. Satan does not exist."

"Anyway, the way I see it, the Lands did some good. People now live in a place they belong. Nothing wrong with that."

"The government did not see it that way."

"Do I look like a guy who gives a shit about what the government thinks?"

Cain thought to inform Sampson, whether he cared or not, that they all were slaves to the big G. Then, he thought better of it.

"I suppose not."

"You made a lot of money with all this crap," Sampson said.

"We're talking about the '90s. Deepak Chopra brought New Age into the mainstream. Oprah discussed psychic phenomena almost daily and had mediums on her show weekly. Wealthy housewives had séance/wine parties. You could have a glass of wine, get Botox injections, and have your future read. Those days were good to me."

"But you lost it all."

"And then some. Then the cult had me arrested, and I have been rotting in here ever since."

Sampson lit a cigar, an Ashton Vintage Sun-Grown. *A rather good one,* Cain thought. *How the hell did he get that in here?*

"Why did they turn on you? I have never been in a cult, but I was in a gang. A gang doesn't turn on its leader unless he does something stupid."

"I pushed the fabric of reality too hard. Some of the members got sick."

"Sick like cancer?"

"I guess you could say that. Some became physically altered."

"Like losing their hair. Losing weight?"

If only it had been so simple. There were side effects when Cain played with reality. There was no way around it. Cain had never wanted to harm the members of the cult—or anyone for that matter. He was a pacifist. But shit happened, as the adage went.

"More like growing an extra head or becoming steam. Or sneezing only to find you no longer have any bones—left a blob to be carried around in a basket. Does that answer your question?"

Sampson did not speak right away; he didn't even blink. Cain thought he might get beaten for how he answered the giant. Then Sampson wet his lips and spoke.

"Shit, guess I'd be damn pissed off at you too if I had to be carried around in a fucking pail."

"Yeah."

"So, there is no Cult of Change anymore?" Finally, a question.

"Oh, they are around. The Cult of Change has a new leader, I hear. A Native American called White Feather. He pretends to be a shaman or some nonsense. But he does not show himself, even to the members. I promise you he does not have the power I do," Cain said. He had no idea what the cult did these days. Since the group left him, the cult was not *changing* anything but their underwear. And he was not too sure about that.

"So, let me ask you this: if all this is real, and you have this power, why don't you think your way into another world where you're not wasting away in this place?"

"I don't have the tools to get out of here."

"And that's why you asked to meet me."

"Correct."

"I can get anything."

"I have heard that before. Many times," Cain said.

Sampson was neither the first inmate to ask these questions nor boast the means to procure the needed tools. All had failed to deliver on their claims. Cain was not too optimistic about this meeting, but what did he have to lose? He had nothing but time, and now that his latest (and last) appeal for freedom had been denied, there was no reason *not* to discuss his situation with Sampson. Cain looked at the Ashton cigar Sampson smoked. Cain inhaled its dark, earthy aroma.

Maybe he could get anything.

Cain explained that if he could get his hands on the needed sacred items, he indeed could get out. The colossal man clarified that as long as Cain took him along, he would procure the said items.

"What is it you need?"

"Essential salts from the mummified body of a Dominican priest who died in the eighteenth century, smokable DMT, and water from the sea of Yam ha-Melah near Israel."

"DMT?" Sampson asked.

"N-dimethyltryptamine. A drug. But I warn you, DMT is strong. Intense," Cain said.

"They haven't made a drug too strong for me."

"If you say so."

***

Within three weeks, Sampson had miraculously procured the necessary items. As the two made their plans, Sampson explained more than once that if this did not work, he, Cain, would wish his only trouble was a life sentence.

That night, Sampson was able to secure a room where they could be alone. It appeared premium, hand-rolled cigars were not the giant's only connection. Cain inspected the items. He scattered the salts around them in a circle, poured the water over them, and loaded the DMT in a small pipe.

"What is this shit," Sampson said as he sniffed the pink-white, crystalline, clumpy material. "It smells like mothballs."

"As I explained, It's a powerful drug in the hallucinogen family. But it's unlike any drug you have ever experienced,"

"Bullshit. I've tripped balls hundreds of times. I've hallucinated some sick shit."

"But this doesn't make you hallucinate, per se. There is a difference between a hallucination and what we are about to experience. This drug shatters the fabricated world and allows one to see the real.

"It's a drug. It can't do all that."

"It's a drug, yes. But it's also God in a pipe."

"Barclay Cain, you are one fucked up dude."

"It's going to get us out of here, which is all you must worry about. Three good hits from the pipe; no more, no less," Cain said. "Do you understand?"

"Yeah, Cain. Even a dummy like me can count to three."

The door shook in its frame as they were about to light the pipe. The guards were knocking.

"Who's sucking who off in there," one guard shouted. Then, the metallic jingle of keys.

"Quickly," Cain said. And they passed the pipe back and forth three times.

As soon as he exhaled the third hit, Cain could see in Sampson's face the pure folly of the man's bragging only moments before. The titan was a boy on a terrifying roller-coaster. The poor bastard did not know the ride had yet to begin.

The room around them passed in a *woosh!* They traveled through a tunnel of intense light and wild shapes. Shapes that did not exist in the reality they knew; forms appeared that were impossibly both a triangle and a square simultaneously. They witnessed figures that were a language rather than a formation to be perceived. Structures that challenged everything one thought was solid and natural as they burst through a chrysanthemum-like mandala.

"What the fuck is this?" Sampson said, his voice had lost all its bass.

"You need to stop thinking. You need to allow it to all unfold."

"Unfold... are you crazy? What are those?"

Cain watched all the creatures move about him and his fellow traveler. These lifeforms came in various sorts. Each appeared of its own species. Some of the beings were fractal. Others were humanoids, animals, or only large faces. Some of the elves were made of forms that held information. More importantly, an exchange occurred, a relationship between the observer and the creatures observed, one moment verbal, the next a kind of telepathy. Everything was a matter of one's mind, beliefs, and intellect that determined how to decipher the communication and extract its meaning.

A bejeweled goblin zipped past. The creature blinked in and out of space-time, then stopped in front of Cain and Sampson, vibrating with energy.

"I can't do this."

"Don't give in to astonishment," Cain said.

But he knew he should have better prepared the man for the spectacle he was witnessing. They were presented with thousands of details per second, unable to secure hold of any of it for more than a moment. The creatures made objects with their voices, singing structures into existence, and then offered these items to Cain and Sampson, like children proffering their art projects to parents.

The creatures danced and got closer. A wild comedy and tragedy in one laughing-crying being. A green child played a smoking flute. A pink baboon held a human head that spoke its thoughts.

When Cain was able to get some footing, he found Sampson reduced to a weeping infant, the formerly intimidating man now curled in a fetal position. There was no satisfaction in seeing Sampson this way. The beast of a man could walk into the most violent bar or ghetto without a second thought, but witnessing this level of reality transformed him into an infant. But there was nothing he could do to help. One was either able to handle this journey or not.

"Sorry, my friend. But this is where we part."

Sampson looked around at the gaggle of creatures.

"Don't leave me alone," he said. "Cain, you can't leave me here!"

"I'm sorry, but your mind has already broken. The only thing for you to do now is surrender. You need to go with it all."

"This can't be real."

"I regret to inform you, Sampson, but this is true reality."

"Cain, you can't leave me here!" Sampson said again.

But Barclay Cain had indeed left him.

PART I
Revolution Calling

CHAPTER ONE

Church Land

S tu Sawyer sat uncomfortably in the pew with his mother, listening to the pastor's sing-song voice, talking non-stop but saying nothing. The jolly man rocked back and forth on his feet before the congregation.

"God has news! Major news! Now, there is only one God, all-mighty. And only one word of God—the Holy Bible. And now…." the preacher said, waving a book. "The sequel! Amen! That's right, two thousand years in the making, finally, the Holy Bible Part 2! As written by yours truly."

The congregation stood in awe. Stu waited for the punchline, but none came. The pastor had actually written the bible's sequel.

Stu Sawyer lived in Church Land. But it had once been a place called New Jersey before the Great Secession. Stu had learned New Jersey had been a horrible, smog-filled place where people were always angry, and making left-hand turns was all but outlawed.

Church Land was as bad as it sounded, worse. The only music available was Christian rock. The only TV programs were preachers or Christian movies with horrible acting and scripts about people doing evil things like smoking grass or having sex before being married. But, of course, they always repented and got right with God.

He and his mother lived in the middle of the Christian part of Church Land—everything was the worst here. If he and his mother *had* to live in Church Land, he wished they could have lived on Catholic Street. His Catholic friends always missed mass and only needed to go to the drive-through confessional in the back of St. Mary's Church. Five minutes, a few bucks, and a prayer or two, and you were good to go.

Stu would wander around Catholic Street with his friend, Feldman, at night and watch everyone file in and out of the Irish pubs. One night, he peeked into the window of a church. A priest was sitting and watching the ball game. He was drinking a giant goblet of wine and eating fistfuls of the hosts-wafers, like they were potato chips, from a vast gold bowl.

Two chubby twins in matching striped shirts, who reminded Stu of Tweddle-Dee and Tweddle-Dumb, passed around the collection plates, scowling their round moon faces at those who let it pass without making a deposit. The preacher reminded everyone to get in on the 50/50 this coming Saturday.

"I thought gambling was against Christianity," Stu whispered to his mother.

"Shhh."

Stu could never see the positive of living here as his mother did. While not a religious woman, Brandy Sawyer welcomed this change as a new beginning. She got a job in a church's accounting department and had made friends. After the Great Secession, most people moved to whatever

Land best suited them. As for Stu, he didn't fit in at all here, but truth be told, he likely would not have liked New Jersey, either.

"I'll be staying late and signing copies of the Bible Part 2 after service—your donations will be appreciated," the pastor said.

"Jesus."

"Stu! Shhh."

He kept giving his mother slanted looks. She'd told him the radiation was working, and she could expect to be cancer-free soon. He was not so sure about his mother's overly optimistic prognosis.

"Would you stop looking at me? I'm fine."

But Stu Sawyer knew better. He knew, despite her assertions, that his mother was not fine.

***

Back at home, Stu sat at the kitchen table, opened the box of doughnuts he bought from "Dippin' Doughnuts" (what he remembered as Dunkin' Donuts, which now never existed), and bit into a Boston cream. At least the Boston cream still existed in this reality. He needed to get motivated. He had work to do on his website. He'd have to get another dead-end job if he didn't generate more ad money.

He'd tried employment before but was always fired in a matter of days, most of his bosses complaining of his laziness and lack of enthusiasm as the reason for his termination. He'd not always been lazy. But since the accident, he'd become unnaturally antisocial.

But there was hope when he founded *The Unknown Daily*—his website.

He bit into a jelly doughnut.

"Doughnuts again, Stuey?" Brandy asked as she puckered and applied florid lipstick. Stu was one of those guys people hated due to his ability to eat anything and everything and never gain an ounce.

"You're going to Catholic Street?" he asked his mother.

"Yes, I'm meeting some friends for a drink."

"Are you up to it?"

"I'm fine," she said, ruffling his hair as she had since he was a little boy.

Stu wasn't so sure. His mother was tired all the time now. She *looked* tired. She'd been going to doctors almost daily recently yet still insisted there was no reason for concern.

Stu knew his mother had worried about him since the night he and Feldman drove around, and Stu had lost control of the Kia and hit a tree, which, he was sure, had never been on the corner.

Feldman had died on impact, and Stu had emerged from the wreck without so much as a scratch. There were no drugs or alcohol involved, but he still had to face Feldman's family at the services. On that day, Stu knew what it must have been like to be a killer on trial. Eyes were shooting poison at him from all sides.

He thought of that tree that defied logic. Was he crazy? Stu Sawyer was not going insane all at once. Losing your mind does not work as it does in the movies. Like all things insidious, madness is a slow, exasperating descent. When did it start, he thought? He was not sure. Suppose you placed a mug of coffee on the kitchen table and got distracted momentarily, only to find the coffee was now in the dining room. We chalk it to the idea that, at some point, we moved it and forgot. But what then happens when these things become more drastic? Occurring more often?

The changes began on a small scale—Stu could not place the exact day he had woken to an altered reality. He'd asked his mother about this, but she insisted he was only stressed, and his problem was psychological rather than paranormal. But Stu could not ignore everything he was experiencing.

It had begun with the spellings of popular items—which had shifted overnight. Then, the changes became more drastic. Stu's favorite cookies, Sprinkles the Clown's Shortbread Shorties, were no more. Stu's internet searches proved they had *never* existed. But he had bought them all the time. He asked his mother about the cookies, but she had no recollection of them whatsoever. Searching the Internet did find a few hits. Blogs and videos of others who also remembered the cookies that had never been produced.

He was not the only person who had experienced the Cain Consequence. Others remembered events differently than those documented in history. His mother had not wanted to discuss this. She thought his interest in the paranormal was odd enough without him trying to convince her he was experiencing something otherworldly.

"So, you like the idea of my being crazy better?" Stu had said.

"Yes. We can work with that, at least. Dr. Duben cannot work with the idea of some flaky occultist messing with time-space and causing what—alternate worlds?. And all for what, to make a brand of cookies disappear?"

"Barclay Cain was trying to bring his wife back."

Stu had always had a nose for the paranormal—all things unknown, UFOs, Bigfoot, Moth Men, the Cain Consequence. He founded a webzine, *The Unknown Daily*. While still finding its footing, the site was becoming increasingly popular among those who believed aliens invented the Internet, time travel was possible, and had a general distrust of the government. The little money Stu had saved allowed him to run his website until he got a few sponsors. Now, with some ad money coming in, and could get by. Stu even occasionally interviewed "celebrities." He'd recently spoken with renowned psychic Anton Snow. Snow had plugged his new book, telling the story of exorcizing a demon from a possessed apartment complex.

Later today, he had an interview with a former child actor, Rex Dolan, about the Cain Consequence as fate would have it.

His mother hummed along to the Christian music broadcast through the house (this was automatic and could not be turned off). The music constantly played. Later was the Sunny Santos program. Today, Pastor Santos would speak of the dangers of pornography and about a place called Porn Land, a place Stu had secretly wanted to visit for years now but had yet to make the pilgrimage to.

Stu fished through the box of doughnuts.

"Stop with the doughnuts."

"I'm hungry," he said, wiping jelly from his mouth and pulling an old-fashioned from the box.

"I got you an Italian hero. It's in the fridge. Why don't you have that instead?"

He stuffed the old-fashioned into his mouth, went to the fridge, and took out the two-foot hero. His mother had bought it for him from Catholic Street, where all the Italians and Irish in Church Land lived.

As Stu unwrapped the hero, Brandy sprayed a cloud of perfume into the air and walked through it. Stu gagged.

"Jesus, Mom, the perfume."

"Stu! You can't say that!"

"I'm sorry. I'm sorry."

"What's wrong," Brandy Sawyer asked her son. She knew him.

"I can't stand it here anymore." he surprised himself.

"Stuey…"

"Can we please not talk about this now?"

Brandy Sawyer looked at her watch.

"Ugh. I have to go. But we are going to talk about this, okay?"

"Yeah, I have to run too. Have my interview."

"Oh, right, that *Happy Jack* guy."

"Rex Dolan."

"Oh, Stuey, be careful. That guy is supposed to be trouble."

His mother didn't know the half of it.

***

The Unknown Daily:

AN INTERVIEW WITH HAPPY JACK ACTOR REX DOLAN ABOUT HIS EXPERIENCE WITH THE CAIN CONSEQUENCE:

By Stuart Sawyer

If you are a child of the '90s, then you remember the show Happy Jack starring Rex Dolan as the title character, a mischievous kid in all kinds of hijinks, much to the dismay of his parents. The show was only three episodes into its second season before being unceremoniously canceled due to poor ratings. But don't tell Mr. Dolan that. In a parallel reality (one he lived through), he claims that the show ran for six full seasons! But he woke one day to this reality where the show tanked.

Rex Dolan has made a few attempts to revive his entertainment career - including a gangster rap CD, Happy No More – which even featured a profanity-filled version of the Happy Jack theme song. As well as a softcore porn movie, Jack Me, but mostly, he has lived a simple life working several odd jobs.

I had the chance to interview Rex Dolan. We met at a local coffee shop to discuss his experience with the odd phenomenon called the Cain Consequence. The Cain Consequence is the peculiar phenomenon where large groups of people misremember the same given thing in the same way. The Cain Consequence was named after Barclay Cain, the infamous occultist responsible for The Great Secession. Barclay Cain originally made headlines when he married actress Veronica Sinclair. When Sinclair died of a drug overdose, Cain used occult methods, presumably to bring his love back. While he did not get Sinclair back from the dead, he did cause The Great Secession, consequently getting himself arrested. Cain recently escaped prison, and rumors are that he is hiding in a new Land called Haunted Land. But this is just conjecture.

Now, on to my interview with Rex Dolan.

The Unknown Daily: Rex, thanks for this interview. Although I only remember the show's one and a half seasons, I was a fan of Happy Jack.

Rex Dolan: Yeah, well, thanks, but no thanks. I lived it, man. Six seasons. Then I woke one day, and everything had changed.

UD: And the other seasons of the show disappeared?

RD: Fuckin'-A.

UD: We at the *Unknown Daily* have done stories on the Cain Consequence before, but I have never heard of such an extreme example.

RD: I'm lucky, I guess.

UD: And what do you say to those who contend you are making all of this up to get back in the press?

RD: Press? This Micky-Mouse Website of yours?

UD: When did you begin noticing the changes?

RD: I took a job a while back doing surveys in malls and shit like that.

UD: Surveys?

RD: Yes, about movies. For a company to decide if it's worth the cost of bringing older movies to streaming services. One of the things we do is show lobby cards of movies and ask people if they remember the film.

UD: Okay, I am assuming if enough people remember a particular movie with enough fondness, it makes it a candidate for purchase from a streaming service?

RD: Shit, Stu, I can't put anything past you. Exactly. And they take a survey for the free movie passes. But there's a trick to see if they are being truthful.

UD: What kind of trick?

RD:In with all the lobby cards, we have *fake* movies.

UD: Fake, how?

RD: We always show them one lobby card for a fake movie. They look exactly like the cards with actors' names and photos. But they are not real movies.

UD: And some people claim to have seen these fake movies?

RD: Bingo.

UD: But some would contend it's simply a suggestion. This does not prove your ideas of things coming and going from reality.

RD: But here's the deal.

At this point, Mr. Dolan rummaged through a massive fanny pack (yes, a fanny pack!) and removed a lobby card. It did look professional. The movie was called Andy and the Astronauts *and starred Bruce Willis as Andy.*

UD: Okay, and someone claimed to remember this movie?

RD: Not *someone*...over sixty people. The most I have ever seen of this kind of thing before was two people. But *sixty* people of the two hundred or so I surveyed say they remember this movie.

UD: I have to say this is odd. But look at the card. It looks like some silly movie that could be real.

RD: But that's not all.

UD: Please, go on.

RD: Of the sixty, forty-four of them remembered the plot. And they all remember it almost exactly the same way.

UD: Wow, that is strange.

 END OF INTERVIEW.

***

"Here, kid," Rex said and stuffed a slip of paper with his login credentials for the movie survey database into Stu's hand. "You can look for yourself. Tell me this is not crazy."

Stu gave Rex Dolan his pay for the interview and left.

CHAPTER TWO

'80s Land

"*The Has Been*? That's the official title?!" Rex asked his agent. 'Agent' was being kind to Jimmy Rose. Rose managed a backyard boxing ring, ran a trucking company, and was an entertainment agent for people no one else wanted to represent.

"Yeah."

"I should have insisted on seeing the script before signing."

"It's not as bad as it sounds."

"Well, it sounds bad. What's the synopsis?"

"Well, the movie's main character is a guy who was a child star. And, umm..."

"A has been? A loser?"

"Umm, yeah. The protagonist goes on a rampage, killing everyone he thinks destroyed his career. But it's interesting. See, the inside joke of the movie is that real-life former child stars will play all the characters he kills."

"Has-beens, in other words. Jimmy, I don't like this."

"C'mon, Rex. It's not so bad. It's actually kind of clever."

"Yeah, clever, and I am the inside joke. Who else is in it?"

"Well, Marc Price—Skippy from *Family Ties* plays one part."

"Christ."

"Oh, and Gary Coleman—well, a *CGI* Gary Coleman, God rest his soul."

"Skippy, a computer-generated Gary Coleman, and me. Wonderful. I assume Potsie cost too much, huh?"

"C'mon, Rex, don't be like that."

Rex ended the call. What a way to finish the day. Little did he know his troubles were only beginning.

***

Rex Dolan woke with a trifecta: A hangover, having to take a shit, and in the '80s. Well, *almost* in the '80s. Queens, New York, had become '80s Land years ago, and while not the '80s, it sure as hell had all the shit from the decade and in spades. And he was supposed to live here with movies like *Howard the Duck*, *Ishtar*, and *Leonard Part 6*? He'd had enough of the decade the first time around. The look—pastels and neon. The Sounds—Poison, George Michael, and The Culture Club. Not to mention the people.

The mayor of '80sLand, Tiffany Gibson, had banned most technology. She had sent around a manifesto warning how people of the past had carried little rectangular digital devices with them 24 hours a day. The devices were called 'phones' because they began as mobile telephones. The manifesto expounded how people had become so addicted to these devices that they could not stop staring into them long enough to pay attention to their schoolwork or jobs, resulting in people dying from walking into traffic, wandering into construction sites, and even walking off bridges and cliffs. It's believed at some point in about 2023, Jesus had come back to earth to save humankind, but people did not look from their phones long enough to take notice. The educational tone of the manifesto led Rex to believe many people did not even remember the technology they had been using until The Great Secession. Of course, Rex remembered, and while people *had* become too attached to their phones, he was unsure about missing the Second Coming.

In '80 Land, the "newest" technology allowed were VCRs, The Atari 2600, and the Sony Walkman. Sure, there were underground dealers who could procure Smart Phones, but the penalty for such devices was severe. Rex has a blacklisted Smart Phone, and the service was surprisingly good (the satellites still existed whether or not people remembered them).

Rex's first thought was to live in 70s Land, where it was perfectly acceptable to smack the backsides of waitresses in coffee shops, smoke anywhere one wished, and expect women to wait on you hand and foot. But, not surprisingly, 70s Land eventually folded because women stopped moving there.

So, he was stuck in this hell. He worked as a security guard these days. He grabbed his cigarettes and a lighter off the end table. Angela stirred, sniffed, and rolled over in bed. God, he hated it when she spent the night. She liked to cuddle and hog the blankets. She woke in a cheery mood and smiled too much. The shit a guy must deal with to get laid was one of nature's cruelest jokes on humanity.

Rex had met Angela eight months earlier, and the two would get together every other week or so for little more than sex. Angela wanted to get more serious, of course. Rex knew she would eventually find a guy who would take her out, want more than sex, and treat her the way she deserved, and he'd never see her again. And he was okay with that.

He liked her enough—she did not break his balls, was cute, and even enjoyed his dark worldview.

He lit the smoke and dreaded putting on his security uniform and facing another day telling drivers to park only in designated spots and checking passes to enter the parking lot.

"God, the smoke," Angela said.

Rex blew the smoke sideways.

"I have to go to work."

"Come here and cuddle with me," she said, patting the mattress. Rex's stomach turned.

"No time right now, babe."

"Before you go, I want to ask you something, but you can't get mad."

"Oh, Christ. What?"

"You're already mad."

"I'm not mad. I'm *apprehensive*. What is it?"

Rex knew damn well when a woman said, "I want to ask you something," she wanted to do something or go somewhere—shit he didn't want to do.

"You wouldn't want to go with me to my friend's wedding, would you?"

"Are you kidding? I thought we had a system. Nice and easy. No relationship trappings, right?"

"I know. But I don't want to go alone. I'll treat for everything."

"When is it?"

"You want to go?" she asked, leaning on an elbow, her eyes widening with hope.

Something like guilt sat like a rock in Rex's gut as he observed the look of optimism on Angela's face. After all, he was getting ready to let down her.

"September 16th..."

"Shit. I have an important audition. No way I can make it. Sorry."

"Can't you reschedule? It's eight months away."

"Sorry, but the entertainment business doesn't work that way, babe."

He watched her eyes instantly get watery and looked away. He finished dressing and left the woman the way he left most people who had the misfortune to enter his life—disappointed.

***

Rex walked into the security office and went directly to the locker room. Before he could make a cup of coffee, Herb, the "team lead," let Rex know he was wanted in Mr. Kopp's office.

"Can I get a cup of coffee first?

"Negative. Mr. Kopp needs to see you ASAP."

"What's this about?"

"We both have to go into the office *right now*," Herb said.

Rex walked into the office, and Herb followed. Mr. Kopp sat behind his desk and regarded him severely.

"Rex, have a seat."

"Something wrong?"

"Yes. I think it's better if you see this for yourself," Mr. Kopp said, turning his monitor around so Rex could see the screen. The man clicked the mouse, and the video played. The image was the break room in this very building. In the video, Rex entered the room. He was on his phone.

"What is this? I didn't know we were under surveillance."

"Clearly."

"I don't get it."

"First, you have a black-market device. But that isn't the real problem."

"What then?"

Kopp clicked the mouse, pausing the video.

"Anything you want to tell us?" Kopp asked.

"No. What the hell is going on? What's the problem?"

Kopp glanced at Herb, who only nodded. Kopp clicked the mouse again. The video resumed. Rex's heart sank as the Rex on the tape fumbled with his belt. Before long, he was playing with himself, eyes glued to his phone screen. Kopp raised the volume.

"You like that? Take those cocks. Take all those cocks-"

"Jesus," Rex said.

"Anything you want to tell me about this?"

Rex's voice on the video continued.

"...got room for one more cock? Look at you surrounded by dick. You love it."

"What's to tell? I'm rubbing one out. And for Christ's sake, can you mute that damn thing?"

Kopp clicked the mouse and killed the sound.

"You think this is appropriate behavior for the workplace," Herb asked.

"I was alone. I had no idea you were recording me. I locked the door. Look at the time stamp on the video. It's my break."

"You contend because it's during your break, it's acceptable to sexually gratify yourself in the office while watching gangbang videos on an outlawed device?" Kopp said.

"It's not a gangbang video," Rex said.

"It certainly is. Look," Herb said, pointing to his computer screen.

"Well, technically, it's a threesome. Not a gangbang," Rex said.

"Nonsense. There is one woman and two men. That's a gangbang in my book."

"No, it's a threesome. You need at least three dicks to one woman for it to officially be considered a gangbang," Rex said.

Kopp looked to Herb.

"Mr. Dolan may be right on this account. In order to be considered a proper gangbang I would contend at least three dicks, per one female, be present."

"Okay, enough! We are getting off-track here. My God, look at this," Kopp said, pointing to the monitor again. The Rex on the video grinned wildly as he pleasured himself, eyes glued to the tiny screen of his mobile.

"Okay, turn the damn thing off, for Christ's sake!" Rex said.

***

Four of his fellow security co-workers appeared to walk him out.

"You need four guys to take me out of here? Are you kidding?"

He was fired on the spot, but Mr. Kopp assured Rex the company was showing clemency by not pressing further charges.

"Pressing charges for what? Jerkin' the gherkin'?" Rex asked. And then the awful news came—Mr. Kopp let Rex know by law, he was required to report Rex to the police as a sexual deviant.

"One more thing to add to my resume," Rex said.

Outside, the scent of artificial grape assaulted him. The amount of hairspray used in '80 Land had caused so many environmental issues that aerosol cans were outlawed. Aussie Scrunch came in a pump. This crap was invented in 1986 and was therefore allowed in 80 Land. However, as a result, the entire place reeked of a sickly-sweet chemical grape.

Rex thought of the *changes.*

It had all begun for him when he had sat to watch his nightly re-run of *The Fugitive.* Everything was normal until Dr. Richard Kimble mentioned he was looking for the *two-armed man.* Rex continued to watch, thinking he had misheard. He eventually called his father to ask his thoughts.

"Rex, what are you talking about? It's always been the two-armed man."

"Dad, Kimble is searching for the *one*-armed man. Don't you remember?"

"Rex, are you using drugs again?"

"Drugs, no. But think about it, Dad. What sense does it make to search for a two-armed man? Every man has two arms."

"Exactly, that's why it's so hard for Kimble to find him."

Rex had spent the next ten minutes convincing his father he was not on drugs and had let it go.

He didn't want to go home. Angela was likely still there, and he couldn't face her now. Rex put on his Members Only jacket, unfolded his aviator sunglasses, and placed them on. He pushed out his chest like a peacock, stuck a cigarette in his mouth, and walked, arms bowed to use as much space as possible on the sidewalk.

Never let them see you down.

Never be weak.

He felt like a walk. He wanted coffee.

He spotted the coffee shop ahead. Two teenagers were outside telling one another dirty jokes. He thought of a joke a buddy had once shared with him:

There is this guy in a bar celebrating his birthday. The man goes into the men's room to have a piss. While at the urinal, a leprechaun walks in and begins pissing next to him. The man cannot help but notice the leprechaun has gold coins stuffed in all his pockets. The leprechaun notices the man admiring his gold.

"From me pot o' gold. I can grant you a pot full of gold if you like," The leprechaun says. "But you must let me stoop you, duke you from behind."

The man notices they are alone. He agrees. The leprechaun proceeds to violate the man's asshole. When he's finished, the man asks where his gold is. The leprechaun replies with a question: "So, what are you celebrating out there?"

"My fortieth birthday." The man says.

The leprechaun zips up and says: "Forty…a wee bit old to be believing in leprechauns, eh?"

The joke fit Rex's life entirely—empty promises and always getting fucked.

He took a drag of his smoke and headed for the coffee shop door. A fat man with a chubby wife and obese son pushed their way out the door as Rex held it open for them.

"You're welcome," Rex said.

The man stared at him, ready for a confrontation. Then, his brows knitted in recognition.

"Hey, where do I know you from?"

"Nowhere…I have one of those faces."

"No, I know you…you're that guy? From that show? *Family Ties*, right?"

"No! He's not from *Family Ties,* dummy," the kid said. The father slapped the kid's head.

"Christ, that friggin' hurt!"

"You don't know hurt, you little shit."

Lovely family, Rex thought.

Rex looked at the kid, a bratty little boy, already soft from a life of junk food and video games. He looked back at the dad, or was it the mom? Both parents had short haircuts and were dressed in similar jogging suits (though neither looked like they jogged unless chasing the ice cream man was considered exercise). He was not too surprised. The adage was true—couples begin looking like one another after a while—morphing into a creepy androgynous lifeform. Eventually, man and woman morphed into two similar a-sexual creatures—turning the couple into sexless siblings. A frightening thought. He was happy he had never married. He finally identified the mother as she wore a T-shirt reading: *I'm a mother. What's Your Super-Power?*

"No, it was *Growing Pains*," she corrected her husband.

"Yeah, yeah!" The man said.

"No…I got it…*Happy Jack*. You're Happy Jack! Whatever happened to you, I have not seen you in anything for a long time."

"Yeah, you were all over TV back then. The talk shows say you got into all kinds of trouble," the mom said.

"What was it you always said?" the father asked,

"*Happy days are here again!*" the boy said.

"Yeah!" the father agreed.

"I read once you were broke. You lost all your money from the show. What the hell happened? How did you waste all the money?"

"I didn't waste it all, tubby. I spent most of my cash on whores, drugs, drinking, and gambling. The rest of it, I admit I wasted."

"Son, cover your ears!"

"*Happy days are here again,*" the boy said again.

"What a crock of shit that was," Rex said.

He flicked the butt to the curb.

"Wow. So angry," the mother said.

"Well, thanks for the trip down memory lane, lard-asses."

He pushed his way into the coffee shop. Little did these idiots know Rex Dolan, who once played in *Happy Jack*, would help save the world.

***

There was something off about the place. Rex was quite sure this café had not been here yesterday. Sitting here was like being on the set of a TV show; everything resembled a coffee shop, but he had the sensation this was a presentation only. A set. A facsimile of something rather than the thing itself. Still, he sat and ordered a coffee. A fat, messy man, wearing the thickest glasses Rex had ever seen, sat alone at a nearby table with enough food for two families. He had a contraption on his face, feeding him oxygen from a tank at his side. The man was mumbling to himself.

"Marge. Bruce. Blanche. Mel. Rose." The obese man noticed Rex looking his way. "Old names."

"What's that, buddy?"

"There are so many old names no one is named anymore," the man said, struggling for breath.

The waitress brought Rex his coffee, gave him a curious look, and walked away. Rex poured milk into his cup and watched the waitress's ass twist as she made her way back to the counter. He took a sip. At least the coffee was good.

"Oh, yeah. Well, I'm Rex. Not too many Rexs these days. No one would name their kid Rex if they loved them."

"I'm not talking about outdated names—I mean names that no longer exist."

"Is that right?"

The man turned back around, ignoring Rex.

"You can't understand. I am smart enough to grasp the concept. But you, forget it."

"Good chatting, wide load. And fuck you very much."

Rex took another sip. And spit. What the hell was this—tea!? His drink had changed between sips.

Change.

Enough was enough. He carefully pulled out his phone and emailed Stu Sawyer, the nerd who had interviewed him. It was time to hit the road. He jumped into his jacket and left. He needed something a little stronger than coffee.

34

CHAPTER THREE

The old adage states one should never work with children or animals. Stu thought of re-writing it—never work with children, animals, *and* former child stars. Rex Dolan proved to be as challenging as he'd been warned. Yesterday's interview had gone well enough, but Stu secretly hoped to get more insight into what he was experiencing himself—no such luck. While some of what Rex had said was interesting (people remembering a non-existent movie), there wasn't enough to go on. Indeed, as several people had warned Stu, Rex Dolan did appear to be craving attention. While Stu may have had an exciting interview for his site, he had no new answers.

Bringing his laptop into the kitchen, Stu used the credentials Rex Dolan gave him and logged into the movie survey database as he ate leftover pizza. He checked the comments about the fake movie *Andy and the Astronauts*.

Sure enough, an overwhelming number of people recalled the plot: Andy and three others took a journey to what was supposed to be Mars. However, they accidentally land on a planet yet to be identified in the solar system. With no way home, they resign themselves to making a life there.

Andy (Bruce Willis) meets and falls in love with an alien woman. But his main objective is to find a way to bring his crew home. They battle and defeat the evil Silver-Head and his army of snake creatures. Eventually, the Space Program arrived to save them. However, Andy decides to stay here, admitting he never had much of a life on Earth anyway. Besides, he and the alien woman are expecting a child.

When his mother poured herself coffee, Stu asked her if she'd remembered *Andy and the Astronauts*. She did not. She placed a bowl of food on the floor for the dog and faced her son.

"What's wrong?"

Stu explained the reason for the question.

"Stuey, this is nothing but people's imaginations."

"How can all this be in these people's imaginations?" Stu asked.

"It's a hoax. What this Rex Dolan is saying is not possible. He's looking for another fifteen minutes of fame."

"But *scientifically,* it's possible," Stu said.

"How?"

"In an infinite Universe, a multiverse, it could happen. The Great Secession was an impossibility until Cain made it happen. Did you ever think you would live in Church Land rather than New Jersey without moving an inch?"

"I read he escaped from prison."

"Right, and did you read how he broke out?" Stu asked.

"They don't know. Cain just disappeared."

"Exactly, mom. He disappeared."

"Yes, but we all *remember* him. He escaped. There's nothing more to it."

"Maybe."

"Stu, you have been overthinking this stuff since the website. I think it's great, and I am glad you enjoy it, but UFOs, Aliens, Sea creatures, Bigfoot. It's all ridiculous. I'm going to have a nap. Love you, Stuey." Brandy scooped the little terrier into her arms and headed upstairs.

Stu thought about how insane his mother must have thought he was. But he knew she was sick and should not add to her worries. So he decided not to talk about the Cain Consequence with his mother anymore.

Now, he needed to find a way to make it stop.

Stu took a bite of cold pizza and sipped his coffee. He played some music as he worked on the site. What kind of life was this? A twenty-one-year-old "man" living with his mother. He hardly left the house as he could do everything for his site from here. The idea of an actual career was a foreign concept to him. He'd all but given up on ever being connected with anyone romantically. Sex was unlikely, considering how he lived as a borderline hermit.

He opened his email to a message from the former child star.

FROM: badasshappyjack77@dataonline.net
SUBJECT: time to stop the Cain Consequence!!!
Stu,

What the fuck is going on? This is Rex Dolan here. Listen, kid. The changes are too much now that Barclay Cain is out. I'm leaving to go through the Lands and find out how to stop this. It's time to do something. It's time for a little less bark and a little more bite.

This outlaw is ready to move. I can't take any more. Road trip! I got the wheels; you pay the gas. If you ain't too chicken shit, call me. Cain is hiding out in Haunted Land. At least, that's the rumor. Makes sense. I'm going to find out what's going on. If you're down, call
666-867-5309.
PS, this is for someone to share costs…no faggy shit!

A road-trip? Should he go? With Rex Dolan? Was it worth it? Did it matter that his mother's Toyota was now yellow (it had been green a month ago) or that his house now had an extra room? But more than that—his mother thought he was going crazy. He questioned his sanity recently as well. It was time to prove he was not mad. He had wished for a way out of this nightmare more than once—dreamed of escaping. Now, adventure stared him right in the face. Did he have the stones to grab it?

There was a metallic crash outside—a garbage can falling. Stu stuck his head against the window just in time to witness as the can on the ground righted itself, and the dog who had knocked it over walked backward, away from the can. A movie scene in reverse. Across the street was a man—or the *idea* of a man. The figure was only an elongated shadow, misty and thin. Each time Stu adjusted his eyes to see the shape better, the thing retreated ever so slightly into the recesses of the trees and darkness as if teasing him.

The man (if it *was* a man) whistled a happy tune in juxtaposition with the creepy scene outside Stu's window. Then, the shadow vanished entirely. The dog ran forward again, this time missing the garbage can.

The world was glitching. Skipping. Rex Dolan was right—this had to stop. Someone had to do something. Was Stewart Sawyer finally the *someone* in a critical scenario? Stu marched back to his laptop.

Barclay Cain was an occultist and not a physicist. Was he truly magic? Did it matter? Science or magic. With technology evolving so rapidly, magic and science were two sides of the same coin. He even once read the infamous Men in Black had gone to investigate the Cain Consequence but had never returned from their quest. Stu believed in the Men in Black. Indeed, he'd received threatening emails (from an untraceable source) demanding he shut down his website more than once.

Stu re-read the email. He could finally get out of Church Land. For once in his life, should he take a chance?

Shit, I'll have to tell my mother I am leaving. What will she say?

She was going to shit. Stu may have been twenty-one, but his mother's concern for him had taken steps backward since the accident. Stu considered not going, allowing things to go as they were. But in the last couple of days, he had noticed more changes. All his underwear were now bikini rather than boxers. Buster, his mother's terrier, was now named *Baxter* and had changed from black with white spots to the opposite.

He was convinced. He was going to Haunted Land (if they could find it) with former child star Rex Dolan. God help him.

CHAPTER FOUR

Pub Land

This was the first time Bubby had witnessed his attorney, Lee Levin, at a loss for words. No small task for the man. Bubby had known Levin for over thirty years. Levin knew the deal—Bubby could not catch a break. Not all of Bubby's ideas were bad—some were rather clever. But no idea—clever or not—worked in Bubby Goldenblatt's favor. Ever. If you look up 'bad luck' in the dictionary, you will not find a photo of Bubby Goldenblatt only because Webster's would have had to pay royalties, which would have been too much good fortune for the world's worst entrepreneur.

"Give it to me straight, Lee," Bubby said. Lee Levin never gave it any other way.

"Bubby, they're suing. I can't talk them out of it."

"Suing for what? It's a plastic turd. How can they sue over a plastic poop joke?"

"The kid put it on his teacher's desk. She threw it in the garbage pail, where it billowed green smoke and sparks.

And the teacher's mother appeared out of thin air! Her mother has been dead for eleven years, and while she will not say it in as many words, the teacher liked it that way. Her mother's ghost won't leave. And more suits are coming. One guy used the fake vomit to fool his wife, and now they have the spirit of Sam Kinison in their home. He's shouting obscenities constantly; they have not been able to sleep more than an hour or two a night. They are hiring the medium, Anton Snow, to get him out at a thousand dollars daily. And at least a dozen people who bought the roach in the ice cube gag are infested with *real* roaches. A retired cop says his rubber chicken came alive and attacked him. He had to shoot it three times to stop it. He shot himself in the foot in the process."

Bubby had founded "Bubby's Boutique Gags" two years ago. He bought a warehouse and factory in China and put everything into production. Unbeknownst to him, the factory was built on a haunted piece of land where the Sing-Sang-Sung (yes, a family name of all the tenses) had been slaughtered. The troubled factory had produced mostly cursed items. Gags that conjured evil spirits and ghosts. Pranks that pulled demons and troublesome imps out of thin air, joke items that shrunk cars or caused rooms in houses to disappear, and even a snake in a peanut can trick that caused the man who opened it to have the runs for eight days straight. Bubby had put all the cursed items in the warehouse and had his new gags produced in a different place, but the damage was done.

"What the hell." Bubby covered his cherubic face with his hands. Levin put a hand on his shoulder.

"It was a clever idea. But bad timing, that's all. Timing is everything. Like *Monkey Mom*, right?" Levin said, trying a smile and almost succeeded.

"Oh, please don't remind me."

Bubby's expertise at failing was not limited to cursed gags. It began decades before with a couple of doomed TV programs. The first was the cartoon he created: *Monkey Mom*. *Monkey Mom* was about a boy who befriended a crazy old inventor. The boy's mother, concerned her son was spending too much time with the eccentric man, sneaks into his lab one night. The mother accidentally gets tangled in a machine, and she and the inventor's troublesome test ape find themselves in the device. The machine is inadvertently powered up, and the ape and the boy's mother switch bodies. Each episode was to be about the boy and the old inventor trying to get the mom and ape together to change them back while hiding what they are doing from the local beat cop and a nosy neighbor.

However, Bubby only made the pilot episode before the show's cancelation. By all accounts, the show should have been a huge hit. But there was a problem—*Monkey Mom* had premiered on Sept. 6th, 1995, sealing its fate. On this same day, another cartoon premiered called *Fake Ape*. And the world was not ready for two ape-on-the-loose cartoons on the same day. *Fake Ape* went on to play for eleven seasons and spawned two movies, a spin-off, and an empire of merchandise. Conversely, *Monkey Mom* was forgotten and was only mentioned here and there in trivia about huge flops in entertainment.

"One thing I never understood—why did you call it *Monkey Mom* when the primate was an ape?" Levin asked.

"Ape Mom had no snap to it," Bubby said, looking into space. "You know my show was better. *Fake Ape* had no moral to its stories. Nothing. *Monkey Mom* had adventure, friendships, family."

"Or the other show you tried. What was it called?"

To Catch a Killer was a reality game show. The show he'd created involved releasing a serial killer from prison (with a tracking device, of course) for people to play the game from their computers and try to track the killer. Much like *Monkey Mom,* the gameshow had only aired once before ending in epic failure. The first killer they freed, a diminutive man called Tuco, was released and never found. Instead, he left behind a string of new murders. Bubby had to live with this horror.

"Let's not talk about TV. So, what now," Bubby asked, rubbing his heavy stubble.

"Bankruptcy. It's all I can suggest."

"There has to be another way…."

"Lawsuits are still coming in from last year's fart bomb debacle. I'm sorry, but Bubby's Boutique Gags is finished," the lawyer said with finality.

"Bankruptcy, huh?"

"I can't see any other way. And I'm sorry, but there is no way I can continue to represent you."

"I understand, Lee. You were crazy to stay with me this long."

Bubby left the law office in search of a drink.

***

He didn't need to go to the pub to get drunk; there were booze and beer taps all over Pub Land. All the offices here had vending machines selling beer, wine, and airplane bottles of harder stuff. Many people complained about all the drunks during the Great Secession, so most boozers moved to Pub Land. Surprisingly, things operated relatively smoothly in Pub Land as most people were on terms with their alcoholism and did not make much trouble.

One need not be Sigmund Freud (whose name in some realities was Sidney Fields) to realize why Bubby was an entrepreneur (albeit a horrible one). At thirty-two, his father had eaten himself into unemployment, so the Goldenblatt family had been poor. One could say dirt poor if they had only been able to afford dirt. Ira "Buddy" Goldenblatt's earliest memories of his parents were dark. His father sitting in the dark, eating himself silly while his mother poured her black rain over her husband and only child. He used to tell his mother not to be so negative, and his mother would reply:

"I'm not negative; I'm a realist, Ira. Life wants you to fail. It's the nature of things, at least for this family."

"That can't be?"

"Look at it this way: imagine you're the landlord of an apartment complex. You rent half of the apartments to drug dealers, pimps, hookers, and sex traffickers. Then you rent the other half of the apartments to normal, hard-working, law-following families. Which do you think would dictate the overall tone of the place? Which group of people would eventually be forced out?"

"I don't get the question?"

"Oh, you get it. But you don't like the obvious truth. The negative *always* dominates. Because negativity is stronger, it always wins, and those who walk around all honey and roses are full of crap."

It had begun raining a few minutes after he'd left Lee Levin's office. Bubby did not have an umbrella. He walked and reflected. Thirsty. His mind hurt.

Bubby could remember being a little boy and coming in from delivering newspapers in the sleet and icy rain, all good cheer despite the work and weather.

"It's miserable out there," he'd said, letting himself into the apartment and slipping out of his wet coat and boots.

"It's miserable in here, too," his mother had said as she scrubbed the floor in enough bleach to make his eyes water. Despite being one of the world's great pessimists, Bubby's mother was one of those old-school women who took her house-cleaning obsession to the point of an art form.

"Any word on Aunt Linda?" Bubby asked. Linda was his father's sister and was diagnosed with advanced stomach melanoma eight months prior. She'd get better for a bit and then be rushed back to the hospital "at death's door" before getting better for a week or two. Rinse, repeat. His mother removed cleaning rags from a boiling pot on the stove.

"She's at the end again. She really should make up her mind and get well or die. It's so inconsiderate to go back and forth like this."

His mother had scoured the counter with steel wool so often she'd smoothed all the right angles to rounded edges.

What memories.

Bubby decided on a not totally disagreeable bar about two blocks north of Lee Levin's law office. Once he stepped inside, Bubby was not surprised to discover this was *his* local pub. He did not know how this phenomenon occurred. But he always found himself in The Starlight Lounge whenever he entered *any* bar or pub. It defied time and space, but he accepted it as part of reality now.

At first, he'd panicked, trying to talk to the customers and workers in the bar, explaining they were all in some time loop. But all that happened was he'd get cut off and have to live this hell sober. So, he learned to keep his mouth shut.

The door opened, letting in the freezing wind and fluffy snow (It had been 72 degrees and pouring rain when Bubby had entered the pub two minutes ago), and a small woman bounced in. The weather was consistently poor in Pub Land. Snow. Sleet. Rain. Cold. Brutal humidity. Sweltering heat (many times on the same day). Harsh weather made it easier to squander your days in a bar drinking without guilt.

"It's neither fit for man nor beast out there. Oh, man. I always wanted to walk into a bar and say that," she said.

She removed layers of coats and sweaters until the elfin girl emerged.

In the meantime, the barkeep introduced himself to Bubby as Pat—as if they had not had this exact introduction countless times. He was the same bartender who was in every bar. His hair and clothes would change slightly each time, but he was always the same "model."

"Bubby Goldenblatt of Bubby's Boutique Gags." Bubby said as he had said so often and ordered a beer, as he'd done as many times. An automatic introduction. But Bubby's Boutique Gags had been long over even before the lawsuits and his meeting with Lee today. No one would pay outrageous prices for high-end, top-tier practical joke products, cursed or otherwise.

Bubby sipped his beer and plopped onto a stool.

Bubby had gotten his nickname at school. Bubby meant grandmother, and because of his gentle nature and aversion to sports or anything too competitive, Ira became 'Bubby.' He had considered fighting the nickname but knew battling would only make the name stick. However, the kids, enjoying his new name, did forget for a while to rib him about his father's weight, and this, at least, was a welcome respite.

His mother told him to fight the kids who made fun of his father. What kind of son allowed his classmates to speak about his father in such a way? His mother thought humiliating Stan Goldenblatt for being as useless as a whore with a Ph.D. was her job exclusively.

"You never fight back," his mother had said.

"I'm sorry. I just *can't*."

He could recall the door opening as his father struggled to get his 400-plus frame into the tiny Queens apartment.

"Something smells good."

"Oh? I had better take the boiling rags off the stove before you eat them," his mother had said.

"I'm starving."

"I've yet to know you any other way."

His mother's face wore a look that would prompt anyone to ask: *is anything wrong*? But Bubby and his father had learned long ago that a considerable number of things were always wrong, and she would have no hard time telling them each and every one. His father had learned only to speak favorably.

"Look at how nice and clean this place is. I would not know how to live without you," Bubby's father told his mother, hanging his coat while kissing the top of his mother's head as she scoured the stovetop. Her gaze never left her scrubbing.

"If you lifted a hand to help, you'd learn how to clean."

"All I know is I had better go before you."

"What the hell does that mean?" his mother asked. Now she *did* look from her cleaning.

"It means I hope I die before you. I would not know how to go on without you," his father explained.

"Oh. And stick me with all the bills! You want that you should go first, so I am the one planning a funeral, dealing with everyone at a shiva, handling all the damn paperwork!"

"No, I only meant-"

"I know what you meant, you lazy sack!" she said.

"Fine!" His father held out his arms dramatically to the sky. "God, this is Stan Goldenblatt at 27-55 Hillside Avenue, Queens, New York. I want to revise my wish. I want that *she* should go first. Thank you. Amen. Over and out. Okay? Are you happy? You die first. Go. You can die now for all I care!"

"You son-of-a-bitch."

The young Bubby then went into the other room as his parents continued to fight. In the movies, when someone was upset, he or she would have a drink. So, he crept to the cabinet where his parents kept the little whiskey they had on hand. He opened a bottle of scotch and took a long pull. He swallowed and winced. He took another and winced a little. He took a third and did not wince at all.

Despite his father's clear order with the all-mighty, in the end, his dad *did* go first. His mother had murdered him. It just took 32 years to complete the task, as dying of aggravation is seldom speedy. His mother (who was always "dying" of something or other) eventually got her wish and died of cancer of the everything a few years later.

Pat, the bartender, polished glasses and then a jar with BEATLES written across it. The jukebox played "A Hard Day's Night ." Pat sang in a thick Irish accent.

"It's been a Hard Day's Night, and I've been working like a fuckin' dog!" The man perfectly sang the line with the added word into the melody.

Bubby wanted to get drunk, clear his mind, and figure out a way to free himself from this space-time nightmare. Mostly, he wanted to get drunk.

The girl put all her coats behind the bar. There was a midget or *little person* as they were called these days ("little person" sounded more offensive to Bubby, but what did he know), dressed and made up like a clown (was *clown* still politically correct?). The clown was alone at a table in the back. His head was resting on the table. He rose momentally and shouted: "Hey, honey, vodka, neat," in a Spanish accent and laid his head back on the table. The clown was a new "character" in this crazy loop.

The girl poured a double and brought it over to the clown. He struggled to adjust himself on the tall stool.

"Need help," the girl asked.

"More than you can imagine," the little clown said.

"Poor thing. It must be hard being so small in this big, cruel world."

"How would you like to walk around face-height with nothing but elbows and assholes?"

The girl took the money for the drink, left the change, and moved away from the angry clown. Today was the first time a little clown was here. Could this "curse" finally be over? Either way, the little fellow gave Bubby the creeps.

Bubby grabbed his beer and headed over to the jukebox. He eyed the selection—the same as always.

"Nothing but the Beatles, Pat?" Buddy asked.

"Yer don't need anything but Paul, John, George, and Ringo. Maybe Pete."

"Who's Pete?"

"Pete Best, the Beatles' original drummer."

"Oh. You know, Pat, you know more about the Beatles than anyone I've ever met," the girl said.

"You sure are a Beatles authority," Bubby said.

"Been told that by folks from Colorado to damned-if-I-know. As a matter of fact, I'm working on a game."

"Game?"

Pat went behind the bar and pulled out a large slab of cardboard covered in crayon scribbles and pieces made of popsicle sticks and construction paper.

"Yeah. I'm making a board game. This is only a prototype, mind you. Okay, the players start on Abby Road, see? They travel through Strawberry Fields. Then, they cross the ocean in the Yellow Submarine. Go to Penny Lane. They answer questions, trivia about the Beatles, to advance from place to place."

"Questions, like *who was the Beatles' original drummer*?" Bubby asked.

"Well, that would be an easy one."

"I guess I wouldn't be good at the game."

"Well, I'm still in the 'pre-production' stages. Hey, look at this. My prized possession," Pat said, removing the jar from the bar.

"An empty jar?" Bubby asked.

"Beatles air."

"Air?"

"Of course. See, this fan went to a show back in sixty-four. He brought this jar here into the concert hall with him. And while the Beatles were playing, he opened the jar and captured some air. Hence, Beatle air."

"Insane," the girl said as she joined Pat behind the bar.

"You have no class. This here is a Goddamn collector's item."

"And you say you didn't collect the air yourself?" Bubby asked.

"I wish."

"So... how could you be sure it's real Beatles air and not an empty jar?"

"Beatle collector's honor. There is an etiquette, you know."

"I see."

Pat turned and busied himself, carefully replacing his game and jar of air behind the bar.

The TV above the bar aired a story about a baseball team Bubby knew had never existed in his reality before today. He moved past two men in matching gray suits and fedoras. Cigarette smoke shrouded their faces beneath the brims of the hats, giving Bubby the impression of an old film noir.

As Bubby settled on a stool. Then, in a gown much too fancy for The Starlight Lounge, a beautiful woman passed him with the fragrance of heaven. Then she disappeared into the crowd. A few young men bellied up to the bar, breaking Bubby's blissful silent drinking. It was nice while it lasted.

One of the men put on a pair of tiny glasses and examined the list of craft beers. Both men wore jeans so tight Bubby wondered how they used the bathroom. Both had huge beards and wore what looked like wooden shoes. They looked like they were trying to dress as elves. Hipsters.

"We will buy you a beer if you can settle a bet for my friend and me," one man said.

"I'll help if I can," Bubby said.

"Okay, is it gay for two men to have a threesome with a woman?"

Bubby was not about to answer such a vulgar question. "As long as you keep your *pinga* to yourself, no problem," said the little clown behind them.

"And," the second man added, "what about having sex with a blow-up doll? Is that gay?"

"Doll? Mmm… *estúpido* but not gay."

"See? Nothing to worry about," the man said to his friend.

"Well, I guess…." the second man said but was clearly unsure.

"So, you agree it's not gay whatsoever for two guys to screw a blow-up doll together. Okay, thanks for settling that."

"Wait!" the clown said. "That is not the question you asked!"

"Oh no. You already said it's cool. If it's not gay to screw the doll and it's not gay to have a threesome, then it's not gay to have a threesome with the doll. Right?" the second man pleaded to Bubby.

"I think the last scenario changes things," Bubby said.

"Oh no. If you answer 'no' to question one and answer 'no' to question two…then you must answer 'no' to question three," the first man said.

"But in scenario three, there is no woman. Now, where is my beer?" the clown snapped.

The two confused men walked away. Bubby was unsure what the interaction had been about but figured something had recently taken place, which left the two men questioning their straight-ness. So the boys had recently tied one on and double-teamed a sex doll—not the worst thing that can happen when alcohol is consumed at great capacity, Bubby considered. But the hipsters were clearly troubled by their intoxicated actions. As George Bernard Shaw famously declared, "Youth is wasted on the young."

"Well, that was one of the strangest conversations I have ever had, and that says a lot," Bubby said to the clown.

"You can only blame yourself."

"How so?"

"It's all happening in your head."

"Sorry?"

"You are dreaming right now," the clown said with a cantankerous grin.

"I'm not sure what you're talking about, my friend."

"I'm not your friend. Look around and tell me this is not a dream," the clown said and wobbled into the crowd.

Bubby sipped his beer and looked around the dark place. He noticed many conversations around him appeared to be only people mumbling. The more he tried to eavesdrop on conversations, the more convinced he became all these people were not speaking but doing a pantomime for his benefit. Extras in a movie.

Is it true? Am I dreaming?

Then he noticed the men in the matching gray suits and hats were not men but...two gorillas. They were still drinking, grabbing fistfuls of nuts from the wooden bowl on the wobbly table, and acting like two men in a normal conversation. No one else in the bar appeared to notice. One of the primates took a long, slow drag of his smoke.

Sick sweat broke on Bubby's face and rolled from his armpits into his shirt. He needed sleep. He swallowed his beer and noticed the cocktail napkin under it. Someone had written something in a feminine scribble in red ink.

Mr. Goldenblatt,

It would be best if you stopped all of this. I know you are frightened. But you are one of the few who can stop it.

Cain is free and at it again. Search the Lands until you find Haunted Land, and stop him, please.

Bubby looked around. What the hell was this? He thought of the beautiful woman he'd seen moments ago. He lifted the napkin and held it under his nose. It carried the mysterious woman's scent.

"You buy me a cerveza…" a voice said behind Bubby.

He spun around on his stool. The midget clown was back. He read over Bubby's shoulder.

"Excuse me –"

"Beer for me?" the little man asked. "You buy?"

"I don't think so. Did you put this here?" Bubby asked, holding the note.

"A napkin?" the clown asked.

Bubby looked, but the napkin was blank.

"I... never mind."

"You are always here, *si*?"

"No. It's my first time in this pub," Bubby said, realizing this was both true and false.

"No, you are always here. Being here every night will ruin you," the clown said, offering a tiny, calloused hand.

"A tavern can't corrupt a good man, and a synagogue can't reform a bad one," Bubby said, taking the man's hand.

The clown jumped back as they shook when the hand buzzer went off.

"Are you a little boy! Act like a man, ming."

"I'm in the gag business these days…well, I *was*," Bubby said, admiring the hand buzzer, a Shwartzman Hand-Quaker 22. Bubby emptied his pockets on the bar: along with a hand buzzer, he also had a plastic vomit, a rubber turd, and a nail with a fake nickel as the head. You nailed it to the floor and watched some poor sucker attempt to grab it. He also had the old dollar bill on the fishing line trick. You watched someone run after the dollar as you inched it away as if the wind were moving it.

"Stupid toys."

"These items here are classic gags."

"You have always been here for years and years. You can't leave," the clown said.

"Of course, I can leave."

"Well, you *can,* but you don't have the courage. Like you didn't dare to stand up for your wife."

"What did you say?

But the clown was gone again. Bubby looked around.

"Looking for someone," a man asked.

"Uh, yes. Did you see a midget clown walk away?"

"A midget clown, you say? Brother, how much have you had to drink?"

"Not enough."

"I hear you loud and clear."

"I can't take all these...changes," Bubby said, more to himself than this man.

"You see it too?"

"Yes. You notice it as well?" Bubby asked.

"Fuckin'-A right," the man said, lit a cigarette, and offered his hand.

"Rex Dolan."

"Bubby Goldenblatt."

They shook. This time, Bubby did not use the hand buzzer. This guy did not look like he had much of a sense of humor.

They discussed the changes over a drink. They also spoke about how some things had become a mash-up of two or more events, becoming one bizarre truth. For instance, the musical groups Bon Jovi and Journey no longer existed as separate entities but as one band called Bon Journey. A horrible super-group poisoning the airwaves with an infernal song called "Separate Ways Dead or Alive."

"Did you ever see the movie *Moonraker*-, Bubby asked but noticed Rex was looking at a newspaper lying on the bar.

"What the fuck!" Rex said too loudly. A few people looked from their drinks or conversations.

Rex, as if in a trance, handed the newspaper to Bubby.

"What?" Bubby asked.

"Another mash-up!"

The newspaper article was about a haunted house in Long Island, New York. Of course, Bubby knew the story— *The Amityville Horror*. They both remembered this happening in the '70s rather than in the present.

"Holy shit, "Bubby said. "But only the dates have changed…where's the mash-up?"

"Look!" Rex said, pointing to the photo. Bubby could not remember the man's appearance—Lutz was the name. But now, the man in the photograph was a beast of a thing— a horrible creature in billowing "MC Hammer" style pants and a Gold's Gym tank top, even though he appeared to have only seen a gym from the outside. The man in the photo stood before the infamous house with the odd bay windows. The man looked familiar, though. The name stopped Bubby at once: Joey Buttafuoco!

"What in the name of God..."

"Yup. Joey Buttafuoco is now the guy from the Amityville Horror," Rex said.

Both events had occurred in the same general location. Could this be why they fused into one puzzling truth? Of course, said events should have been separated by some twenty years. Bubby shook his head.

"May I ask where this pub is?" Bubby asked.

"You're asking me where we are?"

"Where did you enter this pub?"

"80s Land," Rex said.

"I came in from Pub Land."

They read the article as well as the rest of the paper. There were many odd stories—one piece told the tale of a local laborer who had died last week but had no sick days left, so he continued to rise each morning and show up to work, much to the dismay of his co-workers. Another told the tale of an oil executive in Corporate Land with a possessed asshole. It had begun innocently enough—his sphincter only whistling show tunes. The trouble was the smell on some of the Rogers & Hammerstein numbers during the big finishes, which needed copious fluctuation. Finally, the man's asshole took to telling all his secrets. It snitched to the man's wife about the cache of porno on his computer. But Bubby and Rex kept coming back to the *Amityville Horror*. Now, the Lutz family had never lived in the infamous house.

"We have to stop this."

"Yea. I'm way ahead of you, Bubbs. I'm going with another guy to find Haunted Land. It's where Cain is supposed to be."

"But even if you find a way to do that, what if you guys make it worse?" Bubby asked.

"Worse than Bon Journey? Worse than Joey Buttafuoco being back in the news?"

He had a point. Rex handed Bubby a slip of paper. The pub got more crowded, and Bubby turned around to find the man named Rex had disappeared. And Bubby Goldenblatt found himself drinking alone again.

CHAPTER FIVE

Hippy Land

The text message, from an unknown number, read:
VERY CLEVER.
Julia typed: *WHO IS THIS?*
A FRIEND
WHAT WAS CLEVER?
YOU WERE THINKING OF PUTTING ITCHING POWDER IN YOUR ROOMMATE'S PANTIES

The mention of the itching powder put a stop to the would-be prank. A good thing, too, as the itching powder was from a discontinued company. Not only would the powder have had her disagreeable roommate scratching her crotch, but it would also have had said crotch speaking in French for at least three days.

ARE YOU THERE?

Who was this? How did the texter know what she was thinking?

WHAT DO YOU WANT?

YOU WOULD DO WELL TO GO TO HAUNTED LAND. IT'S WHERE A WITCH WILL FIND HER ANSWERS.

A witch? Of course, Julia was a witch, though not by birth. She had been raised a witch, but it was not in her blood. As such, there was a limit to the efficiency she could hope to achieve in her magic. As a result, Julia could cast any number of spells with highly unpredictable results, often making the situation worse. Sometimes, significantly worse.

She turned her phone off, took the itching powder into the bathroom, and emptied its contents into the toilet. As she flushed, a purple cloud erupted from the toilet and was gone as fast as it came.

Julia Faith lived in Hippy Land. A witch could do worse, say to live in Church Land or Corporate Land. Still, this place had its issues. While the land was comfortable and fertile for growing crops, the people who lived here were still starving because everyone was lazy. They could not figure out why nothing ever got done as they all waited for someone else to do all the work. Hippy Land may have been a good idea on paper, but in practice, it was a place where everyone was broke, and no one worked for a living.

Julia got out of her dusty work clothes (she worked as a picker in a warehouse selling herbal supplements that claimed to fix anything from the sniffles to cancer but did absolutely nothing), took a quick shower, and slipped into her Hello Kitty pajamas before sitting to watch TV with her roommate, Bruja.

Bruja and Julia agreed on nothing and were placed in the apartment together simply because they were classified as type 2 witches. Bruja said she did not consider Julia a proper witch because Julia had been adopted into a family of witches.

"You look like an idiot," Bruja said, lighting a long cigarette.

"Something positive to say, as always, I see."

"Whatever."

Julia sipped an iced tea and settled into the chair in the living room. She found herself watching a show called *Cheers, Friends!*. She assumed she was watching a one-off special, but Bruja confirmed Ross, Rachel, Monica, Phoebe, and Chandler had always hung out in the bar in Pub Land (Boston did not exist anymore) called Cheers.

"This is all wrong," Julia said.

"*You're* all wrong," Bruja said, conjuring herself a glass of wine. Bruja looked at Julia suspiciously while Cliff Clavin and Chandler Bing argued about trivial facts. When Julia told Bruja these were supposed to be two different shows, she was met with hoarse laughter.

"You keep on smoking pot," Bruja said. "That stuff turns your brain into mush," she finished and drained her glass of wine.

The grass *was* potent shit, to be sure. One of the few perks of living in Hippy Land was the quality of the grass. Indeed, Julia's dealer often bragged he got his supply from the same guy who supplied comedian Carrot Top his steroids.

Julia took a sip of her iced tea. She took a few deep breaths to relax, but when she exhaled, her nostrils whistled.

"What the hell was that?!"

"It was my nostril, for crying out loud," Julia said, pulling at her nose.

"Now you're picking your nose. God, you are so gross."

"I'm not picking...never mind."

Julia wished she could change her living situation. However, she had no choice. She only came home to sleep and watch a little TV these days, which was still too much for Bruja. After Bruja had slept with her last two boyfriends, Julia stopped bringing men home. Anyway, male hippies were not Julia's type. They tended to be full of crap, playing the earthy organic thing just to get laid. Men were the same no matter the land.

She'd been dating a new guy, Chicky Constantino from Doo-Wop Land, for a few months. He sang with a group (everyone in Doo-Wop Land was in a group) called Micky James's the New Ram-a-Lam-a-Ding-Dongs, featuring Bobby Fontaine & the Joey Black Orchestra, with the Manhattan Heartthrobs & the Timmy Two-Bit Melody Makers, with the Angel Brothers' New Red, Red, Red Hots featuring Billy DiMartino and the Night Sky Orchestra with Jimmy Revino's Brooklyn Revue and the Smooth Sounds Sammy Santini Band. She was careful not to bring him home for fear Bruja would seduce him.

There was a thud on the far side of the room. Julia's ventriloquist's dummy, Mr. Holmes, had fallen from his shelf, his vacant eyes staring at the two witches.

Julia struggled to get out of the worn chair where she had sunk. Bruja watched her fight the chair, a disgusted look on her face.

"Jesus, you need to lose weight," Bruja said.

Bruja was slight, skinny even. But a thin achieved from a steady diet of black coffee, alcohol, and cigarettes rather than anything to do with a healthy and active lifestyle. Julia may have had a few extra pounds, but it didn't bother her.

Julia looked at her phone.

"Expecting a text from a man," Bruja said, laughing—the laugh of a chain-smoking frog—ending in a cough as it so often did.

"So funny. I got a text from someone telling me to go to Haunted Land. I think it may be Barclay Cain. You know he broke free. He's supposed to be there."

"Of course, I know that!" Bruja knew everything there was to know about Barclay Cain. Cain was like a god to Bruja.

"I think it may be him."

"Yeah, right. The great Cain would look for you," Bruja said while keeping one eye on Julia and her phone.

"It could be," Julia said, retrieving Mr. Holmes from the floor.

"Would you keep that thing in your room—it gives me the creeps," Bruja said.

"Who, Mr. Holmes?" Julia asked, holding the dummy. His monocle had come loose and dangled from a string— his painted black hair like icing on a cake.

"Such a stupid thing. You make this place look like kids live here."

"Sorry, I'm like fifteen years younger than you- "

"Eleven…and you'll wish you look as good I do in eleven years. You look worse than me now!"

"Bitch," Julia whispered.

"What's that, freak?"

"Nothing."

"That's what I thought. And put your helmet in your room, too," Bruja said, pointing to Julia's pink moped helmet. "You look like an idiot on that sewing machine with that stupid helmet."

Julia loved her moped. It hardly used any gas and made finding parking a breeze. The perfect mode of transportation, weather permitting. The pink helmet matched the motor scooter's color perfectly.

Julia threw the dummy and helmet on her bed. Growing up the fat kid, Julia had retreated into her world. A world where Mr. Holmes became her best friend—she would never get rid of the silly thing.

"Don't listen to that idiot, Mr. Holmes," Julia whispered into the dummy's ear as though he could understand.

She watched a little more TV, not looking at Bruja, who sat in the recliner, drinking and scratching her crotch (it appeared Julia did not need to put itching powder in her roommate's panties after all).

Probably has crabs, Julia thought.

"What's that?" Bruja asked.

"I didn't say anything."

"I thought I heard you say something."

Bruja was a bitch, but her magic was old pure magic. Julia would have to watch what she *thought* going forward. Bruja may have been an awful human, but her magic was strong.

On TV, the friends who should have been in New York continued to cause trouble in the pub where everyone knew your name. Monica ordered a beer from Sam while Joey walked over to Diane Chambers, gave a sly smile, and said: "How *you* doin'?"

Julia had had enough.

She retreated into her bedroom, lit a joint, and got under the covers. Perhaps she'd wake to the ordinary world tomorrow. Warmth crept into her body. A little calmer now. The grass was providing a pleasant fuzziness in her head. Her eyes became heavy, and she was about to doze off when a *"click-clack"* sound had her ears prick up. She looked to the source of the sound and almost choked—Mr. Holmes was standing in the middle of her room! He pointed to the far wall. As she coughed out cannabis, Julia noticed a door in her bedroom. A door that had not been there this morning—a small and hoary-looking thing that would have been more at home in the side of a tree in a Tolkien novel than her bedroom wall. When she looked back at Mr.

Holmes, he was lying on the floor, limp, where he'd stood a moment ago.

"What the…"

Julia rose and examined Mr. Holmes. He was normal again. Lifeless. Only a toy. She walked to the door, her bare feet cold on the wood floor. She grabbed the handle of the heavy door. The knob was old. Brass or copper. Cold like the floor. She pulled, and while there was a *creak,* the door did not give. She pulled again, and this time the door opened.

Creeeeek

The handle slipped, and Julia fell back on her butt. Her pink polished toes in the air.

"Damn!"

"What are you doing in there?" Bruja asked. She was watching Julia through the crack in her bedroom door. Julia was on the floor, rubbing her ass.

"None of your bee's wax," Julia said, closing the bedroom door. She examined the mysterious new entry in her wall. It opened with another *creak*. Walking through the door, Julia found herself in...

***

WELCOME TO MOTIVATIONAL SPEAKER LAND: Where only Winners Live!

The sign welcomed.

The grass under her feet was too green, too lush. The flowers, trees, sky, and sun were so perfect it had to be synthetic—something from a magazine advert rather than anything organic. The air was perfumed. Julia almost gagged.

"Well, hello there!" a cheery, sing-song voice called. A man stood a few yards from her. He was at least six-foot-five. He had the body of a model, the hair of a rock star, and smiled like a gameshow host. His suit and Omega watch stunk of success. He walked closer, moving like silk on a red carpet.

"I'm Todd Champion, best-selling author of *Cause I Said So* and the sequel, *Cause I Still Said So.*"

"What?"

"Both of my books are currently on the best-seller list!"

"Which bestseller list?" Julia asked.

"The big one."

"Which one is that?"

"Yeah, that's right."

"Huh?"

A man jogging along the golden road stopped and stood at Todd's side. While Todd had dark hair and skin tone, this man was light-skinned and blond. His eyes were blue, whereas Todd's were brown. This, however, was where their uniqueness ended. Other than the eye and hair color, they were twins—two dolls made in the same factory. Ice ran across Julia's back.

"This is Chip Winner, our resident athlete."

"Uh…hello," she managed.

"Morning, Chip. A fine evening for a jog," Todd said.

"You know it, Todd. Only losers allow themselves to get soft," Chip said. Then he looked at Julia and said: "No offense."

"Work until your bank account looks like a phone number," Todd said.

"I wake every morning three hours before I go to work and begin my workout regimen. I drink a paleo, zero fat, no carb, keto, plant-based, vegan, high-protein shake designed for my blood type for breakfast. Look at this," Chip said as he removed his shirt and made his pecks jump.

Chip then dropped to the ground and did fifty no-handed pushups before standing again and looking at Julia for a reaction. He was in fantastic shape, to be sure, but his eyes and glued-on smile were sadly vacant.

"Well, see you!" And off Chip Winner ran, jogging into good health and shallowness.

"If, at first, you don't succeed, try management. Go the extra mile. It makes your boss look like an incompetent slacker!" Todd's smile grew to an unnatural size, teeth like piano keys.

"Huh?"

"Are you a winner, Julia? Do you want more out of life, Julia? More money, Julia? More respect, Julia? Does Julia desire more power?" Todd asked, flashing a disturbing, glowing smile.

"Why do you keep saying my name?"

" '*It's a proven fact the sweetest sound to a person's ear is the sound of their own name,*' Dale Carnegie said that."

"I think it's creepy," she said.

"But are you a winner?"

"Mmm…well… I don't know," Julia said.

"Well, Rome did not create a great empire by not knowing. They did it by killing all people who opposed them," Todd said, arms open as if ready to receive a hug. His perfect hair moved only so slightly in the scented breeze.

A short man in all white and an obscene amount of jewelry waltzed over.

"Julia, this is Sunny Santos. He lives in Church Land but has a radio show here every morning," Todd said.

"Julia, have you accepted Jesus Christ as your Lord and Savior?" the flashy man asked. He adjusted his horrible toupee and smiled. The whites of his eyes and teeth were golden.

"Leave her alone, Sunny. She's looking for real inspiration, not fairytales."

"Jesus Christ is the way and the light. Nobody will see the Kingdom but through Him. And me, of course," Sunny said.

"Christ was a loser," Todd said.

"What?!" Sunny said, taking two steps back and twisting an ostentatious diamond ring around one of his plump fingers.

"He died a pauper. He dressed like a bum- "

"You watch your mouth!"

"He didn't have the brass balls to grab life by the yin-yang and make money," Todd finished.

Sunny stepped into the polished man's face. Todd Champion had about a foot on Sunny, but the shorter man wasn't intimidated—he had the all-mighty on his side.

"You take it back."

"I will not."

"I'll knock those pearly whites down your damn throat."

Julia ran back the way she'd come. At first, she couldn't spot the odd door, and images of having to live out the rest of her days in this dreadful place flashed through her mind. But then Julia found the door floating like a mirage in the air, like a misplaced piece of someone's dream. She jumped through and back into her bedroom.

She ran into the living room. The bizarre TV show was over. The president was giving his State of the Union Address. Only the president was now Dr. Phil! Julia watched for a moment as Mr. President/Dr. Phil told a reporter perhaps he, the reporter, had never gotten over his momma sitting him sideways on the potty when he was little. She ran for the remote and turned the TV off.

Bruja was gone. So was all evidence she had ever lived here. As though her roommate had never existed—a spell, Julia was sure. While she did not mind Bruja's disappearance, she found herself questioning what this disappearance was all about.

Her phone (even though she had powered it off) chimed.

ARE YOU READY TO LISTEN NOW?

WHO IS THIS?

YOU CAN SEE THE CHANGES, CAN'T YOU? GO TO HAUUNTED LAND. FIND ANSWERS. STOP THIS MADNESS.

Then the phone blipped, and the texts disappeared like the exchange had never happened. Julia checked all the settings to no avail. Who turned her phone back on? Bruja? Did Bruja see the texts? She looked back in her room, and the odd little door was gone.

CHAPTER SIX

Rex Dolan had never told anyone about Josh. He'd had the cat for nearly five years now after finding the damn thing wet and starving in a bush near his apartment. Reluctantly, he'd moved Josh in, and the cat stayed put. Sure, why live outside when you can live in a home, get fed, and sleep all day and night? Not a half-bad life. Now Rex had to leave the cat with a friend while he embarked on his journey—damn pain in the ass.

Rex parked his black Mustang half on the sidewalk, lit a smoke, and walked to the door of an apartment belonging to Pip—the closest thing he had to a friend. As he rang the bell, Josh mewed from his carrier.

"Zip it, Josh."

Pip was an obese man-child who ran memorabilia conventions of old TV shows where fans paid to have items signed or for the opportunity to take a photo with the "stars" of yesteryear. Though he hated it, Rex occasionally did the conventions for easy, tax-free cash. He resented sitting at a fold-up table with silly 8x10s of him as Happy Jack. He had come close, more than once, to punching the people who passed his table, shouting, "*Happy days are here again.*" Especially when the cheap pricks didn't even buy anything.

Pip came to the door dressed in his usual shorts and T-shirt. The shirt sported large Japanese lettering and a robot of wild colors and sharp angles. Rex assumed this to be some movie only geeks cared about. The shirt was so tight it threatened to split if Pip sneezed. Pip's mouth looked like he'd been making out with a clown, all red and smeared. Rex knew Pip had not made out with anyone (clown or otherwise) for many years, if ever.

"Rex, come in. Want some fruit punch?" Pip asked, indicating his Sigmund and the Sea Monster cup.

"Fruit punch? Do I look like I am five years old?"

Pip did not respond but took a long swig of the sweet red drink.

The apartment was a venerable museum of forgotten TV and lost pop culture. Posters for everything from the *Six Million Dollar Man, The Groovy Ghoulies,* and *The Muppet Show* hung beside signed photos of Elvira, Vincent Price, and the *Dawn of the Dead* cast. Shot glasses, mugs, action figures, bobbleheads, and other memorabilia threatened to explode the over-stuffed shelves. Pip waddled through the messy apartment, moving records, comics, and VHS tapes, making room for Rex to sit. Josh cried.

Rex placed the carrier on the carpet and opened the door, but Josh stayed put.

"Your new mode of transportation?" Rex asked, pointing to a red and white tricycle resembling a candy cane.

"It's a gift for my niece. Her birthday is tomorrow."

"What in shit is that?" Rex asked, pointing to a new addition to Pip's already crowded apartment—a model train set. A station sign reading HANDLEY stood by the tiny station. A mini conductor in a topcoat stood here as well. A miniature lady in a red dress was the lone passenger on the train.

"A new hobby."

"Jesus, Pip. You need a woman, not more shit to collect."

"Well, I don't collect trains, but I could not resist this tribute to my favorite episode of *Twist of Fate*," Pip said.

"Say what?"

"You are familiar with the TV show *Twist of Fate*, right?"

"Negative."

"Oh, Rex. Have I taught you nothing in the years since our acquaintance? *Twist of Fate* was a show that ran only one season in 1961. A Twilight Zone rip-off like *One Step Beyond* or *Outer Limits*. The show was not particularly good, but one episode—"Last Stop, Handley!" was fantastic."

"About a train, I assume?"

"Yes. The main character wakes on a moving train. But it's not the character's normal train. A beautiful brunette in a red dress strolls past." Pip pointed to the tiny figurine in the train car. "But then he looks away for a moment. When he looks back, she's disappeared. Then the conductor walks past, and it gets good."

"No wonder it only ran for one season. What's the point?"

"The guy hates his job. He hates his life."

"Okay, maybe I can relate a bit."

"Every night on the train ride home, the lady in the red dress passes him and smiles. The conductor keeps saying: *'Last Stop, Handley!' 'Last Stop, Handley!'* But each time the guy moves to the next car to find the woman, she moves to another car, and our man can never catch her."

"And?"

"And the man eventually falls off the train, looking for the beautiful woman, and dies. And he gets buried in the local cemetery."

"And the cemetery is named *Handley*, got it. Wow. Mind-blowing," Rex said.

"Your problem, Rex, is you don't enjoy the more subtle messages art has to offer."

"Right, I'll keep that in mind."

"George Wrench wrote the episode. Originally, he was hired to write for-"

"Who gives a rat's ass, Pip. There are some things I don't need to know. That's the problem with people like you—you must know everything."

"Knowledge is power."

"Yeah, you're a powerful man with your *Dark Crystal* puppets and extensive and rare *Gamera* collection."

Josh's head appeared from the carrier. He moved forward a step.

"What kind of knowledge is it better *not* to know?"

"It's not the *not* knowing but...things like who wrote the "Happy Birthday" song or who invented "eny,meeny,miny,moe". Who gives a shit? Those are questions no one knows the answers to. No one *wants* to know the answers to."

Pip took a bite of a cupcake he'd had resting on a Sex Pistols CD cover. He took a swig of punch.

"Sisters Mildred and Patty Hill wrote the "Happy Birthday" song. And the famous choosing game known as "eny,meeny,miny,moe" originated at the turn of the century in France and was coined by big game hunters Erine Eeny and Moe Miny. They had caught a rare white tiger by its toe in a trap and were deciding whose name should appear first in the headlines-"

"I hate you."

"How long are you going for," Pip asked, changing the subject.

"I'm not sure."

"And you think you are going to find Barclay Cain? The guy is harder to find than Hoffa."

"I'll find him. I'm going to Haunted Land, my man. I know he's there."

"I hope he makes a Comic Book Land."

"Yeah, you'll get laid there."

"I ain't getting laid here anyway. You may get lost or disappear in Haunted Land. I can't take on this cat permanently," Pip said, biting into a Twinkie.

"If watching Josh is going to be a problem, let me know now."

"It's not a problem. I never knew you had a cat."

"Well, I don't—not really. This damn thing won't leave."

"Most people would consider that having a cat."

As if knowing his human and the fat man were discussing him, Josh crept out of the carrier, his little orange head bobbing, examining the surroundings.

"Here is his food," Rex said, pointing to a large bag. "He eats this, and only this food, twice daily—8 am and 3 pm. He gets fourteen shrimp treats at 1 pm and fourteen chicken treats at 9 pm. He drinks water and water only—no milk. None of that punch crap. He drinks water from this glass only. And here's his brush. Brush him every night at 9:30 pm. But do not brush his head or stomach—he hates that."

"Christ, does he get a daily massage as well," Pip asked.

"Don't fuck around. Josh is very regimented. Are you sure you can handle this?" Rex asked.

"I think I can handle it."

"Don't *think*. I need to know you can do this."

"Jesus, Rex. I can handle it."

Josh was entirely out of the carrier now and causally walked around, taking in his temporary home. He batted at something on the floor. Rex bent to see what the cat had found and was now chewing—a green octagon die, something from a geeky role-playing game.

"Pip. What if he swallowed this?"

"I will handle the cat. Don't worry. We'll be fine."

"Anything happens to Josh, and it's your ass."

"Got it. So, I read your interview."

"What did you think?"

"You serious about all this Cain Consequence crap?"

"It's real. You know I have a hell of a memory."

"Well, it depends. When I owe you money, it's great; if you owe me, your memory sucks."

Josh let out a meow and jumped on a chair.

"I told the truth," Rex said.

"You know what my grandfather used to say? 'Never let the truth get in the way of a good story.'" Pip said.

Rex rose with a grunt and scratched Josh behind the ear.

"You don't give Pip here any shit, or he'll eat you," Rex said to the cat. He turned to Pip and said: "Anything happens to this cat- "

"I know…it's my ass. Relax, I got this. Find Cain. Get to the truth. Have fun."

Rex did not think fun would have any place in his upcoming journey.

* * *

As he finished packing, his mother was in near hysterics. Stu sat beside his bags and waited for his ride. He looked straight out the window, avoiding his mother's eyes.

"I do not like this, Stuey, not one bit," Brandy said.

"Mom, stop worrying."

"I hope this is not about my being sick. I am fine, you know."

"It's not. I have to do this."

"Is this about Feldman's death?"

"No," Stu said.

"And why won't you tell me who's going with you? This trip is crazy."

"It's not important. After this trip, I will write a piece to put the website over the top. Then everything will be fine."

Stu was grateful for the distraction of a horn blowing four long, obnoxious blasts from the driveway.

He grabbed his bags and ran out the door; Brandy followed.

"This is who you're going with? Oh no!"

***

It took a lot to make a man like Barclay Cain uneasy, but Zack and The Bat sure came close. Already, he was witness to the evidence of his jumping. Anytime he used his power, there were ramifications. A woman with two heads, who had been a normal, even attractive, lady moments ago, passed him, drinking a bottle of water and passing it between her two heads. The "brothers" had been one man (Zachary Battenberg) before Cain's arrival. Now, they wandered around in confusion. Having had one person's intellect divided between them, they needed to work together to accomplish the simplest of tasks.

They were now Zack and the Bat. Zack was a thin, ridiculously tall man, and The Bat, conversely, was a fat, round man of about two feet. The little guy resembled Uncle Fester—a bald, pale man with a simple smile permanently plastered on his befuddled face. His lanky "brother" was equally pale but had a thick head of slicked-back hair, black as coal. They both wore long wool coats, which appeared from the Civil War era, complete with intricate gold buttons down the side. Battenberg (as a singular being) had once been a prominent investment banker.

While Cain regretted how his bouncing realities affected others, shit happened. He was ready to regain control of the Lands, his rightful position. But first, he needed a team. He strode over to Zack and The Bat.

"Gentlemen…how would you like to earn some money and be a part of a great paradigm shift?"

The two peculiar men looked at one another.

"I will handle this, brother," Zack said.

"No, I will do the talking," said The Bat.

"This stranger does not want to speak to a human bowling ball!"

"Oh, but he will speak with a piece of spaghetti?"

Even though these men were arguing, they were speaking as one—both saying the words of himself and his sibling.

"Gentleman, please. I will speak with you both. Are you interested in making money?"

"What kind of money are you offering, and for what," Zack and The Bat said in unison. They even moved together, one soul in two bodies. Cain did his best to explain. Did they recognize him?

"You're familiar with the infinite monkey theorem?" Cain asked.

"Of course—a monkey hitting keys at random on a typewriter for an infinite amount of time will almost surely type any given text, such as the complete works of William Shakespeare," the creepy brothers said.

"Exactly. However, this is only part of the equation. Along with a replica of Romeo and Juliet, there will be infinite versions remarkably close, say one character off.

And this is what people are experiencing now. A *version* of their reality with minute changes. Some are so slight that they never even notice they have shifted into a changed reality."

"Where do we start?"

"First, I need a place to set up shop."

***

January 8th. Elvis's birthday (a day that was not a national holiday, and this pissed Rex off to no end). An excellent omen to leave on such a day. He pulled up to the Sawyer residence. Johnny Cash crooned over the nosy engine, singing how no matter what women came and went, he was born to be a "Solitary Man." Just like Rex Dolan.

Rex sat in the driver's seat of his Mustang like a king, cigarette dangling from his lips, sunglasses hanging off his nose, and gave four long blasts of the horn. The door to the house opened, and the geek who had recently interviewed him came running with an overloaded backpack. A busty brunette woman followed.

"This is who you're going with. Oh no!" the woman said.

"And what *do* we have here..."

The woman held a little terrier and was kissing its ears and paws. Rex thought of Josh. He hoped Pip and the cat were getting along. The woman was falling out of her tiny dress, thick in all right places. She pulled a pack of smokes from her bosom.

"Stuey, slow down," she said.

"Damn, bet there's gold in them thar hills!"

Brandy Sawyer must have been a D-cup. She searched for a match. Rex flipped his Sun Records Zippo and offered the flame.

Brandy took the light. Rex closed the lighter with a cool snap. Stu's mom was unimpressed. Rex removed his sunglasses.

"How are you, sweetheart?"

"What a classless animal," Brandy said, blowing smoke to the side. She left a bright ring on the filter.

"I'm an animal in bed, sister."

"I'm Stuey's mom. You had better not get him in any trouble, or you'll answer to me. Got it?"

"Mom!"

"Hot damn. What a firecracker. And you," Rex said, turning to Stu, hand out, "gas money."

Stu dug through his pockets and handed Rex a few wrinkled bills.

"Here you go."

"Damn, Stu, you should've told me your mother was stacked like this. I would have suggested she come along."

"Listen here, jerk. I don't like this trip, not one bit. You look like trouble to me," Brandy Sawyer said.

"Oh, I'm trouble, sister. You can count on that. You look like you could use a little trouble in your life."

"You need a lesson in manners. That's what you need."

"Oh, I got what you need," Rex said softly, leaning out the Mustang's window like James Dean.

"Dear lord."

"Don't 'dear lord' me, lady. You don't look much like a churchgoer to me. What's up with that?"

"This is a good place. It's a good place for Stuey."

"C'mon, Stu is a grown man. You can't mother him forever. But I sure wouldn't mind you mothering me for a while. How about a little kiss?"

"I wouldn't kiss you if you were pure oxygen and I were suffocating."

"But you're kissing the paws of that dog, and I bet he just got done rolling turds around in the backyard."

"His paws are cleaner than your mouth."

As if in response, a long, low growl emanated from the terrier, a precursor to a bark. His little face twisted as if mad at Rex for taking Stu away. Rex thought of Josh again. He already missed the little bastard.

Stu went around the back of the Mustang to put his duffle in the trunk, avoiding his mother's eyes.

Brandy hugged her son closely.

"Goddamn, I'm jealous. I wish I were in those mountains!"

"Don't you blaspheme."

"Do you know who I am? I'm a TV star."

"Please. *Happy Jack.* Are you kidding? I would rather watch *Alf.* And I guess many others agree, seeing as *Alf* lasted much longer than your show."

"Actually, *Happy Jack* was on for- "

"Oh yeah, that's right. In another reality, it lasted a lot longer. I read the interview. In another reality, I am married to Brad Pitt."

"Mom!" Stu said.

"Let's roll, Stu. Let's find this Cain character."

"Barclay Cain! That's who you are going to see?"

"It's okay, mom."

Rex had a tough time looking away from Brandy as she hugged Stu goodbye again. Finally, they took off.

Rex pushed at his hard-on. He grabbed the crotch of his jeans and made room for his woody.

"Are you playing a game of two-ball," Stu laughed.

"Nah, kid. Just checking out my prick. I wear my dick on the right side, and it jumped over to the left. You wanna fix it for me?"

"No thanks."

"Good. Now zip it!"

This is going to be a long ride, Stu thought.

***

Bubby was three-quarters drunk when he made his way to a new bar. He had no hard time drinking regularly, but he hardly drew a sober breath for the last two days, the creepy little clown from the other night still in his mind's eye. He was done. Bubby Boutique Gags was his final swing at the plate. It was over.

Bubby parked his Oldsmobile by a massive pile of garbage bags at the curb and walked several blocks before settling on a bar. He entered the pub. Loud, aggressive music played. The bar was mostly empty. The place stunk of stale beer and dead dreams. Perfect. There was a musty dampness to the pub one could practically taste. A monster of a man stood behind the bar. Three tough customers sat at the far end, sneering at him through a haze of blue smoke. These were not the same cast of characters who usually awaited him. The crazy curse was broken!

Bubby walked deeper into the bar and stopped. The clown was here.

"No women. Only white men," said the clown.

"What is this? Are you following me?

"Yeah. *I* am following *you,* but I get to where you are going *before* you. Does that make any sense?"

Bubby didn't bother answering. He figured he was stuck with the midget clown. They approached the bar, and the large bald man eyed them skeptically.

"Two *cerveza*," said the clown as he struggled onto a stool.

"*Cerveza,* you say? Well, fuck me sideways. Let me see some ID," the pock-faced, muscled beast said.

"What bullshit," the clown said, but Bubby stopped him and, despite being in his sixties, pulled out his license and handed it to the man behind the bar.

"We're just looking for a couple of beers, guys," Bubby said, shuffling through his pockets for cash. A rabbit's foot, a packet of itch powder, and the nickel/nail gag fell from his pocket.

"Why are you in here," the barkeep growled, looking at the license, "*Ira*?"

"I'm sorry…."

"Ira?" one of the other men said.

"Fuck me. 'Ira Goldenblatt,'" Pock-Face laughed.

"Call me Bubby."

"I'll call you an undertaker, you Jew bastard."

"What?"

"You and this little beaner here are in Nazi Land," he said, smiling. The men from the end of the bar rose from their stools and slowly strolled over.

"You know what, I think I will leave," Bubby said.

One man went to the door and locked it. He took a long pull off the can of cheap beer.

"It's a little late for that."

All the men held cans of the same beer; all had the bellies to testify how much they liked said beer.

"Look, the Lands are changing all the time now. It's an easy mistake. I'll leave." Bubby said.

It made sense everyone had abandoned this place. After the Great Secession, many reported there was a Nazi Land, but no one knew where to find it (as if anyone in his right mind wanted to find Nazi Land). Like many of the Lands, it occasionally shifted—one of the glitches of the Cain Consequence. Some time ago, all the Neo-Nazis had moved to Nazi Land, but they eventually turned on one another, with no one left to hate. The blonds turned on their dark-haired brethren, claiming superiority. Rumor was that only the most rabid and hate-filled people remained in Nazi Land. Leave it to Bubby to find his way into a bar here.

One Nazi, a painfully skinny man with huge teeth and yellow eyes, looked to the man behind the bar—their leader, presumably.

"I'll take care of him for you. I'll show 'em. Let me cornhole 'em! I'll cornhole that Jew-boy, but good!"

"Relax," the barkeep said to his excited friend.

"I wanna cornhole his ass. I'll do it for you. That'll teach him to wander into Nazi Land."

"Easy, let me think."

"I'll cornhole 'em both, no problem."

"What the hell are you so into this for?" Pock-Face asked his friend.

"Huh? I'm not *into* it. But I'll do it, no problem."

"You're always looking to cornhole everyone. I'd say you're into it."

"No, I'm not into it. It's to show dominance—not sexual. A power thing," he said, yet he appeared to be trying to convince himself more than anyone else.

"Cornhole? You mean make-a-fuckie on me?" The clown asked.

"Yeah, boy. I'm gonna 'make-a-fuckie' on your little ass," the man said, bobbing on his heels with excitement. He undid his jeans. He stood there with a hard-on in his hands, looking to his leader, like a dog looking at his master, waiting for the okay to eat.

"Oh, fuck it. Have at it," the barkeep said.

The man's face widened. He moved toward the clown.

There was a sound like fabric tearing. The man gasped. He stepped back a pace. Two.

"What the hell is-". Then his face went slack. The man grabbed at his crotch. Blood, thick as syrup, poured from between his fingers.

"Are you looking for this?" the clown asked, throwing the man's member on the bar with the sickening sound of raw meat hitting a platter, a bloody knife in his other hand.

One of the other Nazis made a move and squealed, holding his stomach, his intestines falling in grotesque pink-white loops to the ground. Pock-Face ducked behind the bar and appeared holding a .38, pointed it right in the clown's face, and pulled the trigger, but the pistol jammed. He dropped the pistol and ran for the door. The clown threw three small knives into his back before the man was a third of the way to the door. Pock-Face slid lifelessly to the floor. The last Nazi froze for a moment, all the color draining from his already pale face. Then he stiffened, clasped his heart, and fell to the ground with the dead thud of a sack of manure.

The clown managed himself behind the bar, tossed the slick knife on the counter, and drew a beer.

"Those knives. Your size. You're *him*," Bubby said.

"Tuco is my name."

"I'm the one who freed you. I freed a killer."

"You want a beer before I kill you?"

Bubby had no desire to be "gutted" but accepted the beer.

"You disguise yourself as a clown...smart."

So, this was the guy he had freed with the *To Catch a Killer* show. Was it not poetic justice he should die at this man's knife? But what were the odds of Bubby meeting *this* man again? More than mere coincidence. But more importantly than existential questions—how would he get out of this in one piece?

Tuco came back from around the bar to face Bubby. Bubby went into his coat pocket and grabbed the first thing his hand found to use as a weapon—a rubber chicken.

He slapped Tuco in the neck with the chicken. It did nothing in the way of a weapon. However, the blow rendered Tuco off-guard for a moment. A ghost appeared in the corner of the bar—an emaciated man in baggy underwear. The rubber chicken was a cursed item made in the haunted factory. The spirit screamed and regarded the front of his stained underwear with disgust.

"My asshole is on fire! My balls burn!"

Buddy observed the ghost of a man who likely died of syphilis sometime before Fleming had invented penicillin.

"*Fantasma*," Tuco said.

"My balls are raw." The ghost cried.

Tuco took a step away from the apparition and howled in pain—he'd stepped on the upended nickel/nail Bubby had dropped moments before while nervously rummaging through his pockets. Tuco lifted his foot. The nickel was flush against the sole of his sneaker—the nail entirely in his foot. The clown hopped as he picked at the nickel.

Bubby took the moment and ran for the door. He grabbed the knob. Locked! He fumbled with the latch and got out as several little knives stuck into the door jam. He ran the three blocks to his Oldsmobile. He jumped in and took off.

***

Tuco limped and jumped out the door in time to see Bubby pass in his Oldsmobile, black smoke pouring from its rear. He plucked the damn nail from his foot and went back into the bar for another drink. He looked at the floor where Bubby had dropped something other than the nail— a small slip of paper.

> *I am leaving with a kid named Stu Sawyer. We will go through every dam Land until we find Haunted Land.*
> *If you mean business, I will see you there.*
> *~Rex Dolan*

"Haunted Land," Tuco said to himself. "I'm going there, too. Bubby, you're a dead man."

***

They had not been long on the road before Stu bugged Rex to stop for food and use the bathroom.

"Boy, you complain a lot."

"I do not," Stu said.

"No breaks. Relax, kid, or you're in for a rough ride."

"C'mon, pull over."

"Don't be such a bitch," Rex said.

"But- "

"No buts. What we got going on here is a men's road trip, sweetheart," Rex said as he tilted the review mirror and combed his hair.

"Watch the road."

"I got it covered. Don't be such a pussy."

"Don't call me that," Stu said, his voice rising.

"Ha! Easy. Simmer down."

"This car is a mess. It smells."

"Jeez, you're a dainty little thing, huh?"

Stu noticed Rex was regarding him with disapproval.

"What?"

"What are you supposed to be, Bert or Ernie?"

"Huh?"

"Look at the way you're dressed."

Stu looked at his jeans, red Converse sneakers, and striped shirt. Stu was aware he looked younger than his twenty-one years. He knew he looked like a kid.

"I'm comfortable."

"Comfort has nothing to do with it, my man. Me, I'm built for speed. And look at that haircut."

"What about it?"

"It's all uneven. Where did you get that butcher job?"

"I cut my own hair."

"Shit, I should have known."

"Pull over, please."

"Negative."

"But I have to go."

"I got an empty beer can in the back—piss in that."

"But I have to…go number *two*."

"For Christ's sake, can't you fart it out for now?"

"'Fart it out?'" Stu asked.

"Yeah, honey. Fart around the turd for now."

"That makes no sense."

"Not pulling over," Rex said, eyes glued straight on the road ahead.

Stu wondered what in the hell he'd gotten himself into. After a few minutes of wonderful silence, Rex spoke.

"Have you seen any signs of any other Lands?"

"There won't be a sign."

"Not a sign like a road sign. *Signs*."

"No, but we will know it when we see it. We will *feel* it."

"So, Stu, when was the last time you got laid?"

"I don't think that's any of your business."

"That means you ain't had no ass in a loooong time."

"Not that. I don't kiss and tell."

"C'mon, man, we've got a lot of road ahead. We have to talk."

"Okay, but can we talk about something normal?"

"What's more normal than a couple of men discussing getting laid?"

"My ex-girlfriend, I guess that was the last time."

"If you have to *guess* about it, it's been too long, brother."

"Maybe."

"Maintain," Rex said as he let go of the wheel and turned around to grab a beer from the back seat.

"What the- "

"Maintain, mother fucker. Handle the wheel while I get situated."

Stu held the steering wheel steady as Rex opened his beer and lit a cigarette. Rex resumed control of the wheel. He was quiet momentarily, and then Rex's head bounced around in all directions, searching for a portal.

"Nothing."

"I don't think you know your way…we're lost."

"There is no way, kid. We're-."

"A portal! Right here," Stu said.

"Huh, right or left?"

"Left."

"A left here?"

"Right."

"Oh…."

Rex swerved to the right.

"It's a left."

"You said 'right'!"

"Right. You asked, 'left here,' and I said 'right'".

"Right, you said 'right.'"

"I said 'right' to the left!"

"What are you babbling about?"

"Going forward, let's say 'correct' rather than 'right'?"

"Going forward, keep your piehole shut."

Stu rubbed his temples as the threat of a migraine teased in the deep recesses of his brain. No matter—they found a portal. To what Land was anyone's guess.

***

Julia Faith needed money or could not make this month's rent. With Bruja gone, she would have to eat the whole thing. So she had lined up an odd job to make a little extra cash. A man named Bubby had contacted her and asked if she would authenticate a rare book of witchcraft. She arrived at the Pub Land bookstore, where they agreed to meet.

Upon entering the bookstore, there was a commotion, and she watched as two workers tried to calm a chubby, scruffy man. While it was common to see arguments in Pub Land, the man did not look like a troublemaker. He was crying about a book he was holding.

"Tom Sawyer, for Christ's sake. Are you saying you're not familiar with the book *The Adventures of Tom Sawyer*?"

"Never heard of a book with that title. And honestly, it sounds made-up," the condescending young girl behind the counter said, rolling her eyes.

Julia approached the man, knowing this was the guy she was meeting to authenticate a book. Bubby told her his story.

One of Bubby's endeavors had been finding rare books to flip for profit. He'd tracked a first edition of *The Adventures of Tom Sawyer* in close-to-mint condition. He had several potential buyers, one of whom owned one of the last remaining bookstores in Pub Land—this bookstore. But this morning, he'd found the book had changed. Rather than *The Adventures of Tom Sawyer* by Mark Twain, the book was now a ridiculous thing called *The Life and Times of a Schmuck on Wheels* by Alan Smithe. Not only was the novel of the self-proclaimed schmuck not worth the paper on which it was printed, but Tom Sayer had been erased from the world. Research proved Samuel Clemons had never become Mark Twain. Clemons had lived and died a boatman, having never put pen to paper in this reality. But worst of all was a horrible song the band Rush had now recorded in 1981, also titled "Schmuck on Wheels." Bubby had listened in disbelief at the changed song:

A modern-day idiot,
A Schmuck on Wheels
Today is this putz,
mean, mean deal.

After the initial shock, Bubby thought of writing Tom Sawyer himself (the book, not the song), but he couldn't remember much of the story.

Another of the rare books Bubby had come into possession of was the fabled *Necronomicon*. This book, mercifully, remained unchanged. Bubby needed help authenticating the book and contacted the witch.

"Bubby, you have an original copy of the *Necronomicon*?"

"I'm hoping you can tell me."

They sat at a table and ordered lattes. An effeminate-looking man took their order. Bubby looked in his bag to ensure the book had not morphed into something else since this morning. The book remained unchanged, and he handed the book to her.

"Wow."

Julia leafed through a few pages. She checked the inside covers. As she was appraising the book, Bubby checked out *The Life and Times of a Schmuck on Wheels*. Julia looked at the book that should not exist in Bubby's hands.

"I never heard of that one."

"What about *The Adventures of Tom Sawyer*?"

"Of course."

"Do you notice other…changes?"

And that's how Bubby Goldenblatt and Julia Faith realized they were alike.

The man returned with their drinks.

Julia looked at *Schmuck On Wheels* by Alan Smithe. Being a film buff, Julia knew the name Alan Smithe. Smithe had directed more films than Spielberg and Scorsese put together. But Julia informed Bubby that Alan Smithe was the pseudonym many directors used when making a film to which they did not want their names attached. However, now he was an actual person, an author as well as a filmmaker.

"Look, Julia, I'm not a weirdo…you're young enough to be my daughter. But let's team up. I'm heading to Haunted Land and looking for Cain and answers. I met a guy in a bar a few nights ago. He's also going.

She considered leaving and trying to find the truth with this stranger. A crazy thing to consider. But as a film buff, she could not help but notice this reality now had the *Weekend at Bernie's* trilogy released by the Criterion Collection (these movies were now considered arthouse classics). She knew someone had to stop this madness.

"You are seriously going to look for Barclay Cain?"

"Yes."

"I have been looking for another person who noticed the changes for a long time. What are the chances we find each other like this?"

"I agree."

They decided to go together.

They went to both of their places and packed. However, Bubby's Oldsmobile died before they could even get going.

"We'll take my vehicle," Julia said.

They doubled back and got Julia's moped.

"Are you kidding? Will it hold me?" Bubby asked.

"We'll be fine," Julia said, placing a bright pink helmet on her head.

The moped begged for mercy, crawling because of the added weight, but it held as Julia and Bubby headed out to find answers.

CHAPTER SEVEN

The portal danced before them, a glowing beacon to a new adventure. The radiant oval was in the middle of a horde of trees that looked impossible to penetrate.

"Can we drive through this?" Stu asked.

"I can drive through anything," Rex said but removed his sunglasses and regarded the portal skeptically.

"Let's do this," Stu said.

"Fuckin'-A."

Rex checked his phone and was not surprised to see no service. He looked at Stu, whose phone was equally useless.

"I wanted to call my mother," Stu said.

Rex didn't say anything but wanted to call Pip and make sure Josh was okay.

"Stop worrying about mommy. It's go-time, kid."

"Try not to become disoriented. Each Land is its own microcosm and can confuse you until you adjust. The Lands shift and move, so it will be impossible to know what Land we are entering now," Stu said.

"I've been through this, too, junior," Rex said. But the truth was that Rex had never left '80 Land. Stu, too, had never been out of Church Land but knew this from research he'd done for his site.

Rex inched the Mustang forward, and the trees shifted ever so slightly. A bush trembled. Then, the trees before them parted, not unlike the entrance to a car wash. However, they entered a cave of bushes and trees rather than brushes and soap. Eventually, a clearing opened to a street. Rex hit the accelerator. Stu's head swam as they entered. But the re-orienting process took less time than he'd thought.

The bushes and trees at the entrance quickly gave way to more urban surroundings. Rex made a series of random turns. Finally, they found themselves in a populated area. Rex parked the Mustang and got out.

"Let's check it out, kid."

***

Brandy Sawyer checked the time—why was this taking so long? The normally ten-minute drive to the grocery store on Catholic Street was taking forever. Why? There was no traffic or accidents, nothing slowing her commute. At first, she thought she might have taken a wrong turn; indeed, her mind was elsewhere. However, she was passing all the usual landmarks.

She'd gone to her doctor's appointment first, and, as she'd predicted, they were entirely out of options. At only fifty-one, she was not ready to pack it in. Truthfully, she had yet to even find herself. The many doctors she had seen had different things to say—medical jargon about treatments, medications, etc. However, in the end, they had all said the exact two words: *malignant* and *inoperable*. Brandy Sawyer did not have a medical degree but knew when a doctor (or four, as it were) paired these two words together, it was time to begin looking for a deal on a coffin.

The doctor handed her a few pamphlets on how to discuss her prognosis with her family and how to take care of "final arrangements." *Final arrangements. Final costs.* A sweet way of saying *you need to plan your death.* There was a lot to do: financial stuff, legal crap, plans for the house. Even dying was a pain in the ass. She figured in death, as in life, men had it easier. All a man had to do was delete all the porn off his computer and drop dead.

Her mind went to other matters. *How long would Stu be gone*, she thought. Stu may have been twenty-one years of age, but he was still recovering from the traumatic loss of his friend and what Dr. Duben called "survivor's guilt." What was he doing searching for different Lands with a narcissistic sociopath and looking for Barclay Cain? All utterly ridiculous.

"What's going on?" she asked herself. "Where is the damn store?" After over half an hour, she pulled into the familiar parking lot and did her shopping. The ride home took precisely eight minutes and forty-two seconds. What had happened? Had time shifted just as Stu had said it could? Was there actually something to all the hocus pocus he believed?

Brandy Sawyer was putting away the last of the groceries when there was a knock at the door.

＊＊＊

Julia pulled the moped to the side of the road—a Porta-Potty! Her bladder had gotten heavy miles ago, but she had not been able to find anywhere to go.

"I need to pee. Do you have to go?" Julia asked.

"No, I'm good," Bubby said. "But it's been good to stretch out my legs."

Julia opened the door expecting the worst, but the potty was surprisingly tidy. She lowered her jeans and pink panties and sat. Someone had written on Porta-Potty's wall in black marker.

Are you a rich white girl who needs to get back at Daddy? Is Daddy holding on to your trust fund? Do you want to show him what you can do if he does not get his shit together? Well-hung black man for hire. Piss off, Daddy. Show Daddy what's in store if he does not give you your way. Bring this thick dick nigga home! 718-big-black.

"What the hell?"

And the ghostly voice whispered in Julia's ear.

"This is my home. I died here. This is my shithouse. Get out!"

Julia's pee sprayed a fountain of warmth on her knees as she screamed and struggled to her feet. She zipped her jeans and went for the handle only to find the door had disappeared; the wall was now only smooth, uniform plastic. She pounded a dull hollow drum on the walls.

"Get out of my shithouse!"

"Help," Julia cried.

"Julia, are you okay?"

"I can't get out; there's a ghost in here!"

"I am a ghost, alright. And that was my writing. One of the girl's fathers killed me. Shot me dead right here in this shithouse. Now I am a thick dick nigga with no one to dick."

"Bubby, get me out of here."

Bubby fumbled with the door and stopped. A ghost? How would he fight a spirit? He backed off and had to think.

"Bubby!"

But after a moment, Julia had succeeded in kicking out a panel of the Porta-Potty and escaped. She got on the moped, and they took off. What the hell had happened? Was something trying to stop them from getting close to Haunted Land? After a few moments, Bubby broke the silence.

"I'm sorry. I panicked and was no help to you."

"It's okay."

"No…it isn't. Julia, you need to know something about me before we get too deep into this thing."

"What?"

Bubby paused. When he spoke, his voice was small.

"I'm a coward."

"Bubby, I don't believe that."

"No, I need to come clean. I'm a coward through and through."

"I don't care about your past. We are on a new journey. We are renewing ourselves and will become what our destiny has always wanted us to be. I trust you, Bubby. You're no coward. Anyway, a haunted Porta-Potty, we must be close."

"You're a good kid, Julia," Bubby said as they rode on, never noticing the green sedan following them.

***

Tuco could hardly believe his luck as he watched Bubby leave a bar and hit the road. The idiot clung to the back of a scooter, and a girl, her hair and clothes all colors of the rainbow, drove. He had to think fast.

"You have a car, Jetter?" he asked the degenerate with whom he was drinking.

"The name is *Jenkins*. Worrall Jenkins."

"Well, *Jenkins*, do you have a car?"

"Uh, yeah."

"Let's go for a ride."

"I don't think so."

"You don't feel like getting laid?" Tuco asked and grinned broadly.

***

Worrall Jenkins was never one to make sound decisions. His love of drink and excitement usually led him into trouble of one kind or another. He'd met the little clown in a dive bar a few hours earlier and now was driving the tiny creep with the promise of women. Jenkins never said no to an offer too good to be true, no matter how many times it turned out to be just that.

"Are these ladies…are they...er...small, like you?"

"No, they are full-sized," Tuco lied—there were no women, full-sized or otherwise.

"Oh, too bad. I wouldn't mind a little lady," Jenkins said through a grin of diseased teeth.

Tuco put a Newport in his lips and opened the glovebox, looking for a match, but found the compartment full of nothing but yo-yos. Yo-yos of all sizes and colors, strings tangled like worms in a tackle box.

"What the hell is this?"

"Oh yeah, that's what I do."

"Do?"

"Yes…professionally."

"You use yo-yos professionally?"

"Yes. I'm a professional *yo-yologyst*."

"A what?"

"A yo-yologyst. I yo-yo professionally."

"And you make a living doing this?"

"Well, truthfully, it doesn't pay well. It does not pay at all, actually. But I sure do love yo-yos."

"Wonderful."

"Want me to pull over and show you how I rock the cradle or walk the dog?"

"No, I don't want to see any of that stupid shit. Keep driving."

"Yo-yos are not stupid."

"I can't think of anything stupider."

Jenkins sipped from a bottle of E&J.

"Which way," Jenkins asked.

"Follow the moped. And hand me the bottle of Easy Jesus."

"So, my little friend, what was the best piece of pussy you've ever had?"

"Huh?"

"The best. Tell me about it," Jenkins said, sweat forming on his upper lip. "And don't leave anything out."

"You want to know the truth?"

"Yeah, yeah! Tell me."

"The best piece of pussy I have ever had was this little light-skinned Puerto Rican mother fucker in jail," Tuco said.

"Say what?" Jenkins said. He must have misheard the clown.

"You heard me, Americano. Son-of-a-bitch called me *papi* and everything."

That stopped Jenkins's sex talk. The man now only looked at the road ahead, knuckles white on the steering wheel. Finally, after a long and painful silence, he spoke again.

"Oh. But you're taking us to *women* now, right?"

"The best you've ever seen."

The road before them shone. The portal to another land was upon them. The moped with Bubby and the girl went through the portal.

"That's another land. I'm not going through—who knows where we'll end up," Jenkins said.

Tuco shifted his arm, and the knife fell into his hand and was at Jenkins's throat instantly.

"Please-" the man started, but the words caught in his throat. So was Tuco's knife. Tuco left the car in time not to get caught in the hot spray of blood.

CHAPTER EIGHT

The damn place stunk of semen and disinfectant. A young man stood here. He'd edged his hair, beard, and eyebrows flawlessly, giving him the look of something fake, a magazine-airbrushed idea of man rather than something born of a mother. It took a moment for Stu to realize the man was completely naked as he was covered from neck to ankles in tattoos. His colossal penis, which hung to his knee, was also tattooed. His perfect teeth and the whites of his eyes were tinted blue from all the Viagra he had abused.

"Hey, welcome to Porn Land."

"Fuckin'-A," Rex said, lighting a Camel.

"I'm Lance Tagger, mayor of Porn Land," the curious man said and pointed to a sign:

> *Welcome to Porn Land*
> *Lance Tagger: Mayor*
> *Woody Hardon: Treasurer*
> *Dick N. Bush: Chief of Operations*

Lance extended his hand.

"Sorry, braugh, I ain't shaking your hand," Rex said.

"Are you guys passing through or staying?"

"Just passing through," Stu said.

"Holdup, Stu. Let's see the ladies here and not be too hasty," Rex said.

"Well, if you're looking to make a home here, we require you to bring a woman," Lance said. His half-hard-on bounced as he spoke.

"Shit, if I had a woman with me, I wouldn't be looking to stay here, buddy."

"Well…you know…you look like a power-bottom. We may be able to use you. Have you got a contract yet?"

"What are you babbling about? What's a power-bottom?" Rex asked.

"For our all-male films. You could be a great bottom."

"Are you fucked? And even if I *were* queer, I would be a goddamn top!"

"Oh no. We have too many tops as it is. Why be a top? If you are only a top, you may as well be straight."

"I *am* straight, you cock-knocker!"

"C'mon, friend. I'm looking you over, and there is no way you're *all* straight."

"The fuck I ain't!"

Two Asian men approached. Stu was happy to see these guys, at least, wearing clothes.

The mayor introduced them as Long Wang and Mi Dong Hang Lo.

"These guys are our Asian twinks."

"Is this guy a new power-bottom?" Long Wang asked Lance, pointing to Rex.

"Screw this noise. C'mon, Stu, let's move."

They left the mayor and continued driving through Porn Land. After a few miles, Stu complained.

"Rex, I'm hungry."

"Let's get to another Land first. I don't want to eat here!"

"I'm hungry. I'm starving!"

"Power-bottom! I ain't *all* straight! What kind of shit was that?" Rex said to himself.

"Rex, I'm hungry."

"Balls, Stu! I heard you. How about a tube steak smothered in underwear?" Rex asked, clutching his crotch.

"I'm going to faint."

"We only had breakfast a couple of hours ago."

"Right...*hours* ago."

As if on cue, they approached a building shaped like a colossal cheeseburger with a sign reading: *Cheeky Chong's Cheeseburgers.*

"Cheeky Chong's! Cheeky Chong's! Chee-"

"Shut up!"

"But I'm *starving.*"

"Oh for Christ's sake," Rex cried, pulling into a parking spot.

"Hell yeah!"

"You better have cash 'cause I ain't paying."

They parked in the dark parking lot and entered. Once inside, Rex realized Cheeky Chong's Cheeseburgers was a themed burger joint. A *transvestite* theme. The Human League's "Don't You Want Me" blasted through the sound system. Rex, at least, knew this song. He loved this song, in fact, but he would never admit to it.

Stu took no notice of the crossdressers, slid into the booth, and buried his face in a menu.

"What in Christ kind of place is this?"

"Who cares."

An announcement came across the PA: *"Table for two. Three-Ball Billy and Dick Rubbin."*

All the pardons were in incredible physical shape and covered in tattoos like their mayor. An obese crossdresser came over in a flaming red wig and fishy-colored rainbow dress.

"Hi, boys. I'm Sissy. Can I start you hunks off with something to drink?"

"Christ, Sissy. You're a big bitch, huh? How about getting ol' Rex here a beer—hold the AIDS," Rex said. Sissy took a step back and regarded Rex with icy disapproval.

"We don't joke about that here in Porn Land, you dick."

"Ha! Dick. You like dick, huh?"

"Shit, Rex. Knock it off. I'm starving. You'll get us kicked out of here before we even eat." Stu said.

"Don't worry, sweetie," Sissy said, running a long pink nail under Stu's chin. "Sissy here has thick skin to assholes like your friend."

"Yeah, I bet you like 'em thick."

"Christ, Rex!"

"Rex? A hick name for a hick little boy. Nice hair," Sissy laughed.

"What?" Rex asked.

"God, that hair. Does it double as a helmet?"

"What's wrong with my hair?" Rex asked, running a hand across his stiff mane. Glancing around, he noticed how different his hair was from all the other men in the diner. They all had short, carefully edged, perfect hair, like their eyebrows and the beards of those who sported them.

"These guys all look like fags," Rex said.

"Yeah, well, the '80s called, and they want their homophobe back. Wait, tell me you're from '80s Land," Sissy laughed.

"Yeah, so what?" Rex answered. Sissy yelled across the room: "Diamond, get over here…you're not going to believe this."

Another crossdresser came over, as thin as her friend was plump. She wore a pink wig and matching satin jumpsuit.

"Well, look at these two," Diamond said.

"Leave the little one alone; he's sweet. But get a load of this one," Sissy said, pointing to Rex.

"OMG. He's wearing *black* jeans!"

"And a fanny pack!"

"What am I a goddamn joke here?" Rex said.

"What will you have?"

"I see here the *porn stud deluxe.* I'll have that," Rex said, pointing to the menu.

"And I will have your largest burger," Stu said.

Sissy went to put in the order, but Diamond stayed behind.

"Can I do something for you?" Rex asked.

"Maybe."

Rex turned to Stu.

"Eat fast, and we're out of here. Let's find Cain and get this crap all sorted out."

"Cain?" Diamond asked. "I knew it. You guys are looking for Barclay Cain."

"Don't worry about it. My buddy and I have business here. *Dangerous* business." Rex said.

"Is this all about the Cain Consequence?" Diamond asked.

"How did you know-"

"It's about nothing," Rex said, cutting Stu off.

"Oh. Because many conspiracy theorists believe Cain is here. Well, not in Porn Land but…." Diamond said.

"What do you know?" Stu asked.

"I don't *know* anything. Are you boys with the Cult of Change?" Diamond asked.

"Rex Dolan is not with anyone, honey."

"What do you know about all this," Stu asked.

"I notice changes, too. Tell me what you know," Diamond said.

"We can't say," Stu said.

"Can I come along? I want to find out what's going on, too."

"No way," Rex said.

Sissy appeared with their orders. She placed a tiny plate before Stu. The burger was about the size of a half-dollar and made from something resembling bird food.

"Where's the beef?!" Rex laughed. But being he was the only one here from '80s Land, the joke went unnoticed.

"Honey, we don't serve red meat in Porn Land. All the porn stars here need to keep thin. Our burgers contain pea protein, seeds, and sprouts. Served without buns. Carbs, you know. All the burgers are cooked without oil as well. Porn stars hardly eat at all. What if someone has an anal scene?"

"TMI," Stu said.

"Whatever you do, don't order the cream pie for dessert, Stu!" Rex laughed.

Sissy placed a shot of whiskey, a large mug of beer, and a mirror tray, containing what could only be four thick lines of cocaine before Rex.

"Porn Stud Deluxe."

"Holy shit, Sissy. Maybe this place ain't so bad after all. But why is the blow blue?" Rex asked.

"We cut in a little Viagra, of course."

"Shit the bed!" Rex said. He took the shot, did two thick rails in each nostril, grabbed the beer, and downed it in three gulps.

"Fuck me. Another round!"

"Drugs? You're drinking and doing drugs?" Stu said, still examining the "food" before him.

"Put it in park. I know what I'm doing. Stu. You may as well know I have a few vices—the usual suspects. Women, *real* women," he said, looking sideways at Diamond and Sissy, "drugs, booze, gambling, smoking. All real men have vices, kid."

"I don't have any vices."

"That's what you call a sociopath."

"You are a heavy drinker, a drug user, a womanizer, a gambler…you have all the characteristics of the world's great geniuses without the smarts," Stu said.

"Fuck you very much, Stu. Now, Diamond, honey, swing that ass back into the kitchen and let me get another round," Rex said. His mood now much better. He sniffed hard, smiled, ran a finger across the tray, and numbed his gums.

"Sorry, but only one round per customer," Diamond said. "Of course, if you are willing to take me along, I may be able to get you another."

"No way."

"Oh, c'mon. The Mustang you're driving has plenty of room," Sissy said.

"Yeah, sorry, Diamond, but you can't come. I have nothing against your lifestyle. It's only a matter of safety," Stu said.

"Safety?"

"I'd rather not explain," Stu said.

"I think you had better explain," said Diamond.

"Yeah, I'd kind of like to hear this myself," Rex said, sniffing.

"Well trannies, I mean drag-queens, I mean…well, you guys are a fire hazard."

"What?"

"Yeah, you'll go up quickly in a fire. Drag queens are flammable. All those scarves and wigs."

"Who the hell told you that?"

"My pastor."

"Yeah. A fire hazard, see. Stu here is right," Rex said.

Diamond walked away and appeared right away with another beer, shot, and tray. She went around to Rex and rubbed his shoulders.

Rex took the shot. This time, he did one line in each nostril. He dipped a finger in the beer and stuck it in his nose, sniffing hard.

"This is some serious shit."

"C'mon, big boy. Diamond here will make it worth your while. You guys can sleep at my place tonight, and we can leave first thing in the morning. And I have real food at my place," she purred in his ear. Rex froze, the Viagra going to work in his bloodstream.

"Can you ladies give my business associate and me a moment?" Rex asked.

Sissy and Diamond walked away, and Rex leaned into Stu. However, people were at nearby tables, and Rex and Stu went to the men's room to chat.

"Are you kidding me? A bathroom attendant in a diner?" Rex said. Sure enough, an older black man dressed in all white (his dark face in stark contrast to the bright white clothes) stood at a counter of colognes, breath mints, and hair products. Even the man's shoes were a glossy white.

"See this guy here, Stu? This guy is what you call a fly in a glass of milk," Rex said and laughed. The man said nothing, but his bloodshot eyes lasered in on Rex.

"Jesus, Rex!"

The sound of flatulence came from a stall like a machine gun.

"Dude is dropping a duce in that mo-fo."

The attendant approached the stall, put his nose in the stall's door crack, and sniffed.

"What the…"

"Stu, the guy is a shit-sniffer. Perfect job for him. He's addicted to shit stink."

"What have I gotten myself into?"

"Never mind. Let's get to the business at hand. We won't have to sleep in the car tonight," Rex said, went to a urinal, and unzipped.

"Rex, are you nuts? Booze, drugs. And now you want to have sex with her? Or him. I don't know what the right term is anymore."

"What? No! Who's talking about sex? Let's sleep well and eat well. *Eat*, Stu. And Diamond knows something."

"I don't know…." Stu said. But he, too, was reasonably sure Diamond had some information.

"Trust me on this one."

"I know this is a mistake."

"I got this, junior. It's all good."

Rex went to the counter, washed his hands, popped a few mints, splashed some Panty Dropper cologne on his face and neck, and flipped a quarter on the counter. Then, they left the restroom and got back to the table. Diamond and Sissy were still at the server station waiting for them.

"Ladies, come hither," Rex shouted over the music. He did the remaining rails and finished the beer.

"Diamond, you got yourself a deal."

***

Stu promptly passed out on the sofa when they arrived at Diamond's House. Rex and Diamond had a few drinks. After the third double vodka, Diamond talked. She told Rex the Cult of Change, Cain's old crew, was actually trying to *stop* the changes. After the falling out with their disgraced former leader, they saw how misguided they had been.

Was this true? Were the Cult of Change now the good guys? Rex was not sure what to believe. Diamond put on some music.

"Where should we look? No one even knows if Haunted Land exists." Rex asked. He could hear his voice slurring slightly. He found himself thinking Diamond looked surprisingly good. Maybe coming here was a bad idea.

"Well, I don't know about finding Haunted Land—no one knows if it even exists. But Cain is supposed to be in West Land," Diamond said.

"Then I guess we'll go through the Lands until we find West Land," Rex said. "Now, Diamond, honey, how's about another drink?"

***

They were at a turning point, and whichever path they chose would likely ruin someone's life—who knew, in this new world, what the outcomes would be because of their choices? Bubby and Julia had a horrible ride on the moped, but they arrived. They both needed sleep. But first, Julia needed a bathroom again. They searched for a restroom and stumbled upon a kids' soccer game.

Welcome to PC Land

"There must be public bathrooms here," Bubby said. Behind the referee stood a vast wall of trophies.

"Is this a championship game," Bubby asked a father on the sidelines.

"What? No! There are no champions here," the man said, shaking his head.

"What's the score?" Julia asked one of the moms.

The woman turned so quickly that her sporty ponytail flew behind her like a horse's tail.

"What did you ask?"

"Who's winning?"

The mother pulled a whistle from a chain around her neck and blew. The sound was deafening. Within minutes, a group of people surround Julia and Bubby.

"She asked the score," the woman said, pointing to them.

"What is this?" Julia said.

"Who are you all?" Bubby asked the group surrounding them.

"We're security," one man answered.

"But you don't have uniforms," Bubby said.

"We don't wear uniforms; they may intimidate some people. Uniforms show authority and can make people uncomfortable. Now, you cannot ask the score or who's winning. All games end in a tie. What's wrong with you guys?"

"Listen, my friend here needs to use the bathroom. Can you tell us where the ladies' room is?"

"The what?!"

"The woman's room."

"You bastard! There are no gender-specific restrooms here."

Julia and Bubby looked at the growing crowd.

"Go!" Bubby said.

They jumped on the moped, hardly moving quickly enough to outrun the mob on foot. They finally lost the crowd before seeing a door to another Land. Julia drove through.

The doorways from Land to Land were funny things. One could jump through one, end up in a different Land, and get stuck there for hours or a few days before seeing another door. Sometimes, one would immediately find another entrance and jump again within minutes. Luckily for Bubby and Julia, this was one of the latter times. They were, for a moment, in a Land (they were in and out so quickly they did not see a sign with a name) where countless Asian people were singing karaoke.

They drove through another portal.

The sign read:

> *Welcome to Corporate Land: Where the Bottom Line Is King*

Long black streets stretched as far as the eye could see, and towering mirrored business buildings reached into the sky and beyond. The only thing opposing the uniform structures were the ostentatious electronic billboards making the old Times Square look like a country road. There were advertisements for everything and anything but primarily for medications. Pills promising relief of everything from marriage woes to a prescription for a drug, vowing to grant the person the ability to earn more money.

"A pill that makes you earn more money. How?" Bubby said.

Before Julia could answer, they were interrupted by a naked woman who passed out vouchers to bring to your doctor to get a free sample of the pill called *Earnmoreaquil*.

"I don't like this place, Bubby."

"Yeah, me either. Let's see if we can find another Land."

A buzzer rang, and the ground rumbled. The shaking came closer and closer until hundreds of people emerged from the buildings. All were male and wearing identical suits. They all had tiny, skinny bodies with heads at least three times the size nature intended. All had similar Botox smiles frozen on their giant faces. At once, they all spoke but were not having any conversation. Instead, they were all shouting buzzwords, corporate slogans, and stuff not unlike the crap Julia had heard in Motivational Speaker Land.

"Win, win, win!" one of the man-creatures said and bopped on his heels.

"Every dollar I will ever make is right now in someone else's pocket!" a red-haired creature said.

"Whether you believe you can or can't…you are right!"

"The key to success is sincerity; once you can fake that, you have it made."

As the huge-headed monsters noticed Bubby and Julia still on the moped, the creatures approached them.

"Bubby…."

Bubby took Julia's hand. They looked all around. The corporate monsters were closing in.

"Sales! I can sell a Chinaman rice!"

"I can sell stocks to a dead man."

"Over there! A door," Bubby said, pointing to a blur in the distance.

Julia gunned the moped and drove through a portal as it appeared between two of the corporate monsters. They jumped into…

> *Welcome to TV Land, where life imitates mediocre television*

"Oy. TV-Land."

"I hate TV," Julia said. She was thinking of *Cheers, friends!*

"We will get out as soon as we see another door," Bubby said.

The moped coughed and jerked.

"Oh no."

"What?"

"Out of gas," Julia said. Much to her chagrin, the time had come to abandon the moped and walk.

On one corner, two women were cooking on portable stoves. A man stood between them, narrating. "Contestant A is in the lead and on her way to finishing her meal."

The other woman, Contestant B, presumably turned and punched Contestant A in the mouth.

"Oh, and Contestant B is taking things up a notch!"

"Oh my gosh," Julia said.

"Yeah, reality TV is getting worse and worse."

Both women, their meals forgotten, attacked one another. One held a large fork, but she was hit in the face with a hot cast-iron skillet before she could spear the other. The odor of burning skin accompanied her screams.

Bubby and Julia walked on.

A gaggle of intoxicated, middle-aged women passed, cackling uncontrollably. The women were all dressed ostentatiously but clearly from money. A group of fans followed them. The fans wore skirts so short their privates almost showed. All the followers held red Solo cups.

"Reality show housewives," Julia whispered to Bubby.

"Look at the old man with the young girl," a blond said through a face full of plastic surgery.

"You talking to us, bitch?"

"Julia, don't engage them," Bubby said.

"You old pervert," another of the group said.

"Ma'am, if you were twice as smart, you'd be an idiot," Bubby said.

Julia burst out laughing and clapped her hands. The woman flipped Bubby the bird and walked away.

They walked another two blocks undisturbed before bumping into a group of men in camo. The group had a massive cache of electronic gear.

"What are you guys doing? Looks like fun," Julia said.

"We are searching for Bigfoot. Squaching," a bearded man said.

"In the middle of the street? In a city?" Bubby asked.

"We've heard there was activity in these parts –" the man stopped mid-sentence and cupped a hand around his ear.

"Did you hear that?" another of the men asked the bearded leader, though there was no sound. He cupped his hands around his mouth and made a feral sound. They all listened for a response. Of course, none came.

"That way!" the man said, and they all ran, boots clapping the street.

"Amazing. I have tried making TV shows and always failed. These Bigfoot hunters have all kinds of successful shows, and while viewers know they will find nothing in the end, they are always so popular," Bubby said.

"That's true."

"I swear I did it all wrong."

"Poor, Bubby. After this is all over, you will finally find your spot. I know it."

"You're a good girl, Julia."

On the next block, they found a hotel to get some sleep. Bubby insisted on paying for two rooms even though Julia said this was not necessary. They would sleep a few hours and resume exploring. They said goodbye, and Bubby made it as if he were going into his room for the night. Once Julia closed her door, Bubby went in search of a bar. He needed a few drinks before retiring.

***

Haunted Land was not unlike the Bermuda Triangle. However, rather than nestled in the islands in the northwest Atlantic Ocean, Haunted Land was found in a parcel of land between what was once New York and New Jersey— affectingly known as the asshole of the universe. Haunted Land contained every reported haunted home, building, bar, and hotel ever known.

Cain left the creepy Zack and The Bat behind as he checked things out. Here was his secret place. He'd found it over twenty years ago, knowing no one wanted to come here. It was perfect. His brain went cold; there was the presence of ghosts here. Red eyes peered out from the dark (it was always night in Haunted Land). Sounds resembling a cross between a baby crying and a dog's bark echoed from the woods. Most houses here were of the gothic variety, but there was also a demon-infested cottage, a VFW hall run amok with evil imps, and a haunted treehouse full of possessed puppets.

Cain crossed the bridge leading to the building and over the River Black. He opened the office door and wandered around his old stomping grounds. This place was the source of all the power—leave it to the universe to show its irony and make the most vanilla-looking business building the site where its magic was strongest. Most of the doors of this structure led to magic places, Cain remembered from his last visit to this enchanted building. But, learned occultist or not, nothing in this place made sense—even to him.

He had no idea when this place was built or whom it belonged to, but unusual energy emanated from the building. As peculiar as Haunted Land was, the building held even more secrets. For one, he found the rooms much larger than the building could contain. However, what he viewed in many of the rooms was more interesting.

Some rooms fit the building perfectly—empty offices containing a desk or two, but many of the rooms undoubtedly belonged to different structures from far-off locations and even from other times. These doors were portals to magic places. Some were more modern and updated, others belonged to something more colonial. And the deeper Cain went, the stranger it got. Entering one room led him into an office with workers rushing back and forth. There was even a receptionist. The plump black woman was typing on a hologram keyboard as Cain entered.

"May I help you, sir," she asked, looking from her screen (which floated in the air before her—this place was clearly from some not-so-distant future.

"What business is this?" he asked. He was informed the business was called *Loveofyou*. A place where you paid to go into a machine, allowing you to have sex with yourself. Cain was unsure if this unholy act was achieved with mirrors, virtual reality, or magic. Either way, the idea revolted him.

"Who would want to do that," Cain asked.

"You'd be surprised. Are you interested in booking a session?" the woman asked.

Cain turned to head back out, only to find the door gone. However, there was another door on the far side of the office. He ran, went through, and found himself on a beach, the sun causing sweat on his face. He inhaled the salty air. He went through several doors leading to a series of bizarre worlds. Finally, he found his old room. His *archives* room.

He dug through his old files and found a paper he'd written about how easy manipulating people was. He'd once conducted a double-blind study in which he handed fifty students a reading from a "psychic" and asked if the results applied to them. These said things like: "You give too much," and "You always think of yourself last," or "No one appreciates how hard you work."' All the participants had said the reading was uncannily accurate to them. But, of course, all the papers were identical. People were remarkably easy to control.

Cain meditated on his mission and left the building, not before conjuring a Kraken to inhabit the River Black surrounding the building to protect his secrets.

***

Rex woke to the welcome smell of freshly brewed coffee and the sound of the shower running from the bathroom connected to Diamond's bedroom. What had he done? He struggled to recall the previous night's events when the bathroom door opened. Steam billowed into the tidy room, and Diamond's voice, a bit more masculine than last night, called out.

"Feel free to go downstairs and help yourself to coffee.

"Sounds good."

Then, a thin *man* exited the bathroom, wrapped in a towel. He made his way over to Rex and placed a soft hand on Rex's neck. He looked like Diamond's twin brother.

"What the fuck is this?!"

"What?" Diamond asked.

"What in the shit is this?"

"What the hell are you talking about?

"Why are you like that?!"

"Like what?"

"A man!"

"Well, I'm a man, Rex."

"Yeah, but- "

"Okay, you're freaking me out."

"I'm freaking *you* out. Are you nuts!"

"Rex- "

"You swing your ass back into that bathroom and get yourself all dolled up! Rex Dolan ain't no fag!"

Shaken, Diamond ran back into the bathroom and slammed the door shut.

Rex dressed in record time and hurried downstairs, where Stu was still asleep on the sofa.

"Stu, get the fuck up."

"What…"

"Shhh. Get dressed. We're leaving. Now."

"What about Diamond?"

"Don't you say that name. Quick, before he gets out of the bathroom."

"We're leaving without her?"

"Him! And yes, we're leaving without him."

"But you promised- "

"The fuck with what I promised."

CHAPTER NINE

"Rex, slow down! You're going to kill us!" Stu said.

"Zip it, kid. I know what I'm doing. Hell yeah, there's a portal ahead."

Rex raced through the doorway to an unknown Land with the haste of a man trying to outrun the cops. The portal's brightness temporarily blinded them as they entered and were spit out the other end.

"Shit!" Rex skidded. He scarcely missed a black family crossing the street, who made the Huxtables look like gangsta rappers.

"Willikers!" The father shouted.

"TV Land," Rex said, indicating a sign.

"Let's move on."

"Hold on, kid. Let's not forget I'm likely a star here. We'll be treated like royalty."

"Rex, are you kidding? No one remembers *Happy Jack*."

"Is that right?" Rex smiled, placed a Camel in his lips, and gave Stu a little slap on the cheek.

"Yeah."

"We'll just see about that."

Rex parked the Mustang and sprang out. He puffed out his chest and checked out the scene. A man in a cheap suit with a fake tan and saccharin smile approached them immediately. The man was at least in his sixties but was in decent shape and wore a thick hairpiece. He held a long microphone.

"Ladies and gentlemen, please welcome our two newest contestants on *How Would You Survive?*" the man said in an annoying monotone.

"He's a game show host," Stu said.

"I'll handle this," Rex said.

"And who are you, gentlemen? I'm Guy Money, host of *How Would You Survive?*"

"Looks like your lucky day, Guy. You have a celebrity guest. I'm Rex Dolan, star of *Happy Jack.*"

"Never heard of it," Guy said into his mic. He held a stack of index cards in his other hand.

"How does a TV man not know of my show?"

Guy ignored the question and read from one of his cards.

"Rex, you're about to make whoopie with a lovely woman and find, sadly, you are unable to *rise* to the occasion. HOW WOULD YOU SURVIVE?"

"Well, Guy, I excuse myself to the bathroom. But instead of going to the shitter, I head into the kitchen. I grab a bottle of good old hot sauce. I get a good amount on my middle finger and jam it in the old yin-yang. That will get the stick ready for dippin'."

"Jesus." Stu moaned.

"Ten points to the man no one has ever heard of. And you…"

"Stu."

"Stu, you find yourself-"

"What do you mean 'never heard of'?" Rex interjected.

"C'mon, Rex, let's move," Stu said.

"You got it. This clown doesn't know shit."

They explored the Land. Couples and families passed them here and there. All the dads were complete man-child morons, the moms, and children leading the way. *Like TV shows,* Stu thought. Large flatscreen TVs on poles stood on every corner, showing all kinds of TV programs. The whole place was an exercise in artifice, like being on a sitcom set. There was even a laugh track blasting from nowhere. It made Stu's neck wrinkle in gooseflesh.

"See any doors?" Stu asked.

"If I did, you think I'd be pulling my pudd in this shit-hole?"

"But you said you'd be treated like royalty."

"The hell with what I said. You'll soon realize I don't know what I'm talking about. Oh no…"

Rex pulled the sunglasses from his pocket and slipped them on.

"What?"

"Cop," Rex said.

Sure enough, a cop was walking around with a boy of about eight. They headed right for them.

"Gentlemen."

"Officer," Rex said.

"This boy here is an orphan," the cop said.

"That so?"

"Yes, sir. Would you guys like to adopt him?" the cop asked.

"Come again," Stu asked.

"He's a good boy and has taken to you guys. And a same-sex couple adopting a child would be great for ratings."

"We aren't a couple."

"Aren't there legalities about adopting a kid?" Stu asked.

"Mmm…well, on TV, if an orphan likes an adult…they adopt him," the cop said.

"I don't think so," Rex said.

"But if you guys are starring in a sitcom as a same-sex couple…well, an adopted son is perfect."

"What's with all the gay shit. Stu, you're cramping my style."

"Well, there is Diamond- "

"You shut your fuckin' trap!"

"Hey," the cop said, covering the boy's ears. "I'm going to keep my eyes on you two."

"Keep your eye on this prize," Rex said, cupping his balls.

"How's that?" The cop asked.

"Nothing, sir. Thank you," Stu said, pulling Rex.

Finally, the cop and the boy walked away. Stu thought it was only a matter of time before Rex got them into more serious trouble. He didn't know the half of it.

***

All humans have a sixth sense. Perhaps it comes as knowing something is not quite right about the person you're dating or something off about the job you are offered. You go right ahead and get into the situation anyway, only to find out weeks, months, or even years later your original hunch was correct, and you should have run no matter how attractive the offer.

And so, before she even opened the door. Brandy Sawyer knew something was wrong; whatever awaited her on the other side would change things forever. The room went slanted. The air had changed; she was breathing the atmosphere of a different earth. The doorknob was ice. The woman on the other side of the door wore oversized sunglasses and a ballcap, her hair tied back. Still, she was familiar.

"Brandy, don't freak out. I'm here to help you and Stu," the woman said. The woman's voice was a copy of her own, as it sounded in a recording or video.

"What do you know about Stu? Who are you?" And by way of an answer, the woman removed her cap and glasses. Then Brandy Sawyer screamed.

***

They needed to work together, so they would have to learn to get along. But Stu thought Rex would get them killed before they could get deep into their journey. Rex Dolan was loud, crass, and found trouble wherever he went. After spending some time roaming the street, they encountered an older man and a multi-colored-haired girl who appeared as lost as they were.

"Rex?" the chubby man called.

"You know him," Stu asked.

"Huh? Oh, yeah. I met him in a bar the other night. He notices the changes, too."

"Hello, Rex."

"Well, I'll be dipped in shit. How's it hanging, Booty?"

"Bubby."

"Yeah, whatever. This little shit with me is Stu. And who is the little lady?" Rex asked, taking off his sunglasses.

"Julia," the young woman said. Stu thought she looked like cotton candy come to life.

"Who are you supposed to be, Cyndi Lauper?" Rex asked.

"Huh?"

"Excuse him, he's from 80 Land," Stu said.

"Yeah, excuse me. But there is no excuse for my boy, Stu, here."

"How did you guys get here?" Bubby asked.

"We came looking for answers," Stu said.

"Us too! Us too! We're a team! The four of us!" Julia said, clapping wildly.

"Simmer down, sweetie. Rex Dolan is a one-man team."

"We need to work together," Stu said, happy to be with people other than Rex.

"Well, if any of you guys hold me back, I'm out," Rex said.

They decided to go somewhere to talk.

"Let's go somewhere to eat," Stu said.

"You guys should know right off the bat—Stu is always hungry. Don't let his skinny ass fool you," Rex said.

"I did not have breakfast, all because of Rex," Stu pleaded to their new partners.

"Oh, and that's my fault?"

"It sure is. We stayed at Diamond's house and were going to have a hearty breakfast but had to leave this morning in a huff because Rex-"

"Okay, we can find a place. Relax!"

"A bar," Bubby said. "We can get a little drinky drink and something to eat."

As they made their way over to a pub, they were interrupted by a group of women. All spoke Spanish and were upbeat as if caffeinated to the eyeballs, talking over one another, giggling, and falling out of their respective tiny dresses.

"Damn, ladies, how *do* we do?" Rex asked. The women laughed and spoke to one another in Spanish. They looked at Rex again and resumed laughing.

A little man in an old-fashioned suit and bowler hat said: "They are from the Spanish channel. Lovely ladies, indeed." The man spoke in a British accent, and his little mustache bounced around his face as he spoke.

"Hell yeah, the good old Spanish channel. I am not a stranger to that," Rex said. The little man tipped his hat. Rex turned back to his group. The gaggle of women entered a nearby restaurant, leaving behind what Stu imagined heaven smelled like.

"Good day," the little British man said, hopping down the street.

"Folks, as a wee teen, I rubbed 'em out to the old Spanish channel enough times to wax a limo. It's great to get a jerk off on the fly so long as you can nut before the funny old host of the show takes over the screen. Bubbs, Stu, do I lie?"

Bubby and Stu remained silent but shared a look—the dog who crapped on the carpet.

"Charming," Julia said.

"*Happy days are here again!*" a child's voice cried.

"Who said that? Who the hell said that?" Rex asked.

A messy-haired boy stood before them. Though only a boy, he shared Rex's eyes and shit-eating grin.

"It's…."

"Happy Jack," Stu said. "But how?"

"I…what's happening?" Rex said, the color draining from his face like a cup with a leak.

"It's an illusion," Bubby said, touching Rex's arm. Rex shook it off.

"What are you?"

"I'm Happy Jack. *Happy days are here again!*"

"You can't be me."

"Of course, I am not you. I'm Happy Jack; you're a sad man."

"But…but you will be me."

"No way. In TV Land, I am Happy Jack forever and ever. If I become you, I would kill myself—which is what you should do. *Happy days are here again!*"

"Stop saying that, you little prick."

"But… *happy days are here again!*"

"I'm going to strangle the little shit!"

"Rex, no," Julia said.

They all grabbed Rex, and Happy Jack ran away, screaming: "*Happy days are here again!*" all the way.

"Damn kid moved faster than a bunny with a pepper in its ass," Rex said.

"Wonderful image," Julia said, wrinkling her nose.

"Well, that was weird," Stu said.

"Are you okay, Rex?" Bubby asked.

"Yeah, why wouldn't I be okay?"

"The kid…he was you."

"Balls. It was nothing."

"He was a metaphor for your lost youth and dreams. It's okay if that kid freaked you out," Julia said.

"I don't need to be psychoanalyzed by some new-wave dunce, okay."

Stu prayed Rex would behave long enough for them to talk. A guy could hope.

***

"Hello, are you with me?"

"Brandy opened her eyes. She was lying on her sofa and looking at herself.

"How?" was all she could manage.

"It's all true. The stuff Stu writes about the Cain Consequence is real. I am from a different timeline. I'm Brandy Sawyer."

"No…I'm Brandy Sawyer."

"We both are," the woman said. While the woman looked a little less worn, likely from a life with fewer challenges than her own, there was no denying she was indeed another Brandy Sawyer.

"I don't understand."

"I think you do. Or maybe we can never totally understand. Either way, it amounts to the same thing."

Brandy's head was about to explode. So, everything Stu had postulated about the multiverse was real. How could it be? Her twin handed her a glass of water. Brandy took a sip.

"I think I need something a bit stronger."

"You keep the booze in the third cabinet of the kitchen as well?"

"Wow. This is too weird."

"Jameson's, three ice cubes?"

"Okay, I am officially freaked out."

Brandy lay back on the sofa while the other Brandy fixed identical drinks.

"Why are you here?"

"Because Stuey, *your* Stuey, is in serious trouble."

***

The four of them (and Stu was already thinking of them as "the Four," Capital "F") stopped in a bar. Of course, this was a bar from a TV show, but no one could name the program. Bubby and Rex got beer; Stu and Julia ordered coffee and ginger ale, respectively.

Most people in the bar engrossed themselves with a soccer game on the TV above the bar. Stu knew a bit of soccer but did not recognize either team.

As Stu's eyes adjusted to the gloom, he took in the pub's clientele. A veritable aggerate of all nationalities, colors, and sexual identities. Like something on TV, everyone was represented. They all were too young and healthy-looking compared to what you found in any ordinary bar. The obnoxious laugh track went off every few seconds as the characters talked, even though nothing said was remotely amusing.

They found a table, and Stu and the others discussed how most people talk about the Cain Consequence changes regarding nonsense with products or movies. But not real life. Not in essential things. Did it matter that some people remembered Jiff brand peanut butter as Jiffy? So, the Four discussed how it had affected them personally.

"Once, as a girl, I spilled chocolate ice cream on my thigh. I wiped it off, but there was still a pale brown stain in the shape of the ice cream splotch. I showed it to my mother, worried. What the heck was going on? But my mother said I had a birthmark, and I'd had it since birth. I will swear under the oath of the Goddess I never had a birthmark before that moment. My mother looked at me as if I were nuts. I did not want to worry her, so I let it go," Julia said.

"Wow," Bubby said.

"Let's see it," Rex said.

Julia lifted her pink skirt. Rex and Stu both leaned in to see. Julia stopped and lowered her dress.

"Nice try, perv."

"I'm experiencing a lot of changes—all kinds of stuff. I wish a change would happen where my friend didn't die," Stu said, surprised. He had had no intention of sharing this. But he was connected to these people. *The Four.* Stu said to himself and blew on his coffee.

"Oh my God," Julia said.

"That's horrible. I'm sorry. Such a Shanda," Bubby said.

Stu told them the whole story.

"All I want is answers. Why is this happening? More importantly, why are only some of us seeing it?"

"Stu, I can't promise we will get all of our answers or we will be able to stop Cain, but we sure will give it our all," Bubby said.

"That's right, we have your back," Julia said.

Rex shook his head and took a pull from his beer. There was shouting as two men a few tables from them stood and squared off. Quickly, another group pulled them apart.

They ordered food. They ate silently for a while, like people who have known one another for years rather than hours. Stu was grateful the burgers here were made of beef and surprisingly good. Stu may have been much younger than the rest, but they were the Four—he could *feel* it. For the first time, he found people who accepted him. After finishing their burgers, they all compared realities but could not agree on everything. Julia mentioned while she was unfamiliar with *Andy and the Astronauts*, she recalled seeing the movie *Jaws* (many times, in fact). And Dustin Hoffman had most definitely not played the spoiled marine biologist Hooper, which was now the case.

"You guys do realize Barclay Cain will not be easy to find. He's hiding and is the most powerful occultist known. If he does not want to be discovered, we are in for a tough time."

"Okay, so let's find this Cult of Change and beat the answers out of them," Rex said.

"There's nothing to beat. It appears to me we are all on the same side," Julia said.

"I don't even know if there are sides anymore," Stu said.

"Who gives a rat's ass," Rex said, "let's find them and make them tell us where Cain is."

"Someone is changing reality or traveling through time or something," Julia said.

"Time travel?" Bubby asked.

"Time has always been an illusion," Stu said. "Are you going to finish that," Stu asked Julia, eyeing her unfinished fries like a dog looking at a child eating, waiting for the food to drop.

"Be my guest," Julia said, pushing her plate to him. "This is all so exciting," Julia laughed and clapped.

"Chill out," Rex said.

"But I am ready for an adventure."

"This is not about an adventure; it's about stopping this shit. Anyway, time travel is not possible. How can you go to a time that hasn't happened yet?" Rex asked.

"Oh, but it's possible Dustin Hoffman is now in *Jaws*? It's possible Joey Buttafuoco is now the *Amityville Horror* guy," Bubby said.

"Who's Joey Buttafuoco?" Stu asked.

"Be glad you're young and missed him," Bubby said, finishing his beer. "Anyone need a drink?"

"Damn, Bubbs, thirsty?" Rex asked. Bubby went to the bar for another beer.

"Einstein proved time is not real."

"Yeah, until we wake in the morning and Einstein never existed," Rex said.

"God, what a sad thought," Julia said.

"Time is a human invention," said Stu.

"Yeah, right. I'm getting older. My dad is getting older," Rex said.

"Getting older is entropy, not proof of time passing."

"Stu, I have to side with Rex on this one. Time must be real. A clock is designed to keep time," Bubby said, returning with a fresh pint of ale and a shot of something amber.

"Actually, a clock is designed to keep pace with other clocks. Anyway, time sucks because the past equals regret, and the future equals anxiety," Stu said.

"Wow, what an outlook," Bubby said.

"Stu, my man, I agree with that shit. Life sucks, and then you die," Rex said, lifting his beer.

"Wow, Rex, what a negative nelly," Julia said.

"Me? Not negative; I'm just a realist."

"Yeah, a real pessimist," Bubby said, washing his shot with a swallow of beer.

"Well, I am here with a dingbat, a mama's boy basement dweller, and a loser, one who looks to be part alcoholic to boot, so pardon my pessimism."

"You can't be part alcoholic,'" Bubby said.

"What a jerk," Julia said.

A waitress strolled past, balancing a dozen pints on a huge tray. A hairy, fat man slapped her behind, and she kicked him in the shin without spilling a drop.

"We need a plan," Julia said.

"We find Cain, beat his ass, and end it. Simple," Rex said.

"That's not a plan," Julia said.

"I may have some ideas," Stu said.

"Me too," Julia said and clapped.

"Bones and the flake have ideas… I can't wait to hear this," Rex said with a smirk.

"Okay, what's our next move?" Bubby asked.

***

They both sipped their identical drinks and made the same *ahhh* sound as they placed their glasses together on the coffee table. Brandy laughed humorlessly and rubbed her temples. Her first thought was she had finally lost her last marble, and this hallucination was insanity finally completing its job. Her sickness was snaking its way into her brain, at last, feeding on the grey matter and causing the delusion. But this was real. She knew it. So now the question was, how would she keep her shit together?

"Okay, so this is actually happening."

"Yes, it is. I'm sorry."

"I don't even know what question to ask first. All I know is this is my world.."

"That's not true."

"But I have always been here."

"Can you be sure?"

"Of course, this is my world. But with changes. It's all a mistake."

"I'm sorry, but you are in the wrong place. This is *my* reality. Now, we need to get you back to your reality. I am Stuey's mother, his *real* mother. Oh, I know you are his mother, too. But I am *this* Stuey's mother," Brandy-Two said.

"I don't like this."

"You are my Stuey's mother. Or some other Stuey's mother. Anyway, we have to switch."

"I'm not leaving," Brandy said and grabbed her drink off the table.

"We need to switch. Your Stuey is waiting for you in the reality I came from."

Brandy thought this over.

"How do I know you're telling me the truth? How do I know I can trust you?"

"If you can't trust yourself, who *can* you trust?"

"Assuming I go along with all of this—what do we do?"

***

"Find the Cult of Change is the first step," Stu said.

"Even if we find them, how do we know they can tell us where to find Cain or where Haunted Land is?" Bubby asked.

"Yeah, and how do we find them?"

"Even *if* we find them, *and* they know something, *and* we find Cain...then what?"

"We foil his plans," Julia said.

"Foil, how?" asked Rex. "What are you talking about?"

"You know…we foil," Julia repeated.

"Do you even know what foil means?" Rex asked.

"Foil. To prevent something considered wrong or undesirable from succeeding," Julia said and applauded herself.

"Christ." Rex rubbed his head, careful not to mess up his hair.

"Maybe we should have thought this through before coming here," Bubby said.

"I need to use the little ladies' room," Julia excused herself and disappeared into a dark wood door.

Stu and Rex watched her walk away. Her legs were short but smooth and shapely. Her ample bosom jiggled as she walked.

"Damn, she may be nuts, but she has a sweet body," Rex said.

"I think she's more my type," Stu said. "I don't mind if she's not a skinny minny."

"Amen to that, my man. A lot of guys are chicken-shit of a woman with a little meat on her. Not me. Show me a chubby girl, and I will show you a girl with self-esteem issues. And they are the best in bed, my boys."

"I'm not saying all that. But I think Julia may like me," Stu said.

"Really? If I get her once, she won't remember your name, kid."

"I don't think so."

"Guys, Julia is a good girl. And I will not have you speak about her like she's something you take off the shelf like a toy," Bubby said. He drained his beer.

"C'mon, Bubbs, you're going to have to act like a man if you want to work with me," Rex said.

"Speaking about women in such a way is not what makes one a man."

"I agree…it's how many babes you actually *bang* that determines if you're a man," Rex said.

"Oy."

Julia was back at the table now, so the conversation halted.

"Hey, what if we have to fight?" Stu asked.

"Of course, we will have to fight," Rex said. You don't find an occultist or a cult and expect them to give in without a fight, do you?"

"Fight?" Bubby asked.

"And I bet Cain must have an army or something. Followers, I guess," Julia asked.

"There are followers, now? How many?" Bubby asked.

"Of course, there are followers," Stu said. "And a cult must be made of crazy people. And they are an actual cult. That's what Diamond said."

"Who is Diamond," Julia asked.

"He…she is-"

"Zip it," Rex said under his breath, and he pinched Stu's thigh.

"Ouch!"

"You must find Cain and stop him," A voice said.

"Who the hell said that?" Rex asked.

Julia pointed to the TV above the bar. The picture was jumbled, but they could see the outline of a woman. The voice, at least, was clear. But the video bounced around in odd jerking motions.

"Are you guys seeing this?" Bubby asked.

They all were. However, the others in the bar kept cheering—they still observed the game. The image went fuzzy back to normal for a moment and then jumped around again.

"Looks like Max Headroom," Rex said.

"Who?" Julia and Stu asked together.

"You owe me a soda, Stu," Julia said, standing and clapping.

"Christ," Rex said.

"Who is Max Headroom," Stu asked.

"Never mind."

"You must stop him..." the image on the TV said. Then the game was back, and the TV was normal again.

"Well, that was really helpful," Rex said.

"I'm getting another drink; what do you guys want?" Rex asked.

"I'll come with you," Bubby said.

***

"Have you met others of us?" Brandy asked, hardly believing the words as she said them.

"Yes. I have been doing this with different Brandys for a long time, trying to find you."

"What are they…are *we* like?"

"We are alike. For the most part, anyway. I met one of us who was an FBI agent. Another one became a nun in Church Land."

"FBI? A nun? My God."

"Most of us are the same."

"And Stuey? Is he always the same?"

During the bizarre conversation, Brandy almost bounced between being the speaker and the listener, the observer and the observed, as if she were bouncing between her and Brandy-Two's bodies. Sometimes, she found her mouth moving as she was listening. Were they *connected*?

"Again, he's the same for the most part. I met one Stuey who was a real lady's man."

Another version of her being a nun or federal agent was tough enough to swallow. But Stu Sawyer as a player? This whole thing was getting more surreal by the moment.

"We need to get you to the right world. This is my rightful world."

"I'm not leaving Stuey," Brandy said.

"And you won't. We need to get you back to *your* Stuey. I understand this is hard, but I need you to work with me."

Brandy stifled a sob. But then she thought of the disease making fast work of her. Of the limited time she had left in this absurd world.

"Okay, let's do it."

***

Rex and Bubby were at the bar, getting drinks. The bartender eyed them as if expecting trouble. He wiped the bar before them for an uncomfortable time before helping two women at the other end of the bar. Once he was sure the bartender was out of earshot, Rex spoke.

"Bubbs, I will count on you to have my back when things get hairy. Those two are kids, for Christ's sake."

"Have your back, how?"

"When shit goes down. When it gets real. You don't think we will waltz around Haunted Land without trouble, do you? Who knows what we will encounter. We need to get this done—TCB."

"How's that?"

"Taking care of business, Bubbs, Taking care of fuckin' business," Rex said, lighting a cigarette.

"Yeah, I didn't think much about what kind of craziness we are in store for," Bubby admitted.

"And a cult. Those people must be nuts."

"Oh boy."

"You ain't going to flake out on me, are you?"

"I'm not sure how much good I will be in a fight, Rex."

"Well, you better be ready to man up."

"I have to be honest; I'm a lover, not a fighter. And, honestly, I'm not much of a lover, either."

"You need to be ready to do your best. That's all I'm asking."

"I'm not sure how good my best will be."

"What did you think this was going to be?"

"I guess I figured we would find Cain and explain our situation—how the Cain Consequence is disturbing our lives. He'd fix things, and we'd be on our way."

The bartender came over with their pints, took the money, and gave them a distasteful sneer before returning to washing glasses.

"Shit, Bubbs, are you kidding? Has anything ever been that simple?"

"You have no idea."

When they got back to the table, Stu said:

"Julia and I have an idea."

Julia must have stepped outside for a moment while they were getting refills as she reeked of fresh cannabis. Her eyes were glassy, and she could not disguise her smile.

"I can't wait to hear this shit," Rex said.

"What's your idea, guys, Bubby asked.

Julia clapped. "We find the Cult of Change and *join* them. We *infiltrate* them. We see if they are behind everything. And if they are, we stop them!"

"Are you kidding?" Rex asked.

"You have anything better?" Stu said.

"When has my *not* having a better idea stopped me from telling someone else *their* idea is shit?" Rex said.

"Well, let's find the Cult of Change," Bubby said, hoping they were not approaching their inevitable deaths.

PART II
Cain's Cabal

CHAPTER TEN

Booth Templeton had grown accustomed to the finer things in life. And like so many who want for nothing, he coveted the few things off-limits to him. His wealth, charming demeanor, and movie-star looks left him a hit with the ladies but good for little else. His father had made a fortune in firearms, mostly rifles. As a result of being around guns, he was rumored to be as excellent a marksman as he was a womanizer. Guns had made him and his father wealthy, but they had woken one morning and found Texas was now a place called Vegan Land. Once, passionate gun owners lived here, but the people here now had no desire to own firearms, and slowly, their family fortune dwindled. One day, his father had an epiphany—he transformed their factory into a soybean farm, trading steel and gunpowder for seeds and soil. He invested his remaining fortune into producing soy products. Booth's daddy actually made more money producing these ridiculously named products (Ground beefless, phony baloney, soysage) than he'd ever made in rifles. Fortune favors the fortunate, as they say.

But Booth hated this new Land. The women here were not impressed with his money, charm, or looks, and they all stunk of herbs, essential oils, and body odor rather than the heavily perfumed girls to which he had grown so accustomed. Animal shit was scattered throughout the countryside now. Animals eventually took over due to spaying and neutering being considered barbaric and consequently outlawed. Cows freely roamed. Chicken feathers littered everything. The sad corpse of a tiger lay on the ground—a mound of rotting vegetation at its side. People here had tied the tiger because it kept killing and eating the cows—the tiger, chained with nothing to dine on other than the stinking salad, had eventually perished of starvation.

After sleeping with his father's third wife, a cute hippy woman three years younger than he, Booth Templeton was asked to leave the family business and his father's home. Now he needed to find a way to make a living for himself, and since fucking didn't pay (unless he wanted to move to Porn Land), he'd have to figure a way to get paid for shooting guns.

Acquaintances had told him of West Land. He figured someone there would not mind having a cowboy in their ranks. He'd move in and take control of his destiny, reinvent himself.

As he planned his new life, he had tried to grow an old West mustache, but his boyish face would not comply. So, when he went to the costume shop to get his cowboy outfit, he was pleased to find it included a fake bushy mustache and spirit gum to fix it below his perfect nose.

And one day, at the crack of noon (Booth was a late sleeper), he left and, after paying an old meditation master for directions, found a green street leading to a portal. He'd had to go through several strange lands before eventually seeing covered wagons and saloons.

He experimented with several rough-sounding names. Buck Target. Zero Cares. Sandy Beach—but eventually settled on using his real name—Booth.

He found work in a carnival/rodeo performing a rifle show. Despite rumors (most of which Booth created himself), Booth Templeton could not shoot a bull at three paces with a shotgun. But he'd found ways back home to cheat, and much to his delight, the ruse also worked here. He put on his show twice daily, shooting cigars from men's mouths and hitting tiny bells set high on flagpoles. The men with the cigars were plants with loads packed into the cigars, and the bells were set on timers to "ding" on command. It worked perfectly. No one knew what a horrible shot he indeed was. Until one day….

***

Zack and The Bat had asked around. They reported what they had learned to Cain. The trespassers, *the Four*, were looking for answers. They were looking for trouble as well, Cain knew. They wanted to stop the changes from happening. Why else had they come here? He was told the Four wasn't much of a team. A boy conspiracy theorist. Quite possibly the world's most incompetent witch. Unquestionably, the world's worst businessperson. And an arrogant has been child actor with a chip on his shoulder the size of Canada. What threat could they possibly pose? However, given the circumstances, they shouldn't have made it this far. They surely would go no further. Still, now was the time to gather some people just in case. He had already enlisted Zack and The Bat and some others, but no one had any real power. He would need more. As much as he hated violence, he needed a few henchmen in his ranks. Which land should he go to and prepare some people? West Land, of course. West Land was already attracting all kinds of bad apples, people who considered themselves outlaws. He'd go there and gather his new posse.

Cain had a witch of his own. He'd met Bruja, and the witch knew all about him and was enthusiastic to do anything he commanded.

Cain took a moment to send a charm to the interlopers—something to get in their way. He created *get lost* spell and sent it their way. But there was resistance. At least one of them was protected—a *Selected*, perhaps? No, none of them had that kind of old magic. Unless the witch was…. No, it couldn't be. He conjured more power to his hex. He was tired, however. He needed to be careful and conserve his strength. Now was not the time to waste his magic. He hoped the four troublemakers did not get along too far while he gathered power.

He rose from meditation and went to West Land. He entered the general store. The old man behind the counter struggled with a giant sack of something.

"How can I help you?"

"I'm looking to rent a place here," Cain said. "Can you point me toward the nearest real estate person?"

"You're looking at him," the skinny man said. He adjusted his tiny glasses on his pasty, round face. "What do you have in mind, friend?"

"How about the abandoned saloon?"

Every other building in West Land was a saloon.

"Well, you can have your pick. If you have money, that is."

"I have money."

"You have a name?"

"I have money...do I need a name?"

"'Spose not."

"Good. Now, show me my new home."

***

Booth sat on his mechanical horse (meat horses no longer existed as they had all been consumed as meat years ago) and practiced shooting his rifle. He aimed for a finch in a nearby tree and sprayed bullets all over the wood. The finch chirped, undisturbed, as if mocking him. He'd found this place and used it to train, as no one was ever here to see how horrible a shot he was.

He fired a shot at the damn bird and missed by about seven feet—he was getting better! The following bullet went way off course.

"Hey!" Someone yelled. A confused-looking woman appeared from behind a bush.

"I say, where did you come from?"

"Are you nuts, shooting like that? You almost hit me!" the woman said. She looked like she would be more at home in a group of gypsies than in a place emulating the old West.

"My dear, you are speaking to a marksman of the highest caliber. There is no risk of you being shot unless I choose to do so. If that were the case, you would be on the ground with half a dozen slugs in your gullet," Booth said, adjusting his derby on a jaunty angle.

"Is that so? Well, I come from old magic. Strong magic. If you pointed your pistol in my direction, I would turn you into a shrunken head before your finger was on the trigger."

"You are a witch," Booth said.

"I am. A witch working with Barcley Cain."

Booth's breath caught.

"Well, I bet he could use a marksman of my ability in his ranks. I am Booth."

"I am Bruja. I suppose Cain could use a sharpshooter. But I am not sure anyone will need you the way you shoot," Bruja said.

"My dear, judging from your attire and the smell of your cheap perfume, the only employment you are fit for is in one of West Land's brothels. And I daresay you may be a bit long in the tooth for such work," Booth said.

"The nerve."

"I call 'em as I see 'em."

"Why, you little rich boy! That cowboy getup doesn't fool me."

A bird sang from a tree branch. Booth pointed his rifle at the finch and squeezed the trigger.

Click.

Empty.

He reached for his revolver but found his holster empty!

"Looking for this?" Bruja said, holding Booth's revolver.

"I say, it must have fallen while I was riding. The ground is quite uneven here."

"What kind of a cowboy loses his fuckin' revolver?" she said. The pistol matched his rifle, golden and shiny.

"What kind of a *lady* speaks like a common bandit?"

"What kind of *man* rides his horse side-saddle," Bruja asked, laughing.

"An English gentleman," he said and twisted his false mustache (careful to ensure it did not come loose in the sweat forming beneath the false hair), then removed a small cigar from his pristine saddlebag. He flicked a wooden match several times against his saddle to no avail.

"I say, it must have gotten wet."

Bruja removed the lighter from her purse, lit a cigarette, and offered the flame to Booth. He took the light.

"A cowboy does not use such things, but seeing my current circumstance…much obliged."

"Please, don't play the cowboy angle too much, poser. You may fool the others here, but you look like one of the Village People to me."

"That right, stranger? Now, if you would be so kind as to hand over my revolver."

Bruja examined the pistol.

"Is there a reward for this?"

"Indeed, you return my revolver right now, and I will let you live," Booth said in an artificial Western twang.

"You're new here, too, aren't you?"

"Been here a spell. Considering I am the deadliest man with a rifle, this appeared the right place to come."

"And now you have met the deadliest witch with a spell. I can make you ugly as sin or make your cock useless for the rest of your days with a few words. No gun needed."

Booth did his best to keep the fear from his voice.

"Well, seeing as you are working with Cain, I will let you live."

"Gee, thanks. I suppose we're on the same side," Bruja said.

"I don't have a side, honey. I only need to know who's paying. And a word to the not-so-wise: you'd do well to keep on my good side."

"I think you have seen too many Clint Eastwood movies, fancy-boy."

"And you have not seen enough of me to know how far you have walked into the lion's den."

"Seen enough of life to know a daddy's boy who won't survive in West Land for long."

"Oh, I'll be fine," Booth said, finally pulling from his cigar. His face twisted before he hacked. Bruja laughed.

"Ha!"

"Anyway, working with Cain sounds good to me. Take me to him, woman. Hop on up," Booth said, indicating his gleaming mechanical horse.

"I don't need a ride."

"Well, you are not in any shape to walk this land."

"What the hell is that supposed to mean?"

"It means you have seen more than twice the number of cockcrows than I, and I daresay, more cocks than most women."

"You son-of-a-bitch. I should curse your dick."

"You can't keep dick from coming out of your mouth. And I'd wager my last dollar that you have just as hard a time keeping it from entering."

"What is your problem?"

"Climb on, and you can ride with me. Lead me to Cain."

"Yeah, right."

"Suit yourself."

Ultimately, Booth convinced Bruja to climb the mechanical horse and take him to the saloon.

"Put your arms around me."

At first, she declined, but the ground was bumpy, and she almost found herself going topsy-turvy more than once. Then, ever so gently, she held onto Booth, with as little contact as possible to stabilize herself.

At once, Booth moved one of Bruja's hands to his crotch, where his penis was already twitching. Then she pinched.

"I say!"

"Keep your dick to yourself."

They reached their destination without further incident and entered the saloon. Booth recognized the man as none other than Barclay Cain. He'd assumed the woman had lied, but here was the renowned occultist in the flesh. Cain was older than in his photos, but the years had been kind to the man. Bruja fell to her knees.

"Rise, Bruja," Cain said. "I asked you to stop doing that."

Cain was dressed the part of an occultist—long golden robes flowed on him like a metallic sea at midnight. He wore a headdress resembling a cross between a Bishop's mitre and the hood of a Klansman.

"Master, this is Booth. He wants to join us," Bruja said.

"Depends how much you're paying," Booth said.

"Your payment will be room and food for now."

"And what will my work be?"

"To stop a group called the Four."

The saloon was rough around the edges. A creepy pair called Zack and The Bat introduced themselves to him. There were several people already living here. An emaciated old man was wiping tables. A plump, overly cheerful woman stopped sweeping to show Booth to his room.

"Care to join me," Booth asked Bruja.

"Keep dreaming."

***

While the counterfeit cowboy was resting in his room, Bruja decided to take his horse and check out the grounds.

But Cain stopped her.

"How are you good with time spells?"

"Traveling through time? No. I don't have that kind of alchemy."

"I was thinking more along the lines of *bending* time."

"Yes, I can do that. I once made a man think two weeks was an hour."

"Excellent. And what about love enchantments?"

Bruja ran her hand through her scarlet hair, half-closed her eyes, and grinned.

"Of course."

"Wonderful. Here is what I need you to do..."

***

Her first assignment from the master! She needed a few things: Candles (blue, red, yellow, orange). Two poppet dolls (one male, one female). Essential oils (rose petals, patchouli, frangipani, dragon's blood, and chamomile). She could summon a golden vortex if there was no full moon tonight; no problem there. She would do her part to stop the Four.

CHAPTER ELEVEN

It soon became apparent TV Land was where new TV shows were formed and tested. Every fad and trend was heavily represented here. Scripts for "reality" shows littered the streets to the knees. The Four even got stuck for a good chunk of the afternoon in the middle of a staged political rally. The rabid people in the mob were paid to shout, fight, and scream. The chaos was being shot on a low budget, and the same extra actors were used for both political parties. However, the costume and make-up department quickly removed the fake man-buns and added false mustaches as the actors switched sides. It appeared not to matter what was being contested. The people with the cameras reveled only in the hatred and bloodshed.

They were outside having coffee in a park this evening, devising how to approach their new plan, when Bubby removed a flask from his pocket and spiked his cup. He offered the flask around, but they all declined.

"Christ, Bubbs…I've even had enough today," Rex said.

"So, what do we do next?" Julia asked.

"Maybe we should split up and look around. Things will go faster that way," Rex said.

"I don't know about that," Bubby said.

"Why, you think it's a stupid idea?" Rex asked.

"I didn't say it was stupid."

"That's right. Stupid is making a cartoon about a monkey and releasing it the same day as *Fake Ape*," Rex said. "That, my friend, was the world's stupidest idea ever."

Stu figured Bubby now regretted confessing his TV flops to Rex.

Dusk was setting in, but a group got together on a putting green. A few people were filming a show (for a golf channel, presumably) showing putting techniques.

"I miss golf," Bubby said.

"You love golf, huh?" Julia asked. "My dad was an avid golfer. We even buried him with his five iron."

"When I was in the golf club making business, we tried to beat Callaway with a new wedge," Bubby said.

"You made golf clubs? How exciting." Julia said.

"Well, actually, golf *club,* singular."

"You only made one club?" Stu asked.

"Well, the club-making business is competitive. The money you must raise is significant. I only had enough to create one club. I called it '*The Spatula.*' A 100-degree wedge. Golfers complained so much about having trouble getting the ball high on pitch shots. So I decided to go all the way."

"I'm not a golfer, but wouldn't that..."

"Yup. *The Spatula* did one thing perfectly—if you hit it well, the ball flew high and landed right back in its original spot."

"Why would you want to make a shot like that?"

"You wouldn't, apparently," Bubby said.

"Jesus, Bubs. I was wrong about your cartoon. That club was your dumbest idea," Rex laughed.

"I'm not so sure. I once spent a lot of money creating an indestructible piñata."

"Damn, Bubbs, if shit ideas were nickels, you'd be a rich man."

"Rex, leave Bubby alone," Julia said.

"Okay, let's get back on track. Our plan?" Stu said.

"There's no use staying here. I say tomorrow we all jump into the next Land we can find," Julia said.

"Agreed," Stu said.

"Okay."

Guy Money shuffled toward them, microphone in hand, to ask HOW WOULD YOU SURVIVE?

"Let's get out of here before we are on a game show," Rex said.

"I'm going back to my room," Stu said.

"Let's all meet in the morning."

They left before Guy Money could reach them. Bubby decided to stop at the pub for a drink before heading back to the bed & breakfast.

"So, Julia, what do you feel like doing?" Rex asked. "Stu is hitting the hay. Bubbs is going to get tanked. Want to hang?"

"You're really something, you know that?

"What?"

"I'm going to bed, too."

"Am I invited?"

"Asshole." And they parted for the night.

***

Bubby was about four pints in when he noticed a woman looking in his direction. At first, he figured it must be a mistake. He looked away. When he glanced back, her eyes were unquestionably on him.

"What TV shows do you produce," a man on the stool beside him asked. The man looked to be chiseled of stone.

A Greek god in bar rather than riding a cloud holding a lightning bolt. Obviously, an actor.

"No. I'm not in the TV business," Bubby said.

"No? You look like a producer," the good-looking man said.

"What does a producer look like?" Bubby asked.

"Well...er...um..."

"No problem, friend. I know I'm not good-looking enough to be an actor."

"No, it's not that. It's just you look Jewish. So, I assumed you were a producer."

"I see. Wonderful observation."

"I mean...not...err..." the man stammered, grabbed his drink, and ran away. Bubby took a pull of his Ale. The woman swayed over and sat on the now vacant stool.

"Hello." She smiled, the slight mole on her lip rising.

"Hi. Look, I am not a TV producer. So, if you're an actress, I'm sorry to say I don't have any connections."

"I'm not an actress. Can't a gal converse with the only guy in this place who looks like a gentleman?"

"Um, sure," Bubby said.

"You realize someone has hexed you, right?"

"I'm sorry?"

"I can see it in your aura. Someone, a witch likely, placed a glamour on you. Something to make you unable to differentiate the truth from the false."

"I don't feel anything."

"Have you been in contact with a witch lately?"

"Uh...yeah."

"Where did you first meet?"

"A bookstore in-"

"Don't tell me! Pub Land, right?" she said, hand to her temples, eyes closed.

"Yeah, how did you know?"

"We are in Pub Land now."

"Huh? I came into this place from TV Land."

"You never left Pub Land. The witch, as I said, tricked you."

"Why would she do that?"

Again, the woman put her hands to her head and closed her eyes.

"Jules...Julia! Is her name Julia?" Bruja said. She knew how to play men.

"Yes."

"She tricked you, made you believe you went somewhere else. Here, I'll show you," the woman said, grabbing Bubby's hand. Bubby's heart jumped; he had not held a woman's hand in ages. She led him outside. Sure enough, they were in Pub Land. Some things looked different, but he expected this with the Cain Consequence.

"I don't understand."

Bubby and the woman returned to the bar and had more drinks. And they talked—the conversation flowing effortlessly. When the woman leaned in and kissed him, Bubby thought he'd pass out. He had not kissed a woman in more years than he cared to admit.

Then time passed in a flash—scenes of him and this woman as they cuddled and kissed. They held hands and browsed bookstores. They did any number of things that would have made a great montage of some '90s rom-com with Sarah McLachlan's "Ice Cream" playing over it.

Bubby was lost in a most expertly constructed time-loop/love spell.

***

He had never seen so many old people in one place in his entire life. Senior Citizen Land. Tuco observed the relics shuffling through the streets like so many pathetic cyborgs, with walkers, oxygen tanks, and all manner of medical equipment. They lumbered around so slowly they were practically going backward still. However, the naturally old were not nearly as unsettling as the young people who lived here, mimicking the elderly. A young man, who could be no more than twenty, staggered, hunched over with his weight on a cane. Who in the hell voluntarily wanted to live as a senior citizen?

There was a cry from the woods. A man stood, shrouded in the darkness.

"Help me."

"Is someone there?"

"Come closer."

Tuco strode to where the man was. The man was about thirty and remained in the blackness. He had a helmet of stiff hair and a porn-star mustache. He was dressed in polyester bell bottoms and a matching velvet sports coat over a shirt of yellow flowers.

"What Land is this?"

"Senior Land," Tuco said.

"Damn! I'm trying to get to '70s Land."

"Didn't you hear? '70s Land is no more."

"What? Where else can I live looking like this?" the man asked, looking at Tuco through yellow-tinted aviator glasses.

"Change your clothes. Get a haircut and shave off the mustache."

"You think I have not thought of that? I'm a vampire. A *'70s* vampire! If I shave the 'stashe, it comes right back. My master turned me in the '70s. So I can't shave or get a haircut or manscape," he said, opening his shirt to reveal a thicket of dark curly hair.

"Jesus, button your shirt. You're too hairy."

"You don't know, hairy; you should see below deck."

"Keep your pants on, or I will cut you."

"I have been looking for a place I can go without being a joke. Imagine being a vampire and not being able to seduce women because they laugh at your appearance."

"That's funny," Tuco said.

"It's hell. And you should not find it too humorous, my friend. Look at you, a midget clown, for cryin' out loud."

A woman's voice: "You should not get any closer unless you want to get bitten."

Tuco looked at the woman—a tall blond drink of water with a mole above her lip. Her age was difficult to figure out. Still, she clearly had been something in her prime. She looked like a fortune teller in scarves and headdresses. Her aura was purple—a witch.

"Why are you in Senior Land?"

"I'm exploring. I'm staying in West Land."

"West Land? It sounds like I can get away with my look there," the '70s vampire interrupted.

"Forget him," the witch said.

"Forget you, you whore!"

"Is that so, Liberace. Listen, you *CHiPS*-looking mother fucker, *Starkey & Hutch* called, and they want you back."

"You bitch. Fuck you. Fuck you, too, mini clown," The vampire said.

"Better people have called me worse things," Tuco replied.

A tween couple wandered past. The boy had his hands laced behind his back and whistled some long-forgotten song that may have been popular when bread cost five cents a loaf. His partner had one of her arms looped through his, her other arm relying on a cane to stay upright. Indeed, everyone was a senior citizen here.

"This is crazy. Who the hell wants to be old?"

"There is no 'little people' land, so you are shit out of luck," the '70s vampire laughed.

"Stop laughing. You sound like the Count from *Sesame Street*," Bruja said. The vampire scowled.

"Who are you?" Tuco asked.

"I'm Bruja. And I have partnered with Barcley Cain."

"I want to meet him."

"Follow me."

"Yeah, me too," cried the '70s vampire from the protection of the trees.

"You're not invited."

The vampire hissed from the darkness of the woods and cried, "You sons of bitches!"

He did sound like the famous Muppet, Tuco thought as he and the witch hopped through a door.

***

Once they were in West Land, Bruja showed Tuco Cain's ranch. The evil clown reluctantly followed her in. While Tuco ogled at Bruja like something hanging in a meat market, he was still not as bad as Booth. The bogus cowboy did not try to hide that he regarded women as being here on earth for only one reason. But she knew Cain needed more people, and Bruja hoped bringing someone new might put her in good graces with him. It so happened Cain was holding a meeting today.

His rag-tag group of misfits sat in the old saloon, which doubled as Cain's clubhouse and home. Tuco went to the bar, which Cain stood behind, to find something to drink.

"Drink," the little man said.

"He's not a Goddamn bartender!" Bruja said.

"Holy shit, an Umpa Lumpa!" said Booth.

"What did you say, sissy?" Tuco said and removed a machete from his belt.

"Easy, friend," Cain said. "Our resident cowboy here means no harm."

"Si? Cowboy? He looks like a *maricón* to me. And I will mean nothing when I slit his throat."

"Is that right, mini-me? I'll get you a step ladder," Booth said, standing and placing a shaking hand on the revolver on his hip. Bruja laughed.

"Easy now," Cain said.

"I'm looking for work and somewhere to stay," Tuco said.

"Sadly, we do not require a clown of the pint-sized variety," Booth said.

Tuco closed the gap between them. Bruja wondered if she'd made a mistake bringing Tuco here.

"Okay now," said Cain, looking to calm everyone. "What can I get you to drink?"

"Whisky, neat," Tuco said.

"That's a man's drink. This little boy can't handle it."

"Booth, please."

Bruja admired how Cain could calm any situation and speak to anyone on his or her level. Though practically a god, Cain reached behind the counter, removed an unlabeled bottle, and poured two fingers of whisky into a glass before sliding it over to Tuco, who downed the drink in a single swig.

"So, can you use me here?"

"We can use you as long as you don't mind getting your hands dirty," Cain said, pouring another drink for the clown.

"I don't mind getting them dirty, and I don't mind getting them bloody."

"Perfect. Now. You are just in time for our meeting. Please, have a seat."

Bruja found a seat, and Booth immediately took the chair beside her and tipped his hat. His mustache sloped like a dying caterpillar crawling across his flawless face.

"You're all aware of the Cain Consequence, I believe. It's all true. Alternate realities are a fact."

"*Bullshit!*" Booth said with a fake cough—the kind that a disruptive child does in school. He scratched under his false mustache.

Bruja wanted to kick Booth in the nuts but held off.

"One theory about the Cain Consequence is that I accidentally created a time rift resulting in the Lands."

"A side effect of you trying to alter reality and get Veronica Sinclair back. Such a beautiful thing, trying to get your lover back," Bruja said.

"Kiss ass," Booth said.

"I don't understand any of this," a fat man in a shirt riding up his hairy belly said.

"That makes no sense. And why do you talk so dang fancy?" A toothless old woman said.

"I must concur with my dull-witted friend here," Booth said. "It's fuzzy logic at best, Cain." The toothless old-timer was unsure if she was being complimented or degraded and returned to her drink.

"Cain, the little fella is staring at my tits," Bruja said.

"This little fella would like to fuck your brains out," Tuco said.

"I'm already sorry I brought you here. Try to touch me, and I'll put my foot up your ass."

"I'll put my *pinga* up yours."

"I doubt I would even feel it," Bruja said.

"I daresay I believe that to be true," Booth said.

"You pansy! I'm no slut!"

"Come now. You look as though you dunk a dick in your morning coffee."

"You dandy," Bruja said, confronting the man.

"People!" Cain was stuck with a group that could not understand the magnitude of his work. He would have to pick the best of this group as his trusted people. Selecting the *best* of this group would be like choosing the best life preserver from a box of stones, Bruja knew. But they would have to make do.

"None of this makes sense," the toothless old woman said.

"I still don't buy it," a busty old woman sitting in front said.

"It's all possible. And while I am not too crazy about the name, the Cain Consequence is always occurring."

"Horseshit! I have seen you on TV a bunch of times during the '90s—just another egghead if you ask me," the old man said.

"How *dare* you!" said Bruja.

"An egg-head? I am an occultist!" Cain came from around the bar, hands extended in a STOP gesture. Though no one could see anything, Bruja knew Cain was generating energy. The old man grabbed at his jaw. Then, his temples. He kicked out wildly. The little rustic table before him toppled over. He stood, eyes bulging out in a grotesque cartoon spectacle before his entire head exploded.

The group ducked for cover as the man's headless body took two steps forward, unaware he no longer had a brain to direct him as to what to do next. The body must have finally realized it was dead and dropped to the sawdust-covered floor. Blood and brain matter decorated many of the group's clothes and faces. Tuco pulled a small shard of skull from his drink and threw it to the floor before knocking the whisky back.

Even the crickets stopped chirping.

"Anyone else doubt my power?"

All but Bruja froze. She, however, smiled through a face of gore, her teeth and eyes bright in the mask of crimson.

"I am the only man who ever tried to help this world of ours. But, because of this, they arrested me; and forced me to live like an animal. And now that I am free, many will come looking to capture me again. Looking even to kill me. And there is a group called the Four. We must stop them at any cost."

"I still don't understand anything you're talking about," Tuco said.

The whole group stepped back, expecting another display of Cain's power. But Bruja knew the little guy would have to be one of Cain's chosen.

"Understanding how this all works is not essential; what *is* important, however, is we are at war."

"So why not use your power to stop all of your opposition?" Booth said.

"Because the results are erratic. The last time I tried with my old group, the Cult of Change, some grew old overnight. One man turned into a three-hundred-pound baby. Another had his mouth and asshole reversed. But, Booth, if you'd like me to try, I am happy to do so. Let's hope nothing terrible happens to you. "

"Uh, no thanks."

"You have all learned of Schrodinger's cat? It's the idea that one places a cat in a box with a vile of poison. The cat exists both alive and dead until one opens the box. However, this answer is not a fully realized conclusion to this equation. You may open the box to find said cat dead or alive. But you may open the box to find a dog. Or a gorilla."

"Or maybe you open the box to find a Spanish midget clown for our amusement," Booth said.

"*Si*, or this gay-bar 'cowboy' on his knees surrounded by dicks," Tuco said.

Cain rubbed his temples. What a group he'd been cursed with.

"A crude example, but yes, the concept is the same. Infinite possibilities. Now let's eat," Cain said.

Zack and The Bat came around from the kitchen, placing large plates before the group: Steak and french fries.

"Meat. Thank God," Booth said. "Having lived in Vegan Land for so long, anything other than soy is heaven! I was not expecting this."

"What were you expecting?" Cain asked.

"Gruel," Booth said. Everyone laughed, the mood lightening now that bellies were being filled.

"Do you have salad or grilled chicken," Bruja asked. "I'm trying to lose weight.

"Sorry, no," Cain said.

"Well, I know of a low carb, zero fat, high protein, gluten-free diet: the 'all dick diet,'" Booth said. He and Tuco fell out.

"Cain, he's staring at my tits again."

"Jesus," Cain uttered under his breath.

***

Cain split his group. The majority of them he tasked with finding the Cult of Change (who was also rumored to be in West Land, but so far, Cain had not been able to track them). Cain let them all go and asked Tuco, Bruja, and Booth to hang back. When all the others were gone, he spoke.

"I will be honest: the Cult of Change, while a problem, is not the smartest and has been hurting themselves more than me. More of a threat is the Four, and I want them stopped. Stopping these interlopers should not be too much trouble for a witch, a sharpshooter, and the deadliest man with a knife. Despite what the media had purported and what many believe, I am the good guy in this mess."

"We know that," Bruja said.

"And what's in it for us?" asked Booth.

"Ah, when all of my opposition is out of the way, it's my conjecture I will be able to blur timelines, influence alternate realities, and *manufacture* the changes."

"What does that mean?" Tuco asked.

"It means once you eliminate the Four, I can give you three, whatever reality you desire."

This appeased them. Tuco and Booth left the saloon.

"Bruja, may I see you for a moment?" Cain asked.

"Of course."

"How is our little plan going?"

"Perfect. He thinks minutes are hours; hours are days for him."

"And the love spell?"

"Working like a charm. He's weak."

"Excellent. Now, I'd like to speak to you about your old roommate. There is something I need to tell you about Julia Faith."

***

Bubby woke early in the morning to find his girlfriend crying.

"Baby, what's wrong?"

"Don't call me that!"

"What? What's happening?"

"Leave me alone."

"Baby-..." Bubby could not remember her name. Had she even told him her name? Of course, she had. They had been together...how long now? Six months? Seven? Yet, could not remember her name. His mind was cloudy. He could hardly remember how he'd spent the last six months other than with his love in this apartment. But how? He must have left the apartment. He must go somewhere. But there was nothing.

"Why don't you leave me alone, you loser."

"What's happening?"

"She's his daughter! HER! The great man's daughter!"

"What great man?"

"Cain, you idiot."

"I don't understand," Bubby said.

"Of course you don't."

She was drunk and curled on the bed. Bubby let her be and stood lifeless. Of course, this had been too good to be true. Her eyes closed, and she mumbled the name *Julia* several times. Then she was snoring.

He slept on the sofa and woke later to an empty apartment.

He wiped away tears. Blackness, an old friend, enveloped him. Who was he kidding? How could she have loved him? He left the apartment and walked the streets of Pub Land. But it didn't look like the Pub Land he had lived in for years but a rough copy of it.

He went to the bar.

***

"Where is he?" Julia said, her head bouncing in all directions. Bubby had not shown up for breakfast as planned. They checked his room, the lobby, and the lounge. Bubby was nowhere to be found.

"Maybe he got lost," Stu said.

"Or drunk," Rex said.

"No. Bubby would not get lost. And he's not drunk, idiot."

"Now what?" Stu asked.

"We have to find him."

"Oh great," Rex said. "Now we have to babysit this guy?"

Rex had been in an even worse mood than was normal since his Mustang had run out of gas and had to leave it abandoned.

At Rex's insistence, they would check all the bars in the area.

They entered the bar. Though it was morning, a few people were drinking. One was Bubby.

"Unbelievable," Rex said. "He must have stayed in here all night."

Bubby was at a table alone, looking like he'd used his face to mop the place. They walked over.

"Bubbs, what the fuck?" Rex said.

Julia put her arms around him. "Thank God you're okay."

"I…what?"

"Bubby, you were supposed to meet us for breakfast. What happened?" Stu said. But Stu noticed the lost look in Bubby's eyes. Julia detected his aura—a curse.

"Who are you guys?" Bubby asked.

CHAPTER TWELVE

"A love charm?" Stu asked.

"Yes, and something else, a glamor."

"Bullshit. He's drunk, is all", Rex said.

"What are you guys talking about?" Bubby asked. Stu was inclined to agree with Rex that Bubby's condition had more to do with being overserved than hexed. But there was something in the way Bubby tried to form words and eventually gave up. His vacant stare convinced Stu this was more than mere intoxication.

"Bubby, you have to trust me, okay?" Julia said. She put her hand on Bubby's forehead and chanted. After a moment, Bubby's eyes cleared.

"Julia. What happened?" Bubby said, his eyes tearing.

"I'm sorry. Someone used a love charm on you."

"Stu? Rex?"

"Yeah, Bubbs. Can we go now? You've wasted enough of our time."

"Don't be a dick. This charm was strong."

"Wait. How long?" Bubby asked.

"You were gone all night."

"Night? But I was with her for months."

"I knew it! A time glamor. Oh, poor Bubby. You must be so confused right now."

"Can we get going now?" Rex said.

Julia explained how a spell had warped Bubby's perception and made him believe ten hours had been months.

"I can't remember her name. I don't think she ever told me. I forget what she even looked like."

"Nothing wrong with that, Bubbs. You're better off forgetting women. Do you remember the sex, at least?" Rex asked.

"Oh. Shut. Up!" Julia said.

"Okay, back to the plan. We get the hell out of TV Land," Stu said.

And that's precisely what they did. They traveled through TV Land's seemingly infinite number of streets (this land was huge due to how vital TV was to so many people). They searched for a place where they would not be troubled by obnoxious reality TV stars and stupid sitcom dads.

They stayed for a while in a place called Millennial Land. Money had been outlawed in this place, and the inhabitants expected everything to be free, resulting in constant riots. Luckily, most of the people who lived here were skinny and weak. And their attempts to cause damage and do bodily harm to each other were all but useless. The women looked like boys; the men resembled skinny children dressed as lumberjacks for a costume party. So mostly, the people here settled for protesting some cause or other and complaining a lot.

They found lodging and met in the bookstore's coffee shop to discuss how to find and infiltrate the Cult of Change. Bubby got them a table as Rex ordered their drinks.

"I'll hold the table. Get me a double espresso with soy foam," Bubby said.

"A what?" Rex asked.

Julia asked for an almond milk café latte. Stu requested an iced mocha with stevia.

"What the hell are you guys babbling about?"

Rex strode to the counter and looked over the girl.

"Let me get a coffee regular, honey," Rex ordered.

"A coffee with honey?" the girl behind the counter asked.

"What? No! A coffee regular."

"I'm sorry, sir. I don't know what you mean."

"Rex, you're not in the '80s. Coffee is more complicated now," Julia said.

"How do you complicate coffee?"

Bubby stood and shouted: "My friend here will have a venti coffee with two white table sugars and a splash of full-fat cow's milk."

The girl brought them their drinks.

"Jesus Christ," Rex said. "Those are coffees you guys have. They look like ice cream sundaes."

"Sir," the manager, a man who could not have been long out of high school, said, marching over. "You cannot use the name of the Christian deity here. It may offend some customers whose beliefs do not match your own."

"Fucking-A."

Rex removed the cover of his coffee and blew on it. Julia grabbed some foam with a straw and sucked it. Bubby looked at his feet, still embarrassed over the love spell for which he'd fallen, Stu thought.

"Do you guys remember Dr. Phil from TV was the president for a few weeks?"

"I remember Mr. President/Dr. Phil," Bubby said. "Thank God that change did not stick."

They met here the next three mornings. The place they stayed was cheap, and no one here bothered them. They spent a few days brainstorming, but Stu wondered if they were unconsciously stalling, fearing what would come next in this unpredictable journey.

But one day, the bookstore became a pet shop specializing only in rare rodents.

"So, what's our next move," Stu asked, tapping on the glass tank housing a two-headed purple hamster.

"Fuck if I know," Rex said.

"Well, we're dealing with an infinite number of parallel universes. Imagine going to one of the timelines where everything we did was successful rather than failure," Bubby said.

"Let me take a guess: you want to make your stupid ape show a success or something like that," Rex said.

"Something like that," Bubby admitted.

"Right, and you would not try to find the reality where *Happy Jack* lasted for five seasons," Julia said.

"Six. Anyway, we're chasing our tales. We're bouncing around and getting nowhere."

"I'm not sure that's true. Think about it…the witch who hexed Bubby. Why? She must have done it to stop us. Or slow us down, right?"

A TV in the store showed the news. The newscaster was talking about the Cult of Change.

"Listen," Julia said and pointed to the TV. The anchor was a carbon copy of the gameshow host from TV Land.

> *…The Cult of Change is considered dangerous. No one knows what the enigmatic leader is doing or what he looks like. But he is a man known only as 'White Feather'…"*

"White Feather?" Stu said.

"That's it. Let's find White Feather!" Julia said. "We find him, we can join the cult…figure out what they're doing."

"But we don't know what to look for. The TV said no one knows what he looks like," Bubby said.

"Sounds like he's a red-skin," Rex said.

"Rex!"

"Pardon the hell out of me. An *injun*."

"Oh, my God."

"Sorry, honey, an *Indian*."

"Native American," Bubby said.

"Whatever."

"It's worth a try," Bubby said.

They asked around about the Cult of Change and White Feather, but no one knew a thing. They thought they might have found a lead a few times, but the people in Millennial Land were all know-it-alls, and they soon realized their few tips had them going in circles. At one point, they seriously considered packing it in. But then, one new change was Vanilla Ice's rap career became long and fruitful rather than a '90s flash in the pan. This alone outraged them enough to continue.

They finally found a portal and, after jumping through it, found themselves on a new street in a different land. They followed the green pavement. They found themselves in an abandoned industrial park.

"I don't believe it," Bubby said, pointing to a boarded-up warehouse in the distance.

"What?" Stu asked.

"Oh my God. I *think* that's my old gag factory."

"That's not possible. You said the factory was in China," Julia said.

"Yeah, and I live in perpetual '80s. Bubbs here found himself in the same bar miles apart year after year, and we are in a manufactured reality of Lands right now…I would say 'not possible' should go out the window," Rex said.

Bubby staggered toward the building.

"Hold up," Stu said, but Rex and Julia chased Bubby. Stu followed.

***

The old warehouse was the lone structure on the street, like the first construction built in a place then abandoned due to lack of funding. Bubby stopped at the door. He held the heavy padlock hanging from the door in his left hand. His right hand fumbled through his coat pocket and produced a key of rings. Bubby selected a key and put it into the lock. And despite all logic, none of them were surprised to find Bubby's key fit the lock. There was a satisfying *click* when Bubby turned the key and unlocked the door.

The inside of the warehouse was a veritable gag graveyard. Bins of hand-buzzers lay discarded, the corpses of so many things a child's hand would never hold. A box of fake vomit had spilled across the concrete floor, lifelike enough until you noticed each was a perfect copy of its sibling right down to every chunk and bubble. Lines of rubber chickens hung from a clothesline, a sad queue to nowhere. Bubby spun a spindle of toy guns.

"Wow! This is amazing," Stu said.

"Yeah..." Bubby said thickly.

"What the fuck, Bubbs? Are you crying?" Rex asked.

"Hey, asshole! Leave him alone," Julia said.

"What are these," Stu asked, pointing to what looked like a candy bar display.

BUBBY BARS.

"Oh, that was my short-lived endeavor into the low-carb meal replacement business. It flopped," Bubby said, wiping at his eyes with a handkerchief.

"Christ, Bubbs. Your business card should read: *'Bubby Goldenblatt—everything I touch turns to shit, '*" said Rex.

"Hey, dick, fuck off," Julia said.

"Damn, you have some fire in you, Julia."

Stu was examining one of the bars.

"Oh, I wouldn't eat those," Bubby said.

"Why not?"

"Well, I succeeded in making them low-carb. But learned nut butter and beef jerky was not exactly a palatable combination."

A loud sound of flatulence rang out.

"Pig!" Julia said, looking at Rex.

"What? That wasn't me. It came from Stu."

Stu held the deflated whoopie cushion.

"Careful, please!"

"A whoopie cushion. Cool," Stu said.

"Not any whoopie cushion; a Steinman 2000. Best damn whoopie cushion ever made," Bubby boasted.

"You know, Bubbs, you should have gotten into the sex toy business instead. They always sell and cheap as shit to make," Rex said.

"Oy! I could only imagine what would have happened with cursed sex toys."

The windows were boarded up, letting in little natural light. Navigating around the crowded factory was tough. There was a metallic crash as Rex banged into a weight bench.

"Shit!"

"Be careful," Bubby said. "Please…some of these items are cursed. Don't touch anything,"

"Bubbs, what's with the bench?"

"I'd tried working out for a while," Bubby said.

"Yeah, looks like you've been doing diddly squats!" Rex laughed.

Stu snaked through a display of squirting flowers, knocking over a shelf of plastic ice cubes containing fake insects.

"Careful, please," Bubby reminded.

"You know, Bubbs-" Rex said but was cut off by the wet blast of another whoopie cushion. The prolonged flatulence was followed by a *hiss*—like air slowly released from a balloon.

"Ha!" Rex held the whoopie cushion. "I love these things."

"Are you nuts!" Bubby said. "I told you some of them are cursed."

A sound like Bosh painting coming to life rose from the corner of the warehouse. Silver mist rose and folded in on itself.

"Bubbs, what the fuck?"

"Oh no. Guys, get together. A conjuring! A spirit is growing. It can be the worst creature from the darkest corner of hell." Bubby said.

Green smoke surrounded the whoopie cushion. The flies in the fake ice cubes twitched. The rubber chickens danced and clucked from their nooses.

A voice sounded from thin air but was largely unintelligible, like a broadcast from a radio with a bad connection.

"…the fuck…bitch…I…what the hell."

"Oy gevalt."

Stu almost ran as a figure materialized in the corner of the room, grabbing atoms and protons from the atmosphere and assembling itself. The voice was getting more detailed as the entity became more materialized.

"What the shit is this?" the man asked. An old black man dressed in dark jeans and a matching denim shirt stood there. Even the patchwork bucket hat on his head was matching denim. The apparition took a pack of smokes from his shirt and lit up.

"Who are you?" Julia asked.

"I'm Diggs," the spirit said, blowing out smoke and adjusting his tinted glasses. Clearly, he'd expired in the 1970s.

"Bubby, what the hell is this?" Stu demanded.

"A ghost."

"Mr. Diggs, you may go back to the afterlife," Stu said, "this was an accident."

"Hell nah, I'm gonna hang out here for a while," the ghost said, smoothing out his long handlebar mustache.

"But Stu is right…it was an accident," Julia said.

"Yeah, and so was my marriage, and the only way I finally got out of that mess was by dropping dead," Diggs said, blowing out ghostly smoke.

"So now we have a ghost with us?" Rex said.

"Well, maybe we can use a ghost," Bubby said.

"And how the hell could this pimp help?" Rex asked.

"What you say, boy? Who is this Chachi-looking mother fucker? Huh! This pimp will grab you by your hair and snap yo' back, boy!"

Diggs, ghost or not, looked like he could do it, too.

"Diggs, maybe you can help us even if you're not alive. What do you do?" Bubby asked.

"Huh?"

"For a living."

"I'm dead, mother fucker. What the hell do you think I do?"

"He's worthless," Rex said.

"Boy, I'm gonna fuck you up," Diggs said, taking a step closer and tugging at his mustache.

"Let's all take it easy," Stu said thickly.

"Boy, what the hell are you eating?" Diggs asked.

"Bubby, these are not half bad," Stu said, finishing off one of the Bubby Bars and stuffing several others into his pockets.

"Gross," Julia said.

"Diggs, I meant to ask what you *did* when you were alive?"

"New York cab driver."

"Well, there you go, he'll be a lot of use to us," said Rex.

"Son, if you can drive a cab in the Five Boroughs, you can do any damn thing."

"I'm sorry, but I don't see how a dead black cabbie can help us?" Rex asked.

"And exactly what does his being African American have to do with anything?" Julia said.

"Oh, please. Let's not get all politically correct here. We are in a fantasy land for crying out loud. Let's hit the road," Rex said.

"What about him?" Stu asked, pointing to Diggs.

"Yeah, I ain't staying in this place alone," Diggs said. "Them rubber chickens give me the willys."

"Pretend they are *fried* chicken," Rex said.

"Oh my God!" Julia said.

"Boy, ghost or no, I'm going to wax that ass."

"He ain't coming with us," Rex said. "Let's go find the cult."

"Cult? Are you talking about them Cult of Change jokers?" Diggs asked.

"Yeah, you know them?"

"Ain't nothing to know. That cult is a bunch of fools – and *white* fools, at that. They say there's no fool like an old fool. But the truth is, there's no fool like a *white* fool," Diggs said.

"Oh, and what exactly does their being white have to do with anything?" Rex asked. "Excuse me, Julia, will you complain to Diggs here for the racist comment?" Rex asked.

Julia only looked away.

"Julia, maybe you can bring him back to life," Stu said.

"A witch cannot bring the dead back to life. The body is gone."

"Who the hell said I want to come back to life?"

"You like being dead," Stu asked.

"Didn't say I like it. But it beats being alive. When I was alive, I worked my ass off for money and was taxed left and right. They tax every damn thing. They even tax your toilet. They tax your hemorrhoid cream. They tax your toilet paper. How many times can you tax a man's asshole?"

"Do you know where they are, the cult?" Bubby asked.

"Sure, them numb-nuts are in West Land. How the hell does-" but he was cut off by a voice coming from nowhere and everywhere, another supernatural radio transmission.

"Diggs! Where the hell are you? Get your boney ass over here before I smack the black off it!"

"Oh shit…the wife…see ya'll another time," Diggs said and vanished.

"What the heck was that?" Stu asked.

"Shit, even in the afterlife, women are a pain in the ass," Rex said.

***

After dinner, Cain gathered his core group—Booth, Tuco, and Bruja. As troublesome and selfish as these three were, the sad fact was they were the best he had. Cain had to make do as the rest of his group were primarily drunks and the elderly. He gathered them around and told them they were heading out on a job.

"We are going on a mission."

"Where are we going?" Booth asked.

"You will know when we get there," Cain responded.

"A cowboy doesn't hit the road without knowing if there's a bounty on his hide," Booth said, adding a false depth to his voice.

"I can't listen to him with that fake twang anymore," Bruja said. "And your mustache is falling off."

Booth removed a cigar from his leather pouch, and as he placed it to his lips, he adjusted the mustache on the sly. He lit the cigar.

"Are we going to get to cut someone's heart out," Tuco asked, grinning.

"The little guy wants to fight," Booth said, coughing.

"Not if everything goes as planned. But we may need to *intimidate* someone."

"Oh yeah, this is the right group for that," Bruja laughed.

"As I told you all, there are interlopers here. Sadly, I'm beginning to think they may not be as stupid as I first conjectured, and they are getting closer to things I would rather they stay away from. They should be no problem for you three, but we need to get some *insurance*. Gather up, all. We're going to see a man called Pip."

***

As they left the warehouse, Bubby regarded his forgotten dream in a daze. Julia's small, cool hand slipped into his clammy one.

"C'mon, let's go," Julia said and pulled him.

"What a waste this all was."

Julia looked at Bubby. She knew he was regretting something more significant than this unsuccessful business. Regret had such a weight to it.

"You know this is not real, right?"

"Oh, I know. But the failure it represents is real enough."

"We need to move. I bet this is a trap. We must be getting closer. The curse on you, this hallucination—someone or something is trying to stop us. It was a good sign—the Devil does not tempt those souls he already owns."

"That makes sense. I bet you're right. Still, it's hard to look at this."

"That may be true. But you know what is also true? All of it has led you—led *us*—here. To this place. At this time. Bubby, I may be the world's worst witch. But fate led me here with you all—even Rex," she said and smiled.

"You believe that?"

"I believe it. Everything we all went through to this point will make sense soon. This is our destiny."

"Okay. I'm all in. You convinced me. Let's do this."

"Really?"

"Of course. You're a smart girl."

"I don't think anyone has ever said that to me?"

Rex yelled from where he and Stu stood a few yards away.

"C'mon, Julia, let's move! Bubbs could have knocked you up by now."

"God, what a charmer."

"I know this is not the warehouse—I had it dismantled long ago. This place is only an interpretation, like the kid in TV Land was not Rex. Some things are not even completely right. In the corner—the spilled paint was *blue*," Bubby said. The mess was old but clearly green.

Julia watched as the dried mess in the corner turned its color from green to blue before their eyes. "But it still hurts to see it."

"Guys! File out, now!" Rex said.

"Okay, Julia, let's go," Bubby said, squeezing her hand. She touched Bubby's cheek, and they left the warehouse. And as they walked away, the warehouse faded into nothing, like so many of Bubby Goldenblatt's dreams.

***

Pip was engrossed in an old VHS of *Godzilla vs. The Smog Monster* when there was a knock at the door. Pip struggled to free himself from the crater he'd created in the sofa with years of undisturbed movie viewing. He finally managed to rock his way to his feet as the knocking became frantic.

"I'm coming, for jeepers sake!"

Pip yanked open the door. The man standing here looked like a professor. His half-moon glasses perched low on his hooknose. His tweed jacket rumpled. Pip thought the man would make an excellent Dr. Who.

"Yeah."

"Mr. Pip, my name is Barclay Cain."

"Okay…." was all Pip could say. It *was* him. He was older than when he was last known, but it was him. He had more wrinkles, and his hair had receded to a classic widow's peak, but he had gained no weight and retained a youthful glow.

"May I come in?"

"I don't know you…so you can't come in."

"But you know *of* me, I presume."

"Still, you can't come in," Pip repeated. Cain was not a vampire, so the whole *not inviting him in* thing may not mean anything. But it was worth a shot.

"Uh, but I am already inside, Mr. Pip."

Pip's field of vision jumped, reality swam, and he found himself back sitting on his sunken sofa, and indeed Cain was now standing across from him.

"What the holy heck just happened!"

"Do you have a background in the mystic arts?"

"Uh, no."

"Then it's a little hard to explain," Cain said, walking around and taking in the museum-like apartment.

"You are quite the collector. Impressive."

"What do you want?" Pip asked, but clearly, this had to do with Rex's quest for Cain.

"Sweet train set."

"What are you here for? What do you want with me?"

"Relax, Mr. Pip, I am a friend."

"Get out," Pip said and pointed to the door.

"I'm sorry, Mr. Pip. You appear to be a decent enough man, and I honestly do not mean to upset you—I truly hope you believe that. But I cannot leave. Not until I get what I came for."

Pip struggled to his feet. He was grossly out of shape but decided he would not have much trouble getting the fragile man out of his apartment. Pip closed the gap between them.

"Don't you touch him, fatso," said a harsh female voice. The woman appeared behind Pip. She looked to him like a gypsy—all her sheer clothing in purples and grays. Armlets, bracelets, and charms jingled as she moved closer. She sneered, regarding him as if he were something that fell out of a dumpster.

"How... where did you come from?"

"Thanks to the great Cain, we move outside of time and space, fats."

"Now, Bruja, no need for name-calling," Cain said.

"You, too, out! Both of you."

"Can I cut him, please," someone asked.

"No cutting. Pip here is our friend, ain't that right, Mr. Pip?" Cain asked.

What a nightmare. It had to be. A three-foot clown with a sardonic grin and a gleaming blade staggered toward him.

"I'm dreaming. This is a nightmare."

Bruja reached out and pinched a few inches of Pip's belly fat.

"Ouch!"

"This is not a dream, tubby."

"I'm calling the cops!" Pip said and headed for his phone on the coffee table next to Hostess wrappers, half of a joint, and a joystick.

"I'm your huckleberry."

Bruja rolled her eyes as a cowboy sauntered from the kitchen, pistol in hand. With the other hand, he placed a small cigar in his mouth, lit a match on his holster, and brought it to the cigar. But the man coughed and almost dropped his revolver.

"What is this? What do you want from me?"

Bruja leaned in close to Pip. She smelled like candy and sickness. The witch whispered in his ear.

"The beast."

"He's not here," Pip said.

"Oh, Pip. I was truly hoping we could be friends," Cain said. "You are aware of the Cain Consequence and know what it does. Do you realize I can make timelines cross? I could cross a line in your past to make your present quite different from what it is now. I could go back to when they bullied you. I can change it. You are a smart man, Mr. Pip. Can you imagine where you would be right now if all of those bullies had not stolen your future from you?"

The idea was tempting. But Pip had seen enough movies. The promise of an evil genius was never as clear-cut as it appeared. There was always a heavy price for such dealings.

"I don't want anything from you."

"I see."

Cain raised his slender arms like a scarecrow, and the air was sucked out of the room. Everything shifted. One moment, Pip's hair was long, then short. He was in green slacks and then white shorts. At one point, Pip found he was actually in shape (and he almost shouted, *stop!*). But he held fast, knowing he would forever be in Cain's pocket if he accepted anything from the occultist.

"Oh, dear. You're a tough one," Cain said.

"Let me slice it out of him," the evil clown said.

"Have at it, Tuco."

The clown's face twisted into a grotesque rictus, all teeth and faded paint. The witch chanted something, and Pip went stiff.

"I can't move."

"A spell," Bruja said.

And the clown cut through Pip's shirt.

"Oh, C'mon. That was a one-of-a-kind *Killer Klowns from Outer Space* baseball jersey."

"The shirt is the least of what you are about to lose," Tuco said, slicing into Pip's soft flesh.

Pip lost consciousness.

***

Pip was made of tougher stuff than Cain had thought. Tuco worked his knives, but Pip never talked. Not when the clown cut his face. Not when the knife moved around his back. Not even when the clown brought the blade to the man's genitals, but Cain had called the clown off at that point. Indeed, Cain had spoken with Tuco and ordered him not to do any damage from which Pip could not quickly recover. Still, Pip took it heroically. The cuts were primarily superficial, more like burning papercuts than anything. Rivulets of blood trickled down Pip's fat rolls. Bruja went from room to room, looking for what they had come to collect. So far, she found nothing but junk food, stacks of books, and an appalling amount of porno.

"One last chance here, Mr. Pip, then I will let Bruja cast another spell over you."

"There is no such thing as a witch," Pip said.

"Okay, Pip. I was hoping it would not come to this," Cain said. "Bruja, do that voodoo that you do so well."

"Huh?"

"What does that mean," Booth asked.

"Was that English?" asked Tuco.

The dramatic was lost on this crowd, Cain knew.

"What I am saying is go ahead and show us what magic you have," he said.

The witch chanted, her voice becoming disturbingly thick and masculine. There was a high-pitched whistle as the train set came to life. The lights flickered, followed by a jarring *pop!*

Pip grabbed his stomach. He then hunched over. Then he *shrunk*. The sound of bones folding onto themselves filled the room. Cain winced. Pip screamed and disappeared.

"Now what?" Booth asked. But as if on cue, there was a long, low *meow* from the basement.

"I think we found what we were looking for."

"What is that?" Tuco asked, pointing to a red and white tricycle. He pushed the pink bulb on the horn, creating circus music.

"Can we go now," Booth asked?

"I'm taking this," Tuco said.

"Let's go."

CHAPTER THIRTEEN

It resembled the movies *West World* and *Blazing Saddles*, a half-baked facsimile created by those unfamiliar with the terrain it copied. Stu could only liken it to a theatre set. Most people here looked more like suburban middle-class folks ready for Halloween than real cowboys and cowgirls. The whole place reminded him of being in a funhouse composed of only paint and chalk. The stars scattered across the dark sky were more like something created for a planetarium than anything found in nature. But they had made it. West Land.

Dust rose as horses pulled covered wagons. However, these sights were not anything from the Old West. The horses were mechanical, and the wagons these robots pulled were all the colors of the rainbow: pink, purple, lime-green (some wagons were all three), and other wagons were colors that did not exist in the natural world. One such wagon stopped, and its driver, a man at least seven feet tall and thin as a rail, held a bottle of glowing emerald liquid.

"Ladies and gentlemen, my name is Bishop. This elixir here is the best, the *only* tonic you will ever need. It can cure colds. It can help you lose weight. And men...if you are having trouble in the bedroom, a cotton ball soaked in this and applied to the sphincter will solve that problem as well," he boasted and held the vile high. Its green contents sparkled in the moonlight like something magical or toxic. Stu thought it was likely a bit of both.

"Yeah, right. Bet your green shit has nothing on the blue coke from Porn Land," Rex said.

"The blue what?" Julia asked.

"Rex did these drugs in a diner in Porn Land, and then-"

"Zip it, Stu!"

"Uh, never mind."

"He's a snake-oil salesman," Bubby said.

"Not at all, my chubby friend. This stuff here can even help in changing things. Reality is a delicate thing, you know."

"So, you're with the Cult of Change?" Julia asked.

"Indeed, my colorful lady friend."

"Well, shit the bed, my man, we are looking for you guys," Rex said.

"Is that right, stranger," Bishop said. He placed a purple top hat on his head, making him appear to Stu like an acid trip's version of Abraham Lincoln.

"What the hell is that," Rex asked, indicating a yellow monkey hanging on Bishop's shoulder.

"This is Mr. Giggles. Say hello, Mr. Giggles." The monkey threw a nut that bounced off Rex's forehead.

"That little shit."

"Sir, we are looking for the Cult of Change; it's true," Bubby said.

"Well then, follow me."

"How far is it," Bubby asked.

"Far, you ask. Well, there is no such thing here, friend. In fact, we are already here," the macabre man said. And he was correct. They all found themselves in a different area, though no one had taken so much as a step.

"How did you do that?" asked Stu.

"And herein is the answer, my young friend; I did not *do* anything. Indeed, it was done to us. This is how time and space exploitation work. People look at UFOs and wonder how they move the way they do. But they do not move at all. Instead, they bend the space around them, which, in turn, brings them to the desired location. Understand?"

"Another asshole speaking in circles...just what we need."

"Rex!" Julia said.

"Now, now, young lady. I understand every group has its rabble-rouser. I can handle this simpleton," Bishop said.

"What the hell did this geek call me?" Rex said.

The Four regarded their surroundings, perplexed. They had moved an indeterminate distance in an instant. Was it a quarter-mile? Forty miles? Were they in a new universe? Stu sensed he knew what Bishop was hinting at. This place existed outside of time, outside of space. Reality here was a delicate thing indeed.

"Welcome to the Cult of Change," Bishop said. The odd monkey thing, Mr. Giggles, perched itself on Bishop's shoulder, eating curious nuts and berries from the tall man's hand. Bishop took a swig from the bottle of green liquid he was peddling and grimaced.

"Time to infiltrate," Stu whispered to the others.

"First, we have to get settled here," Bubby said.

Julia walked over to Bishop.

"Sir, is there someplace where we can stay, a hotel or something?"

"My dear girl, you're in luck. I just so happen to be the proprietor of the finest lodging in West Land."

Julia re-joined her friends.

"Okay, who's got cash?"

A festive horn blared, and Bubby pulled Julia from a tricycle pedaled by none other than Tuco. Bubby froze. The peppermint-colored tricycle hit a puddle and splashed mud on Bubby. Tuco looked at Bubby and held a sizeable gleaming blade as he passed. Leaving them behind in a cloud of dust and a horn with the sound of a circus.

***

The place was called the Thursday Inn. Bishop informed them the hotel was so named because every day here was Thursday. The rooms were clean and cheap. However, the catch was you lost the other six days of the week for every day you stayed here.

"What a crock of shit," Rex said. But considering what he'd seen already, Stu did not doubt a building here could be the same day of the week every day.

"This place is crazy," Stu said as they piled into the lobby.

All manner of oddities roamed the entrance hall. The bellhop, a man with a face on the back of his head, asked if they had any luggage. A woman with seven eyes greeted them at the counter and checked them in. Each of her eyes was like a window into a still stranger reality. In every eye lived a tiny person—like a minuscule human looking at them through a doll house window. All these "people" had a say, too, it appeared. The woman's voice and mannerisms repeatedly changed as each of the inhabitants of her body took their turn controlling their host.

"Which of you is *The Selected*," the woman asked.

"Sorry, what does that mean?" Stu said.

"One of you has great power. But does not know it."

"Yeah, right. Thanks," Rex said, grabbing the room keys from the mystic woman. They managed to avoid any interactions with the freaks here as they climbed the two flights of stairs to where the rooms were.

"The magic here is strong," Julia said.

"Right, that and a quarter will get you a phone call," Rex said.

"Okay, so they only had two rooms. How are we doing this?" Stu asked.

"Stu, you and Bubbs in one room, and I'll stay with Julia," Rex said.

"Yeah, right!" Julia said.

"Rex, Stu, and I will make do with one room. You take the other room, Julia," Bubby said.

"Thank you."

"Cock blocker," Rex said.

They agreed to wash up, get some much-needed rest, and meet at 7 PM for dinner. The elevator *dinged*. Bishop exited, ducking, and strode into the hall, kissing Mr. Giggles on his little yellow head.

"You all found rooms without trouble, I assume?"

"Yes, thank you."

"Bishop, I have a question," Stu said.

"Yes?"

"Well, if every day here is the same. Then why didn't you make it the *Saturday* Inn? After all, Saturday is better than Thursday."

"Oh well, we chose Thursday because, on Thursdays, we have pudding for dessert, of course."

"I see. Well, why not move pudding day to Saturday, and then you could have made every day Saturday *with* pudding?"

"Bishop's eyes bounced in thought. He bit his lower lip. He scratched Mr. Giggle's head and smiled.

"But we have pudding on Thursday."

***

At 7 PM sharp, Julia knocked on the door. Stu answered and let her in. Rex was dancing around, his face twisted into a grimace.

"What's with him?"

"He's trying to get in the bathroom, but Bubby is-"

"Bubbs is taking too Goddamn long!" Rex said and pounded the door.

"One minute," Bubby pleaded from the other side.

"Hurry in there, Bubbs. I gotta move stool! Hy turd is turtle-heading over here!"

"You got a real way with words," Julia said.

After Rex had "moved stool," they all left the room. They had not walked far when Rex yanked his sunglasses from his pocket and slipped them on.

"Oh shit," Rex said.

"What?" Julia asked.

"Well, well, well…Stu. You and your buddy made quite the exit the other day, huh?"

"Diamond," Stu said. "Hello. This is Bubby and Julia. Guys, this is Diamond. We met her on our way here."

"Hello," Diamond said, looking around them to see Rex hiding behind Bubby.

"Oh, hey. Diamond…what's new?"

"Oh, nothing. I had to get here on my own. My ride left without me."

"Oh, yeah. Sorry about that. Stu and I had an emergency and had to leave in a rush."

"Rex, you do realize, Rex, nothing happened between us," Diamond said.

"How's that?"

"You were drunk and passed out at my place. You understand we did not sleep together, right?"

Bubby and Julia turned toward Rex. Julia was unable to contain her smirk.

"Yeah, of course. Okay, we need to go. Take care, Diamond," Rex said, pushing Julia, Stu, and Bubby toward the dining area.

"Who was that?" Julia asked.

"Just move," Rex said.

Entering the lodge's restaurant for dinner, Stu spotted a poster advertising WHITE FEATHER: HOLY MAN. Of course, the sign did not have a photo of the Cult of Change's enigmatic leader. The advert warned there was to be no recording equipment or cameras of any kind. Stu had no idea why the man kept his identity hidden. That in and of itself was suspicious.

"Check it out," Stu said.

"Maybe this is our answer," Julia said.

"Yeah, yeah, yeah. You think everything is our answer," Rex snapped.

"Something has to be what we are looking for around here,' Bubby said.

"Wow, Bubbs, you're a regular Sherlock Holmes. Me, I'm a regular *John* Holmes," Rex said and grabbed his crotch and laughed. Rex's disposition appeared improved, Stu noticed. Stu knew finding out he had not had sex with Diamond was the cause of his newfound, easier mood.

"Charming."

"Stu, what do you think?" Julia asked. "Want to go to White Feather's rally?"

"He's worth checking out," Stu said, looking at the poster.

"It's worth a try," Bubby said.

"Okay, we'll go tomorrow afternoon," Julia said and clapped.

"Let's eat."

***

The Thursday Inn was undoubtedly haunted. There was no other way to explain all the uncanny things occurring within its walls. As Julia had mentioned, the place had an aura of magic. Over the next twenty-four hours, Stu learned this was where science gave way to enchantment—where rooms relocated overnight, and the clocks struck thirteen. The guests staying here were an astonishing cast of characters who made Bishop and his monkey appear commonplace.

One man living here was called "Even Steven," who, like his namesake suggested, always ended up even in anything he did. If he burned a twenty-dollar bill, he would find another within minutes. Authorities had banned him from all of West Land's casinos and card games. Not that he ever made a profit (he only ended up even). But he would kill time drinking free whisky and playing roulette or cards with the other players, having no chance of ever taking his money. He'd lose a hand, win a hand, lose a hand…

There was the mousy Mr. Dingle staying in the room next to theirs, who was never seen without his tattered suitcase. Everyone knew the suitcase was empty, but Mr. Dingle pretended the case was full of money. He had read a book about the Law of Attraction, and despite his constant whispering of 'this suitcase is full of cash,' the bag remained empty.

An enormous woman on the floor above them, known as Adipose Delilah, bounced around the halls, howling day and night. Blessed (or cursed) with a spell of never aging, she would remain thirty years old forever, but with the dreadful side effect of gaining twenty pounds yearly rather than aging. Whispers among the other guests here asserted she was Bishop's lover and, try as he may, since hearing the gossip, Stu could not stop thinking about how such a tall, slim man and an equally short and overweight woman could possibly have a sexual relationship. But human resolve was powerful—particularly where coupling was concerned.

Pompy was an elderly man who walked the halls hunched over his metal detector. He was warned about this because he kept ripping through the carpet and floorboards of the hallways in search of the gold his detector assured him was here, only to destroy the floors, occasionally bursting the water pipes in the process, but never finding the promised gold.

Stu could not wait to leave the Thursday Inn.

CHAPTER FOURTEEN

Speculations were that WhiteFeather had a "legion" of followers, but when they got to the clearing where his rally was taking place, a horde of scarcely thirty people was gathered here. The congregation stood before a hanging sheet on a cheap plywood stage. A massive man with a tiny head stood in a wood shack selling mugs of beer. The gray sky threatened to split open and downpour at any moment. The ground was mushy with last night's rain.

"What do we do, join them?" Stu asked.

"I don't know."

"Okay, follow me and try to act natural," Rex said.

"Follow you?"

"Yeah, Stu. Follow me. I'm an actor, remember?"

"You *were* an actor."

"Well, I am the expert here."

"Okay, how do we act naturally?" Julia asked.

"What do you mean?"

"What do I know about acting natural?"

"Christ, guys, do I have to do everything around here?"

"What do we do?" Julia asked.

"Pretend we're talking."

"We *are* talking," Stu said.

"Keep talking."

"What should we say," Bubby asked.

"Anything."

"That's too much pressure," Stu said, mopping his face with a handkerchief.

"Say 'peas and carrots, peas and carrots,'" Rex said.

"What the hell does that mean?" asked Julia.

"An old theatre trick. It's what you say when pretending to talk in the background of a scene."

"Why peas and carrots?" Bubby asked.

"Who the hell knows!"

A few of the odd people glanced in their direction.

"Shhh."

The group was mainly elderly and malformed, the latter rumored to be a result of whatever experiments the cult had been involved in back when Cain was still its leader. A three-legged man danced in the mud; his vestigial third leg dangling inches above the ground. A half-man/half woman (like something from an old circus—his/her gender split right down the middle) sang operatically in Italian between gulps of beer. A woman carried a drunken, green-skinned man with a shock of pink hair.

The afternoon was giving way to dusk, and the lights above the stage dimmed. A shadow appeared from behind the curtain. The crowd cheered. A man with a tiny hat and giant mustache strode to them.

"Can I help you?" Rex asked.

The man lifted himself on one leg and let loose with a fart lasting a full ten seconds. The man smiled, tipped his hat, and walked on.

"Wonderful," Julia said.

"Let's go join the crowd. Approach with caution," Rex said.

They made their way over. A naked old man did a jig in the dirt, spilling from both mugs of beer he held in each hand, shouting: "Woo-hoo! Woo-hoo!" He stepped on Rex's foot.

"Shit! Watch it, Gramps. You almost took off my toes."

"Gramps, your ass! I'll have you know back in the day, I once banged two of Frank Sinatra's backup singers—at the same time!"

"Congrats, old-timer."

"Gross," Julia said.

They nudged closer to the makeshift stage. Stu went to a man in a red tuxedo selling hot dogs while Bubby bought beer from the man with the tiny head in the shack. He got a few and passed them out.

"Well, howdy there, pretty lady."

A cowboy, sporting a horrible false mustache and holding a bottle of something green (the stuff Bishop sold?), looked at Julia like she was for sale. Stu instantly felt grimy being in the cowboy's presence.

"Hi there yourself, cowboy," Julia said.

"And you are?"

"Julia."

"Name's Booth. Charmed to make your acquaintance," he said, tipping his hat. Stu thought this guy was as much a cowboy as he was an astronaut.

Julia's voice was higher and girly now.

"Christ," Rex said.

The crowd's roar got louder, and Stu could not discern what was said between Julia and Booth. Eventually, the cowboy led Julia away.

"See you guys in a few," Julia said, beaming.

"I don't like this," Bubby said.

"Me either," said Stu, eying the cowboy as he and Julia disappeared.

"Me either," said Rex. "Who the hell is that putz?"

"See, you care about Julia, too," Bubby said.

"Yeah, if she's looking to get laid, what's wrong with me?" Rex said.

The light behind the stage grew brighter, striking the sheet and stretching the shadow of the person who appeared behind it.

"Why is he hiding behind the curtain?" Stu asked.

"Shhh! The holy man is speaking," a woman said, "what nerve!"

After a dramatic pause, White Feather's voice boomed from behind the sheet; he used a PA system complete with reverb for an ominous echo effect.

"*The white man does not understand that to go forward, one must look back,*" the voice said. "*If you don't live life, life will live you! You do not know where you're going until you're going where you do not know.*"

The crowd roared in approval.

"What the hell? He's rambling," Rex said. However, White Feather's followers did not want any voice other than their leader's.

"Shhh!"

"Shut up!"

"Down in front!"

"Let's get closer," Rex said to Stu and Bubby.

***

Julia took a sip from Booth's bottle. The stuff stuck in her throat, menthol-like. Eventually, the thick liquid plunged into her stomach, where its warmth spread to her head. The drink was alive, wiggling in her gut like a tapeworm. Then, a pleasant heat spread across her brain. What was in the elixir?

They had walked a bit, and between her horrible sense of direction and the effect of the drink, Julia was not sure exactly where they were. The sound of White Feather's voice, while still audible, was far away. The best she could figure, they were now somewhere behind the stage.

"You know Julie, you're a lovely girl."

"It's *Julia*."

"You're with the cult?"

"Not exactly."

"So, who are the three losers you're with?"

"They are my friends, not losers. Not even Rex."

They chatted for a while; discussion flowed easily with Booth. He knew exactly how to keep her talking. But after a time, Julia wondered if he was genuinely interested in getting to know her or if he was just another good-looking, smooth talker. She suspected the latter.

"So, what are your plans for the rest of the evening?"

"Spending it with my friends."

"Right. C'mere," Booth said, putting his hand on her chin and pulling her in for a kiss.

"Not so fast, cowboy."

"Why not?"

"I'm not looking for *that*."

"Sure, you are."

"Confident, are we?"

"That's right. Look, no one is around. How about a quickie?"

"How about you jump off a cliff."

Booth's eyes clouded over, and his pleasant smile weakened. Julia wanted to be as far away from Booth as possible, and now.

"You know what…I think I'm going to find my friends," She said, her voice weak. Booth's hands were like a vice on her shoulders.

"I don't think so."

***

"If you don't control your destiny, your destiny will control you!"

"Yes, White Feather," a man in the back shouted.

Bubby looked at Stu and Rex.

"If you don't change 'em your mind, your mind will never change." White Feather said, then went into an offensive *"hay-a, hay-ya"* chant.

"What is this," Stu asked.

"Shut the fuck up!" a tiny old woman said, her uppers coming dislodged in the process. The false teeth fell into the mud. The old woman grabbed the teeth and shoved them back in her mouth without so much at wiping them off.

"Enough of this horseshit," Rex said.

"What are you doing?" Stu asked.

"Watch and learn, kid. Watch and fuckin' learn."

"Oh shit."

***

Booth had Julia pinned against a stockade fence, the rough wood pressing into her back. His hand mashed her breasts. Julia was too sedated to move. How the hell had she allowed herself to get into this situation?

"Get off me," she said, sounding slow and dull.

"C'mon, relax and enjoy the ride."

"Get off!"

"Ha!"

Booth fumbled with his belt.

"I'm warning you…"

"You're warning *me*? Oh, you're adorable." Booth had his penis out and was now trying to undo Julia's jeans.

Julia spoke in an ancient and forgotten tongue. Booth first thought the mumbling was due to her numbed state from the narcotic elixir. Then, he was convinced she was having an epileptic episode. He backed off. Julia's eyes rolled in their sockets, and she finished the incantation—a curse to turn the beautiful man hideous. But as was always the case, her spell backfired.

While Booth remained unaffected, the members of the Cult of Change, watching White Feather's speech, shifted.

And then came the screams.

***

Rex walked through the crowd to the front of the stage and yanked the curtain, exposing White Feather. The 'white' in his namesake became apparent instantly. Behind the sheet was not the Native American shaman everyone expected but the whitest man Stu had ever seen. He looked like an upper middle age insurance salesman—a plump, ruddy-faced guy in a short-sleeved dress shirt with his gray-yellow hair parted to the side.

"What is this?" the old man who'd bedded Sinatra's singers said, face reddening and throwing one of his mugs at the man on stage who pretended to be a shaman. Then, the old man's head grew twice its size with a spinetingling *crack*.

"This is fuckin' bullshit!" the old granny said as her legs and arms elongated and bent at a new joint, leaving her walking on all fours like a giraffe.

The crowd continued to turn.

"Kill him!" a fat woman, who was turning a bright orange, shrieked, glaring at White Feather.

"He's an imposter!"

"Easy," White Feather said. "We smoke-em peace pipe." Again, he went into the *Hey-a, hey-a*. However, his nervous face belied the happy chant. "*Hey-a, hey-a....*"

"What the fuck?" The giraffe-granny said.

"He's a fake!" someone said through a newly formed beak.

"A fraud!"

"He's a white man! Nothing but a white man," a white man screamed.

"A charlatan!"

The angry mob closed in.

"Let's get out of here before this gets out of hand," Bubby said.

"You knew he was a fake," one of the mob said.

"Have you guys ever watched *Happy Jack*? I'm him," Rex said. "Little Rex Dolan...remember me?"

"It's not working, Rex," Stu said.

The mob closed in. Right when they were indeed about to be torn apart, Bubby fumbled through his jacket and pulled out a pistol.

"You have a gun," Stu asked.

"That ain't his dick," Rex said with a smile.

"Now, everyone...back."

The people did as told. But Stu thought here in West Land, it stood to reason some of these people would also have guns.

"You heard the man...stand back," Rex said.

"Let's get out of here," Stu said, hands raised to the crowd.

"We're leaving," Bubby said.

"Yeah, guys, let's get away from here," White Feather said, appearing behind them.

"Huh, who invited you to come with us?" Rex said.

"Yeah, that's right. You guys leave White Feather here," someone yelled.

"That's right...we'll deal with this faker," Granny said through a wicked smirk.

White Feather lowered his voice: "You guys can't leave me here; they'll tear me apart. They think I did this to them," he said, pointing to a man who now had feet for hands.

"Let's move," Bubby said, and they, along with White Feather, backed away.

After a moment, they spotted Booth shaking Julia, tearing at her clothes.

"Hey!" Bubby shouted. Booth first turned to face Bubby, ready to fight. He stared at the revolver in Bubby's hand and ran. Julia was crying.

"Julia, what happened?" Stu asked. But he knew what the cowboy had tried to do. Julia cried, face flushed. The cowboy had torn her clothes. Julia clutched the rags together at her bosom.

Julia ran into Bubby's arms. Stu looked at Rex, who, for once, did not have a wise-ass comment. He even removed his leather jacket and draped it across Julia's shoulders. They gathered themselves together and left the fairground.

Once they were a mile or two away, White Feather spoke: "Thank you. I owe you."

"What's your story?" Stu asked.

"Name is Tom White. I'm actually not a Native American shaman."

"You don't say? I would never have guessed," Stu said.

"We saved your ass, buddy. Now you help us." Rex said.

"How can I help you?"

"You can tell us what's happening with the Cult of Change. Are you guys making all these changes?" Bubby said.

"*Making* the changes? I'm sorry, I don't understand." White Feather said.

"Are you guys working with Cain again?" Julia said.

"You have it all wrong. We're trying to *stop* him."

"You expect us to believe that?" Stu asked.

"Hey, look!" Rex shouted and pointed to a large tree. A thin, tidy-looking man stood half-hidden behind a large oak tree. He appeared to be talking to himself.

"Holy shit, it's Cain," Stu said. But before they could approach, Cain disappeared in a cloud of mist.

"Cain, where?" White Feather asked, looking in all directions. "Oh, dear. I must tell you guys-"

"Get the son-of-a-bitch!" a green-scaly old woman yelled, pointing to White Feather (or was he plain old Tom White now that his ruse was exposed?).

And WhiteFeather took off.

CHAPTER FIFTEEN

The Cult of Change was a gaggle of freaks now. Then, finally, a man with three heads spoke:

"Who did this to us? Was it White Feather?" one of the heads said.

"I don't know," Stu replied. "But it wasn't us."

"We know that. You exposed the fake. We thank you," the second head said.

"But when we find who changed us into monsters….they are dead!" the third head said in a deeper voice.

"See you guys back at the lodge," a squat man hopping on one thick leg said.

When they were alone, Stu spoke. "What was White Feather going to say?"

"Who the hell knows," Rex said. "And by the way, Bubbs, when did you get a gun?"

"I got it when we were in my warehouse."

Bubby aimed the gun at Rex and pulled the trigger. A small banner unfurled with the words BANG! In red.

"A gag from the warehouse! Bubbs, nice going," Rex said.

"Guys, I need to tell you something," Julia said.

***

Stu had thought this place could not get any stranger, but he was wrong. In the two days since the debacle at the White Feather rally, the Thursday Inn went from being an eccentric dream to a full-on supernatural shit show.

Julia had informed them that it was indeed her spell that was the cause of this madness. The magic she'd used to turn Booth into something revolting had backfired and was directed at the cult members instead. The Cult of Change members had gone from being peculiar to something straight out of a sideshow's nightmare. Bishop was taller than ever, banging his elongated head everywhere he walked. His monkey-thing, Mr. Giggles, however, mercifully remained unaffected.

Mr. Dingle, who was never seen without his old suitcase, was now utterly raving mad. He no longer told tales of his suitcase being full of money. But considering the trouble he now had lugging it around—clearly, the case was no longer empty. Several people complained there was constant chatter coming from the suitcase. Eventually, Mr. Dingle opened the case to reveal a twisted naked man therein, contorted in a way physics would never allow. The case's occupant, a replica of Mr. Dingle himself, was remarkably alive. The man in the suitcase turned out to be the physical manifestation of Dingle's critical voice, constantly degrading the already neurotic Dingle, reducing the confused man into an obscenely drunk loon begging the twisted version of himself to "shut up!" often leaving him crying as his doppelganger screamed insults late into the night.

Adipose Delilah had taken to abusing candika, a drug concocted of equal parts of a resin made of Bishop's elixir and the dust of dried bodies of the poisonous balubalu centipede. She would get high on the potent narcotic and run through the halls naked, singing Iron Maiden songs until the wee hours.

That night at dinner (the meat of some unknown animal), Julia admitted confusion about how her spell had gone wrong and had transformed the cult members. It had been two days since the incident at White Feather's rally. Bishop was in charge for the time being. However, as White Feather had hinted, it did appear they had no real agenda. They belonged nowhere, so the peculiar Thursday Inn had become their home.

The Four were seated next to a group known as the Unemployed Impersonators. At first, Stu believed their group's name must have been some play on words. However, observing the obese, bearded man dressed as Madonna, a black Elvis, and an eighty-year-old Asian Lady GaGa, he realized the group's name was literal. Julia looked at her handiwork around the mess hall, her eyes brimming with tears.

"I can't do anything right. I still don't understand—I did not feel the magic in the least. I never even *finished* the spell because that...cowboy was all over me."

"If you never finished the spell, then how did all this happen," Rex said as he pointed his fork to a three-foot being with no arms or legs rolling across the floor toward the carving station.

"I don't know.

"I don't get it," Stu said. "Why don't witches cast spells for everything? Money. Love. Fame."

"You don't get it. It's the same as asking why every man and woman is not in perfect shape or has a doctorate; *work* is involved. A money spell requires an enchanted green duck's egg laid at exactly midnight under a full moon under the north-most tree of a haunted wood at least one hundred years old. And that's only *one* ingredient. There are hundreds of ingredients to a money spell."

Stu stopped writing on the napkin he'd grabbed and put his pen back in his pocket—he would not be evoking a money spell any time soon.

"I guess that makes sense," Bubby said.

"Yeah, but I am the worst witch ever."

"No, you're not," Bubby said.

"Anyway, they think it's something White Feather did that caused all this," Rex said. "You're off the hook."

"Are you kidding?" Julia said. A few people stopped eating and looked over.

"Julia…" Bubby said.

"I am the one who did this to all of them! Me and my shitty spell!"

"Oh shit," Stu said.

People stopped in mid-bite. Spoons and forks fell to the ground.

"It was them!" a giant baby-man said, pointing at their table.

"Guys…I think we better go."

*****

Movement. Swaying. He opened his eyes, and his head wanted to explode. Pip looked to and fro. The train was utterly deserted. The sign said: LAST STOP, HANDLEY. What was this? The train must have lulled him to sleep, but a train to Handly? How? Pip peered out the window at the vaguely familiar landscape. The grass, trees, and bushes. All of it was phony.

Pip stood unsteady. He'd never taken trains. The last thing he remembered was those strange people in his apartment.

From the corner of his eye, something moved. A woman in a red dress wandered to another car.

"Excuse me."

But she was gone. The conductor passed. He was dressed like something out of a steampunk comic book, complete with a monocle and topcoat. Familiarity washed over Pip. He moved as quickly as his bulk allowed, from car to car, attempting to get the conductor's attention. Finally, he caught up, staring at the man's back.

"Excuse me!"

The man turned, and Pip froze. The conductor looked like something from the failed Barry Levenson movie *Toys.* The plastic idea of a human being.

"What is this?"

"Last stop, Handley!"

"Oh my God," Pip said, calling a deity he'd never believed existed. He stared through the train window again. He looked beyond the deception of trees and barns, and there, in the distance, a giant version of the interior of his apartment.

Pip realized the woman with the odd group who had broken into his home was not lying. She really was a witch.

***

Escaping the Thursday Inn unscathed was no easy task. Bubby had to explain to the cult Julia was distraught and drank some of Bishop's elixir and did not know what she was saying. Ultimately, they were allowed to leave intact, but leave they must.

Now, walking along an empty dirt road, the Four attempted to regroup.

"Well, we spent some time with the Cult of Change, and I have to say I am convinced they are not working with Cain," Stu said.

"They also do not seem to be the bad guys," Bubby said.

"There is no good or bad here. Don't you guys get that?" Rex said.

"So, where do we go now?" Bubby asked.

"I think it may be time to throw in the towel," Rex said.

"There is no home anymore," Stu said. "I don't believe things can go back to normal now."

"What if we are chasing our tails?"

"We're close. I know it," Julia said.

"Close to what? Close to going nuts? Close to getting killed? Close to spending the rest of our lives in this shithole?" Rex said.

The ground rumbled, and they turned to see Bishop's rainbow wagon stopping beside them. The wagon was lopsided—Adipose Delilah sat beside Bishop. On Bishop's lap was White Feather. The two men were trying to even the weight distribution of the wagon as best as possible. It wasn't working. Adipose Delilah puffed on a long wooden pipe, throwing out a dazzling green smoke that sparkled in the moonlight.

Julia crept behind Rex.

"No way...don't hide behind me."

"You're a real gentleman. You know that."

"Hello. Can we give you a ride?" Bishop asked.

"You're not mad at us?" Julia said.

"Dear witch, your spell didn't do this. I needed to run before I could tell you," White Feather said. "But there is only one person with that kind of power..."

"Cain! Cain did it! He was hiding on the grounds when it all happened," Stu said.

"Cain was hiding behind a tree. I thought he was whispering or something. He must have been chanting the spell that did this to you guys," Julia said.

Bishop pushed at White Feather. The two men wrestled to get comfortable.

"Damnit, man. I can't take you on my lap much longer—you're squashing my family jewels."

"What is that?" White Feather asked. "Are you catching wood with me sitting on you?"

"Certainly not!"

The monkey, Mr. Giggles, bounced at his master's shouts. Adipose Delilah cackled opiate-laced laughter.

"They are taking me back to the lodge now that they know I am innocent," White Feather said. "We have work to do. We are going to try and create our own Land. I think Elvis Land" is a good idea.

"Amen to that, brother," Rex said.

"Climb aboard," Adipose Delilah said.

They filed into the wagon. They all got to one side of the wagon to help distribute the weight. It helped but little. The monkey got busy throwing nuts and berries into the air and catching them in his mouth. Mr. Giggles gestured to throw a nut at Rex and opened his mouth wide, showing him what to do.

"Holy shit. You guys see this?" Rex asked, mirroring Mr. Giggles and opening his own mouth wide to give the monkey a good target. Mr. Giggles threw a nut right into Rex's mouth. Rex chewed and smiled. Mr. Giggles hopped about.

Julia removed a half joint from her purse and lit up.

"Would you rather have some of this," asked Adipose Delilah, indicating the smoldering bowl of candika.

"If it's made out of that elixir...no way!"

Rex continued opening his mouth and taking the thrown nuts. "This monkey is amazing," Rex said. Stu had never seen Rex this excited.

"I hope you all realize we are on the same side," Bishop said, guiding the mechanical horses. Delilah laughed and puffed her pipe.

"He's cute," Adipose Delilah said, looking at Rex.

"We do. But now our only hope is to get to Cain himself," Stu said.

"He may be anywhere—he disappears well," White Feather said.

"I wouldn't look for him," Bishop said.

"Cain disappears where?" Rex asked.

"May I have a kiss," Adipose Delilah asked Rex.

"Only if you tell us where Cain is," Rex said, chewing a nut.

"Barclay Cain is *rumored* to hide in Haunted Land," Adipose Delilah said. She grabbed Rex and brought their mouths together. Stu winced as he realized she was giving Rex the tongue. When Rex finally managed to break away, he spoke:

"Fuckin'-A. Then that's where we're going—Haunted Land," Rex said.

"But to get into Haunted Land, you need more magic. *Strong* magic. You will need an incantation from a dark and unholy manuscript. The *Halla-Halla Ruins*, or the *Skull of Santos*. Or a book like *Malleus Maleficarum* or the *Necronomicon*," White Feather said.

Julia looked at Bubby. He pulled the *Necronomicon* from his pocket where it had been since he first met Julia to authenticate its veracity in what felt like a lifetime ago.

"Haunted Land?" Bubby said. "I don't like the sound of that."

"Son-of-a-bitch!" Rex said. Mr. Giggles bounced enthusiastically.

"What happened," Stu asked.

"Him," Rex said, pointing to Mr. Giggles and spitting. "The little bastard got me used to the nuts and, when I was not looking, threw a turd into my mouth!"

"Oh, Mr. Giggles," Bishop said, smiling. "He likes to joke."

"Joke?! Some fuckin' joke," Rex said, wiping his tongue on his sleeve.

Bishop took them as close as he was willing to go to Haunted Land. White Feather gave them vague directions, and Bishop dropped them off at a saloon. Adipose Delilah grabbed Rex on his way out of the wagon and even managed to give his crotch two quick squeezes before he broke free.

They went inside to have a drink and prepare for their journey to Haunted Land.

***

The Crotch Rot saloon was as appetizing as it sounded. A hairy man at the bar spat tobacco juice on the ground as they headed for an open table. A quintet of rough hillbillies played (of all things) *strip* poker. All of the men were at least shirtless and sported huge and hairy man-tits. The most emaciated and elderly player stood, completely naked, dancing a jig, spilling his beer on a fat nude man full of gray hair. The man stood, looking like a polar bear, and socked the dancer, who spun around twice and continued dancing.

The Four found a table.

"What are we all drinking?" Rex asked.

"I'll take a club soda," Stu said.

"No fuckin' way," Rex said. "You have to get booze here, Stu; this is West Land, for Christ's sake."

"I'll get the drinks," Buddy said as they settled at the wobbly table.

"Give me four redeyes," Bubby told the bartender.

"What the hell are you talking about," the barkeep said. Bubby was not surprised to see he was Pat from Pub Land.

"Mmm…Four whiskeys, please," Bubby said.

The bartender gave him a slanted stare, poured the whiskey, and returned to wiping glasses. Bubby brought the drinks back to the table.

"L'chaim!"

"Maybe before discussing all of this, we should say a prayer," Julia said.

"I think that's a fine idea," Bubby said.

"No thanks. Rex Dolan relies on Rex Dolan and not the Easter Bunny, Santa Claus, or God."

"I have to agree with Rex. I don't believe in any imaginary super-being," Stu said.

"But you believe in aliens, Bigfoot, ghosts, the Loch Ness Monster, and the Chupacabra?" Julia asked. Apparently, she'd read some of Stu's recent articles.

"There's more proof of all of those phenomena than there is of the existence of God. Hell, we even met a real ghost—Diggs. But there is no God."

"Stu, what a horrible thing to say."

"Do you believe praying can make a difference?"

"Of course. I knew a woman once who prayed away her cancer," Julia said.

"I call bullshit."

"Rex is right. Think about it—how many bald men are there? If you are right, why are there so many bald men?" Stu asked.

"I don't get it."

"Well, if praying can cure cancer, it should be able to make a bald man grow hair easily. But you never hear of this. Why? Regrowing hair is something you can see and touch; it's tangible. Cancer is less so. Most people are praying but also taking the traditional cure from doctors. Then, they heal and attribute it to the praying. Nonsense."

"Fuckin'-A right, Stu," Rex said and finished his drink. "People think praying is magic or something. Nonsense."

"All I know is magic is real," Julia said.

"Give me one example," Stu said.

"Us. The four of us finding one another."

"Purely chance. If you see magic in that, you can see it in anything and everything."

"Exactly," Julia said. "I see magic in everything."

"Me too, Julia," Bubby said.

They were interrupted as the poker players at the other table erupted in cheers. One man removed his stained underwear, twirled it on his index finger, and flicked it into the air.

"Okay, so, the Cult of Change. We were with them for a while, and they are not smart enough to be doing anything. Diggs was right. They are a bunch of nut jobs," Rex said.

"But they were all pleasant," Bubby said.

"Great. *Pleasant* nut jobs."

"Are we truly considering going into Haunted Land?" Bubby asked.

"Damn right. I'll grab another round," Rex said.

"I don't think we have a choice," Stu said. Despite himself, he longed to return to Church Land and his mom. "You know, this stuff is not that bad," Stu said as he drained his whisky.

Rex returned with more whisky and two large buckets of stinking buffalo wings. "Check it out!"

"What kind of western place has hot wings?" Bubby asked.

"Who cares," Stu said and stuffed a greasy wing into his mouth.

"Dig in."

Bubby ate as well.

"God, how can you guys eat that crap? It will shorten your life," Julia said.

"Yeah, so it will shorten our lives. Drinking will shorten our lives. Smoking will shorten our lives. Eating this will shorten our lives. By what, five years? The last five years are the worst five years of your life anyway," Stu said.

"That's right, Stu," Rex said, sucking the soft meat off a wing.

"Stu, I think you are getting a little buzzed. Maybe you should take it easy," Bubby said.

"Bubbs...simmer. Stu is fine. Ain't that right?"

"Yeah, me fine. I mean...*I'm* fine," Stu slurred.

They had another drink. And another. Julia was staring into her glass.

"You okay," Bubby asked.

"I'm sorry, guys. I messed up."

"What are you talking about? Cain deformed his people, not you," Bubby said.

"Not my spells failing—I am used to that now. I fell for that Booth asshole, and I almost fucked everything up," Julia said.

She never curses, Stu thought.

"It's fine. As long as you are okay," Bubby said. Julia took his hand.

"It's not fine, Bubbs. She almost got us killed. She almost got herself raped."

"Rex-"

"Don't 'Rex' me. We have to get out of here alive, right?"

"It won't happen again."

"It better not."

"Have you guys thought maybe these changes have been going on forever?" Stu asked, changing the subject.

"Like what? Julia asked.

"Like slight modifications, we'd never notice. Say a change happened, altering a lyric on the third song of Cher's second record. Who'd notice?"

"What a scary thought," Bubby said.

"A scarier thought is there would be some people who *would* notice that change," Rex laughed. They all laughed.

Rex looked at his feet when they stopped laughing, appearing far away.

"Rex, you okay," Bubby asked.

"I wish I handled my career differently," Rex said in a dragging drone, the booze slowing his thoughts.

"How so?" asked Julia.

"Shit, I don't know. I should have kept acting. Or never acted at all. Never at all would have been better. My mother wanted to be an actress when she was younger. But she met my dad and got married, and I came along. So, she pushed me into acting for as long as I can remember. She said she knew I had a gift. I believed it. But now I think I was a normal kid pushed into it all."

"Wisdom always comes too late."

"Amen, Bubbs. You're a fuckin' philosopher. Has anyone ever told you that? I guess the 'little guy' is creeping into my mind again," Rex said.

"Little guy?" Julia asked.

"I once read a psychology book—yes, I read, don't all look so shocked. The author said we should think of our negative thoughts, the voice telling us we are not good enough, as a little guy in our mind. And if we shine a light on him, he scurries back into the darkness."

"I like that," Bubby said.

"But you know what the problem is, Bubbs," Rex said, his eyes empty.

"What?"

"It's the little guy who runs the show."

"How depressing," Julia said.

"Well, in case you have not noticed, I'm a depressed bastard."

"Maybe if you met a woman or dated a little, you'd be happy," Julia said.

"Please. I have tried. I tried computer dating before Queens became '80s Land and the technology ban. What a shit-show."

"Why?" Stu asked.

"The first tip about computer dating, boys—if the pic the woman uses for her profile is of her face only…she's a heifer," Rex said, draining his glass.

"Pig," Julia said.

"But I found one woman. Pretty. Kicking bod. We dated a few times, and it went okay. But then she dropped a bomb."

"Married?" Stu asked.

"Married would have been fine. *Better* than fine. A married woman does not expect commitment. She had Parkinson's. So, I stopped calling her."

"Oh boy," Bubby said and got another round, though he thought Stu was already over-served.

"And here's the capper…she got mad at *me*! Here, I was doing the responsible thing, and she still got mad. Just like a woman."

"I'm sorry. *You* were doing the responsible thing, how?" Julia asked.

"I knew I couldn't handle it, so why get involved only to disappoint her in the end? Look, I'm an asshole, I know that, but I'm not stupid. I know I'm too selfish to deal with someone who will become so needy. So, I got out before we got serious. Is that so bad?"

"Well, I guess she saw it differently," Bubby said, returning with another round.

"Bubbs, don't you get all high and mighty on me."

"Wow. And to think I was starting to feel for you. What a swine," Julia said.

"Swine, why?" Stu asked.

"Are you listening to your buddy here, Stu? He stopped dating a woman he liked because she was sick," Julia said.

"Right," both Stu and Rex said together. Bubby looked away.

"And you don't see a problem?"

"No. Rex got out because he knew the situation was not for him. He got out *before* anything serious happened. What's wrong with that? He only dated her a few times. It's not like he left a wife for getting sick," Stu said.

"Thank you, Stu," Rex said.

Julia turned.

"Bubby?"

"Oh no. *Tishar ba mazavcha.* I'm not getting involved."

They ordered more drinks. Julia got a soda this time, but Stu enjoyed the whiskey now that his taste buds were dulled.

"So, Haunted Land is the next stop. I bet we find the answers there," Stu said.

"Oh, I don't know about this," Bubby said.

"Shit, I'm not a-scared of any Haunted Land. Bring it on," said Rex.

***

The air outside the saloon was thick with humidity and stunk of mold and raw sewage. In the distance, the dampness caused a mist. The dirt roads were empty. Stu stumbled a little and laughed.

"Careful," Bubby said. "Let's get him to bed."

"What the hell are you four doing now?" a voice behind them asked.

"Diggs!" Julia said and ran over to the specter.

"Hey, y'all. Sorry, I ran off before, but that wife of mine is worse dead than she was alive."

"Wives still have men by the sack even after death. Well, that seals the deal for me. Never. Getting. Married," Rex said.

"Right. Like they're lining up to walk down the aisle with you," Julia said.

"Hey, Diggs, I have a question. I may be drunk, but I always wondered if ghosts were able to—" Rex started.

"I know your damn question, boy, and we ghosts have other shit to do than watch the living in private," Diggs said.

"You can read minds?" Stu asked."

"Hell, no, I can't read minds, but I know what this nasty white boy was gonna ask. He wants to know if ghosts watch when the living are yanking their cranks, whacking the weasel."

"Ewww," Julia said.

"Is that what you were going to ask?" Stu wanted to know.

"Mmm…no. I…uh…wanted to know…mmm…if ghosts eat," Rex said.

"Yeah, right."

They walked the fake dirt road toward where White Feather said Haunted Land was. Diggs floated behind. Stu stopped, caught by something hanging in the window of a general store. Next to an advertisement for live music next weekend was a traditional "wanted" poster.

"Would you look at this shit," Stu said, pointing to the WANTED poster. It read:

WANTED Dead or Alive: The Malevolent Four – for crimes against time, space, and humanity in general…

The accompanying sketches were crude but were clearly the four of them. "Son-of-a-bitch," Rex said. "Look how fuckin' fat they made me!"

In the illustration, Rex sported a double chin he was only beginning to develop in reality. The poster also had their names wrong. Julia stepped over and read the sign:

"It calls me 'Julie.' It has Bubby as 'Buddy.' Stu, it got your name right and referred to you as the leader of our posse."

"I'm the leader!" Stu said.

"What the fuck," Rex said and bumped Julia out of the way. "Look at this shit! And my name!"

Julia continued to read:

"Rex Dolan, aka. Happy Jack, aka. Happy Jack-Off, aka Jack-Off Dolan," She giggled.

"Jack-Off Dolan," Stu said.

"Stu, zip it!" Rex said and ripped the poster off the wall.

"I don't think that's going to do much good," Bubby said, pointing to the lengthy road. The same poster hung everywhere. Someone had littered every surface with the damn things while they were in the bar.

"And what is this 'The *Malevolent* Four' stuff?" Bubby asked.

"Someone is framing us," Rex said. :Making us look bad.

"Who?"

Julia dug through her pockets and placed a joint into her lips.

"Anyone have a match?"

"Yeah, my ass and your face," Rex said.

Bubby pulled a book of matches from his sportscoat. He lit Julia's joint. The sweet herb filled the air.

"This shit is slander," Rex said, pointing to the posters.

"This is bullshit. How come I ain't in the poster," Diggs asked.

"I don't know," Julia said, reading the fine print of another poster as she exhaled smoke.

"*I* know why…they left me out of the poster 'cause I'm black."

"You're not really black," Stu said.

"Come again?"

"Do ghosts have ethnicities?"

"Ghost or not, son, my ass is black,"

"I don't think it's a race thing," Bubby said. Maybe they can't see you because you're a ghost. Plus, you were not with us when we came here."

"It's 'cause I'm black."

"Wait! They actually *do* mention you," Julia said, reading more of the fine print.

"What does it say?"

"It says….umm...huh...I..."

"Well," Stu asked.

Julia cleared her throat once. Twice.

"Mmm…it says we, the Malevolent Four, mmm... 'may be accompanied by the ghost of an *uppity nigra* called Diggs.' I'm sorry!"

"'Uppity nigra'! Awesome!" Rex said.

"That right, 'Jack-Off Dolan'? Oh, and do your friends know you tickle your asshole with your left hand while jerking off with your right?" Diggs asked.

"I *knew* it!" Rex said.

"This is bad. Someone is setting us up," Stu said.

"Man, I want to get my hands on the cracker who made this goddamn poster!"

A blue flash cracked the sky like cartoon lightning. A *bang* of thunder followed, and a voice cried from all around, like the world's best surround sound.

"Diggs, get your bony ass back home!" Diggs's wife's voice bellowed from the sky. "Right, the hell now!"

"Son-of-a-whore. See ya'll."

And Diggs was gone.

But the Four had a problem. A *major* problem—they were wanted now. Stu thought this new development would make the remainder of the journey interesting in the worst possible way.

Bubby pulled a bottle from his coat pocket.

"Bubbs, my man!" Rex said. "Where did you get that?"

"I bought it from the barkeep before we left."

"That's my Bubbs, always thinking."

"Well, what's an 'old alcoholic' without a bottle?"

"Look, Bubbs, I didn't mean it the way it sounded."

"It sounded like the truth, so no worries."

They walked and passed the bottle around. They agreed to check out Haunted Land in the daylight the following morning. No one was crazy enough to go there at night. Two hours and many drinks later, they found themselves deep into West Land.

"I fucking love you guys," Stu slurred.

"We love you too, Stu," Julia said.

"That's right," Bubby added and smiled.

"Ha, that's my boy," Rex said and put his arm around Stu. "I'd kill or die for you, Stu," Rex said.

"Oh, boy. Rex is drunk," Julia said.

"What the hell is that?" Stu pointed to a filthy blond wig rolling through the dirt road in the wind.

"Goddamn, it's a tumbleweave!" Rex said,

"It does not look like a tumbleweed," Julia said.

"Not a tumbleweed—a tumble*weave,*" Rex repeated. "It looks like a couple of *sistas* fought, and someone lost her weave."

A house lit in red caught their eye.

"Son-of-a-bitch," Rex said. "Julia, give us boys a minute here."

Rex, Stu, and Bubby walked a few feet away.

"What's up," Stu asked, his voice heavy with drink.

"No. Rex, absolutely not," Bubby said.

"Don't 'no' me, Bubbs."

"What is this," Stu asked, pointing his chin to the glowing red house.

"Boys, what we have here is a good old-fashioned, all-American, authentic Western whorehouse," Rex said, smiling larger than Stu had ever seen.

"No," Bubby repeated.

"Fine, Bubbs, you can stay outside. Stu, you feel like getting your pecker wet?" Rex asked.

Stu looked at Bubby.

"This is a bad idea, guys. These women are being exploited," Bubby said.

"Right on," Julia called from the distance. She had been eavesdropping on the conversation.

"Are you kidding? If anything, they are exploiting *us,* Bubbs. C'mon, Stu, let's do this."

"Tishmeri al atzmekha. Be careful, Stu."

"He's with me, no problem. You girls wait out here. If Stu and I are not out by next Saturday, forward our mail."

"What mail?" Julia asked.

"Let them go, Julia. We'll be waiting here for you guys," Bubby said.

Rex put an arm around Stu as they entered the brothel.

***

Bruja entered the common room to find Tuco and Booth gathering supplies.

"Where are you two assholes going?" Bruja asked.

"A face like a sewer and a mouth to match," Booth said.

"Bite me, pansy."

"We're going to see if we can find the Four, and you are not invited, little lady."

"Si, you are not coming," Tuco added.

"Really, junior. Are you guys taking horses? Because I wonder how you will fit on one, tiny?"

The men looked at one another.

"Well, he is certainly not riding bitch with me," said Booth.

"If there's a bitch it's you. I would be on top of you," Tuco said.

"What?"

"I don't want to. But *if* we were to…you know…I would be on top," Tuco said.

"Jesus Christ. Can we all please try and act like outlaws for once?" asked Booth.

"Yeah, some outlaws you two make. A cosplay cowboy and the Mexican version of Baby Huey," Bruja laughed.

"Yes, and the last thing we need is to add an over-the-hill witch to the mix. Now, let's get rambling," said Booth as he and Tuco left the saloon.

"Assholes," whispered Bruja. And she let them get a head start before following.

***

The inside of the brothel smelled of jasmine, sex, and trouble about to boil over. Half a dozen women stood against a purply velvet wall: four white girls, a small Asian woman, and a curvy black woman. The madam, a massive woman of indeterminate age, asked which woman they wanted.

"Rex, we're low on money," Stu warned.

"Stu, my man, I need to get laid. You do, too."

Rex motioned the bartender to give Stu a shot of bourbon and a beer. He asked if they had the 'porn star deluxe' as he's had in Porn Land, but the barkeep scratched his dented head and said nothing. Rex ordered himself the same as Stu.

"Rex, I think I've had enough."

"Never mind. Drink up!"

Stu took the shot and quickly backed it with a massive swallow of the beer.

"That a fuckin' boy!" Rex said and slapped his back.

The madam asked again which woman they each wanted. Stu's chest tightened, but he didn't panic.

"I'll take the colored one," Rex answered.

"'Colored'? What color would that be?" the black woman asked.

"He does not mean any offense. He's from '80sLand," Stu said.

"Even in the '80s, he'd be an asshole," the woman said and took Rex's hand.

"And you?" the madam asked Stu.

"Oh…I don't know. I don't want to offend anyone."

"He'll take the little cute, chink-a-dink right there," Rex said, pointing to the small Asian woman in a bodystocking. She had blood-red hair and eyes like a serial killer.

"Hi, honey," The woman said, in a thick accent, and put her arm around Stu. She gave Rex a pissy stare. Her voice was high and hinted at crazy.

"C'mon, Stu, let's do this," Rex said. They were led through a hall and taken into separate rooms. Stu already regretted this.

***

Bubby and Julia found a bench outside the brothel. They sat, Bubby drinking from his bottle and Julia pulling from her joint. Julia moved in close and rested her head on Bubby's arm. Comforted by her closeness—Bubby thought if he'd ever had a daughter, he would have wanted her to be Julia. He imagined a world of possibilities for this young woman. But she was so unsure of herself. Bubby wished he could make Julia see herself through his eyes: capable, beautiful, strong.

"So, do you have any family or a boyfriend back home?" Bubby asked.

"I don't have any family left. As for a boyfriend, I have been seeing someone for a few months, but I think I may need to end it."

"I'm sorry to hear that. Why?"

"Problems."

"What kind of problems?"

"Do you want to know?"

"Of course, why wouldn't I?"

"Well, it's sexual."

"Oh…never mind."

"No, I want to ask you about it. Stu is too young, and Rex…well…."

"Julia, I am not so sure I want to hear about your sex life."

"Just one thing, Bubby. I want your opinion on something I think is strange."

"I know I am going to regret listening to this. Proceed." Bubby braced himself. He was no good at advising in general. Advice on anything *sexual*, well, he could not think of a worse person for the job.

"Okay, so I am dating this guy from Doo-Wop Land, Chicky Constantino."

"Right."

"Well, the first time he tried to make love to me…I went to his place. I knocked, and he yelled to 'come in.' I walk in, and this trail of rose petals leads from the door to the bedroom. I know he thought he was being romantic. So, I followed the petals to the bedroom, and he was lying in bed, wearing a red silk robe."

"What did you do?"

"I burst out laughing."

"Oy."

"I couldn't help it; he looked so ridiculous. Needless to say, nothing happened that night."

"How did he take it?"

"He was a basket case. Why is it men always say women are crazy and emotional…like men aren't?"

"Oh, we are emotional. We just sit in a closet and have our breakdowns where no one can see us. As for crazy, we men can go neck and neck with you gals."

"But a few weeks later, we finally made love for the first time. Did I mention he's thirty-two, my age, and only recently moved out of his mother's house."

"That's not too strange these days. Living on your own is expensive."

"Hold on. So, we had sex for the first time. It was fine. No major fireworks, but fine."

"Okay…" Bubby said. He knew there was more to the story.

"But when it came time for him to…to…."

"Yes?"

"You know. At the end…when it was time for Chicky to…"

"*Finish*?" Bubby offered.

"Yes! When it came time for him to finish, he shouted as he…as he…."

"*Climaxed*?"

"Yes. Boy, Bubby, you're easy to talk to. When he *climaxed*, he shouted."

"So, he shouted. I guess that's not too odd."

"But it's what he said as he came."

"Julia, I shouldn't hear this."

"But I need your opinion. Chicky shouted, 'I WANT MY MOMMY!' as he came."

"Oh…"

"I don't have much experience with men, but that's not normal, right?"

"Oh, Julia, who's to say what's normal anymore."

"Bubby, please."

"Well, I do not like to judge, but I would have to say run, Julia. Run for the hills."

Julia smiled. She rubbed the back of her hand against Bubby's stubble.

"Thank you. I knew I could confide in you."

"I'm honored you feel that way. But one favor..."

"What?"

"No more about your sex life."

They sat silently, enjoying one another's company for a moment.

Then, from the brothel came a bloodcurdling scream.

***

Stu laid back on the vast crimson bed, wondering who lay here last and if he would catch lice, crabs, or something worse that existed only in this strange land. But the drink calmed his nerves, and he put the fear of microscopic parasites, alien or otherwise, out of his mind. His heartbeat quickened as he watched the woman preparing to service him, electrified by the thought of the contact to come. His pulse throbbed in his neck and temples as well as below. Rex had been right about one thing—it had been a long time since he'd been with a woman—a *long* time.

"So where are you guys headed?" the woman asked (Stu realized he did not know her name. This felt wrong, but he was too embarrassed to ask now). The woman rubbed his shoulders.

"Searching for Barclay Cain. We are going to Haunted Land."

"Oh, be careful there. There are many things out there: enchanted cottages, evil witches, dark creatures, and haunted houses, of course." She warned. Stu could only catch some of what she said because her accent was so pronounced. She laid Stu down and pulled off his jeans. She wore only the erotic bodystocking, showing off her perfect little body, her dark, erect nipples poking through the fishnet. Stu's head swam with whiskey and heat. He thought he might pass out.

Stu did not have much experience with women. He'd had sex only twice in his life. The first time, with a pimple-faced young woman he'd been introduced to by Feldman, was a messy and awkward affair. The second time, with the same woman, was less awkward but just as unsatisfying.

"No problem for us; we're the Four. Maybe you've heard of us," Stu said. The whiskey and impending sex had him talking with a confidence he seldom ever had before. He was beginning to sound like Rex.

The woman climbed onto the bed, pulled Stu's boxers off, and grabbed his shaft. He was not sure he could handle all this.

"Can I lick your *bralls*?" she asked, inching down on him. Momentarily confused, he finally realized "*bralls*" was *balls*. She was kissing her way from his belly to his crotch.

"In the universe's history, has any man ever answered 'no' to that question."

"What? I don't understand. 'no'?" she asked.

His hard-on throbbed.

"Never mind."

"Okay." She moved away from his nether regions.

"No! No! Lick my balls, please!" Stu cried, surprising himself. Rex would be proud.

The Asian woman put a condom on Stu with her mouth and worked him over. He reminded himself to thank Rex for convincing him to come here. After the foreplay, the woman got on top of Stu.

"You want soft, medium, or strong?"

"Uh…Strong, I guess."

Once she put Stu inside, the little woman bucked like mad. And Stuart Sawyer held on for dear life.

***

"Get ready, brown sugar; you're about to get a whole lotta Rex Dolan up in ya."

"I sure hope I can handle it," the woman answered, unimpressed.

"Have you ever watched the show *Happy Jack*?"

"Jack, what?"

"Nothing."

The woman lay on the bed. Rex stood in the corner, looking into the front of his jeans.

"You ready, baby?"

"Uh...yeah. One a minute." Rex turned his back on the woman.

"C'mon, honey. The clock is ticking."

"Do you have any hot sauce?"

"Hot sauce? What in the hell are you talking about?"

"Nothing, Rex said and wished he had some of the blue coke from Porn Land. He got undressed, feeling more like he was about to be examined by a doctor than enter into an erotic encounter. After an uncomfortable amount of time and an embarrassing number of tries, it was clear he would not be able to perform.

"Son-of-a-bitch!"

"It's okay. It happens."

"It doesn't happen to *me*."

The woman pointed to Rex's flaccid member. "Apparently, it does." She worked Rex over with her hand. It was working.

"Hell yeah! Keep it going!"

Right as he was about to explode, a blood-curdling scream shot through the brothel.

"Holy shit," the woman said and stopped what she was doing.

"Son-of-a-bitch, don't stop…please...keep tugging," Rex begged.

"I think that's your friend screaming."

"Goddamnit, Stu!"

***

This was incredible. Stu thought he might lose himself. Then, a pain like nothing he'd ever experienced shook him from his bliss. Stu heard the scream for a few seconds before realizing the shriek came from him.

The poor Asian woman looked as if she didn't know if she should scream or shit. Stu's screech was so other-worldly. The fishnet bodystocking had managed to get tangled around Stu's scrotum. Stu grabbed the woman's hips to stop her from jumping off him (likely taking his favorite, if seldom used, parts with her). He held to the poor woman for dear life. He was caught but good.

"God, please don't move!"

"Okay, you need to relax."

"Relax? My shit feels like it's in a bear trap!"

"Is it *brawls* or *cocker*?"

"What?"

"You catch your *brawls* or *cocker*?"

"I'm caught. What difference does it make? Are you an idiot?"

Her English may not have been perfect, but the woman must have known when she was called an idiot because, as Stu said the word, the little woman jerked her hips and pulled him with her. Stu saw stars. It became clear both his "*brawls*" and "*cocker*" had been caught. When it came to awkward situations, Stu Sawyer never did it half-assed.

"I'm sorry! I'm sorry!"

The door flew open.

"This better be good…I was just about to-"

"Help me, Rex. Please."

"What the fuck, Stu…can't you even get laid without a problem?" Rex said, tugging on jeans.

"Oh shit! White boy caught his shit! Everyone, white boy caught his nuts!" the woman with Rex said.

"She's right. Your shit is turning purple," Rex said. Stu could not bear to see if it were true, but the pain between his legs testified to the comment's veracity.

Julia appeared at the door and gasped.

"Look away. Julia, look away!" Stu cried.

"Oy!" Bubby said. He was peeking through his fingers.

"Someone...get me loose."

"I'm not getting in there," Rex said.

More women, including the madam, appeared in the doorway.

"Make them go away! Stop looking at me," Stu said.

Julia stepped forward yet did her best not to look directly at the scene. Stu turned the color of a ripe tomato.

"I'm going to try a spell," Julia chirped.

"A spell? What the hell are you talking about?"

"Dammit, Stu, just lay still."

"Oh, God!"

"Okay, I need to get into a meditative state."

"Meditative state, your ass, his balls are turning blue," Rex said.

"Oh, God..."

"Okay, *Goddess of lust and blessed of glee, take thy nuts and prick and set them free.*"

They all got quiet momentarily, waiting to see what would happen.

Nothing.

"It should have worked. I felt the energy move around us."

"Oh, for Christ's sake," Rex said.

While nothing happened to help Stu, a symphony of cries from many other rooms filled the halls.

"Oh no," Julia said. "My spell backfired."

"Rex, I'm about to lose my dick!" Stu screamed.

"What the hell do you want me to do?"

"Help him," Julia pleaded with Rex.

"Look away, Julia!"

"Rex, get me out of this. Save my nut-sac!"

"Are you kidding? I'm not touching you."

"Rex!"

"Why me? Why not Bubbs?"

"Oh no. You were the one who got Stu drunk. You are the one who convinced him to come into this place," Bubby said.

"Son-of-a-bitch!"

Rex pulled a knife from his jacket.

"What the hell are you doing?"

"I'm going to cut you free. What do you think?"

Once Rex got close, he realized how caught Stu had become. But Rex swallowed his pride and got to work.

"Get him out! Get him free!" the Asian woman said, tired of straddling Stu.

"Oh, God. Be careful. Careful!"

"Stu, be still, or you will lose a nut."

"Guys, what if I lose a nut?" Stu asked, turning to Bubby and Julia.

"Shit, I got a buddy who lost a nut in an atomic wedgie incident in high school, and he's fine," Rex laughed.

"Rex!" Stu wailed.

Rex got the blade close. Stu jumped as cold steel skimmed his scrotum.

"You're grazing my sack."

"Lay still, for Christ's sake."

Out in the halls, the cacophony of cries continued.

"What the hell is going on out there," the woman Rex was with asked.

"Easy does it, Rex. You have the blade right against his schmeckel," Bubby said.

"Christ!" Stu cried.

"Even He can't help you now," Rex said.

"Oh my God!" Julia cried.

"Put the knife away. I'm scared."

"Damn, you sure got tangled. How the hell were you guys fucking?" Rex asked.

"He wanted strong. I ask. He said strong," the Asian woman said.

Rex put the knife in the stocking and cut. Stu whined but was free in minutes.

"Thank you! Thank you!"

"Yeah, thank me. Now we both have blue balls. I was right there when you did this." Rex said. He turned to the black woman. "Any chance of finishing me off?" Rex asked.

"Get your crazy white asses the hell out of here!"

***

Booth squinted into the orangey night sky. It was good to be riding with a posse, albeit a posse of two, even if Tuco rode the red and white tricycle because, as Bruja had predicted, none of the mechanical horses were small enough for him. Booth took a long pull from his bottle of redeye.

"Send the bottle down here," Tuco said.

"This drink is too strong for a person your size."

"Your ass, *pato*!"

"You can't handle this stuff; you're half my size."

"Half your size but twice the man. Now, don't make me cut you."

"How would you like to bet?"

"Bet what?"

"How many holes I can put in you before you fall."

Tuco hopped up and grabbed the bottle.

"Hey!"

Tuco took a pull from the bottle and spat.

"Fuckin' iced tea! You are a world-class poser."

They came to the brothel and found the Four here. Booth wanted to shoot the '80 guy, but Cain had been adamant—do not kill anyone. Indeed, he preferred they not even *hurt* them. Booth had no idea how Cain would do all he set out to accomplish with such a pacifist perspective.

"Well, would you look'e here," Booth said. It was the colorful girl, Julia, with her friends in front of the brothel. The young guy with her was red-faced and cupping his crotch.

"What do you want?" Julia asked.

"You know what I want from you, honey. I'll get it, too. Why don't you ditch the old man, the kid, and Breakfast Club and come ride with a cowboy?"

Rex took a step forward. The clown had his knife out instantly, and even though it took the "cowboy" much longer to unholster his revolver, Rex figured he could hit him at this distance, lousy shot or not.

Bubby went for his fake gun, but before getting his hand in his jacket, a tiny knife hit his hand. Bubby grabbed his hand, blood trickling between his fingers.

"Bastard," Julia said.

"Sweetie, come with me for an hour, and I'll leave your friends alone. Easy peasy."

"Not a chance," Bubby said.

"What happened to your friend? He couldn't handle the pussy in there?" Tuco said, pointing at Stu, who was still favoring his crotch.

"Yeah, he was taking your mother in there, but her shit is rotten, and it messed my boy up," Rex said.

Tuco aimed a knife right at Rex's heart and then ducked.

"Did you see that?"

"See what," Booth asked.

He was about to make one of his smart-ass remarks when something buzzed past his sunburned ear. Then, something else from the other side. Booth aimed both his pistols at the sky.

"What the hell was that?"

Tuco waved his derby as if fighting off a mosquito.

But what the sky was full of was more the size of birds.

"Oh shit, ming," said Tuco, *"pinga volando."*

"What?" Booth asked.

"Flying cocks," said Tuco as a penis with wings swooped down and hit him in the mouth.

"Son-of-a-whore! Flying dicks!"

"Let's get the hell out of here!" Rex howled as the gaggle of dicks swarmed Booth and Tuco.

"These are full-grown, too!" said Booth. "They have scrotums and everything."

The airborne abominations bobbed in the air, unable to take to the sky like newly born birds. Not only did each prick have wings, but each also sported a hanging set of balls heavy with seed.

One flew low and bumped against Tuco's ass.

"What the fuck!"

Booth waved his revolvers and fired nine shots in the air, missing every last one.

"Hey, man, exactly what kind of cowboy are you?" Tuco asked as he got off the tricycle and produced a large blade.

"I can't get a shot. The pricks are yawing all over."

Two more dicks hit the clown, one in the face, the other in his ass.

"*Maricón*!"

"Watch it now. They are trying to pollenate,"

"They want to pollenate in my ass!"

More of the soaring creatures appeared. Tuco rolled on the ground in fear as more pricks still made their way over to him.

"They are flying all hither and thither," Booth said.

A substantial ebony cock hovered in Booth's face, a perverse hummingbird. Tuco slowly lowered his left arm, and another knife fell from his sleeve into his hand. Once he had the blade in his grasp, he moved like lightning (damn, he was quick). But the hovering dicks were too fast. The black cock yawed to the left, avoiding the blade, and rubbed its swollen, pink head on the clown's cheek.

Tuco rubbed his face where the cock had connected.

"Cocksucker! What kind of town is this shit?"

"Oh, no, I think it's my spell...it worked but not how I had hoped," Julia said, looking at the nightmare in the sky. The spell had worked—sort of. While Stu had remained stuck, Julia's hex *had* worked. The screams from within the brothel's rooms at the time made sense now. While Julia's jinx, meant to free Stu's dick, failed to find its intended target, it released the dicks of all the others in the brothel.

"Holy shit, this is amazing. Being attacked by dicks," Rex laughed.

"You think this is funny, you fool," Booth screamed at Rex.

"Fuckin'-A, it's funny."

Two dicks fought one another to get to Booth's rear as the cowboy swirled around and fired his pistol twice into the sky. Both shots missed their expected target. Tuco swung his knives wildly, missing as well. He then alternated between throwing small knives with one hand and swinging a machete with the other. Nothing connected with the swarm of dicks.

"What should we do?" Stu asked.

"We should leave," Bubby said.

"Yeah, let's get out of here before those...*things* turn in on us," Stu said.

"But I am responsible for this," Julia said. "I should fix it."

"You want to get a butterfly net and gather pricks? Be my guest," Rex said.

"Okay, let's go."

Rex turned to Booth and Tuco.

"Later, boys. Enjoy the sausage party!"

"Bastard! We'll get you yet. I'm going to kill you all. Except for the little bitch. She and I will have a good time before this ends."

But before he could finish his thought, one of the smaller pricks flew into his mouth. He choked and got the thing out. It hovered in a zigzag, like a stunned bee.

Soon, the bogus cowboy and midget clown were overwhelmed by the flying phalluses. The dicks were buzzing faster and faster, bumping and grinding into the men.

"Son-of-a-bitch! I fear they are going to bust nuts momentarily," Booth cried.

"Help!" the clown cried.

"For the sake of God! They are ready to explode!"

The flying monsters whirred faster still. Having been removed during the sexual act, each of them was eager to finish their deed.

"Oh my. Are you boys in trouble?" said Bruja. "You need some help?" She had followed them.

"Your magic is not wanted here," Booth said. Bruja noticed Julia and her friends getting ready to leave the scene.

"I should have known only one witch who could screw up such a simple spell," Bruja said.

"I was trying to help."

"Idiot," Bruja said.

Bubby took a step forward as if sleepwalking.

"You...."

"Bubby, what's wrong," Julia asked.

"She is the one I loved. When I was gone."

"You bitch. You feel like a big witch?" Julia said.

"What would you know about being a witch?"

"She's twice the witch you are. And ten times the human," Bubby said.

"Is that right?" Bruja asked. Then she softened her features. "Bubby, come to me, my love."

Bubby wobbled as if in a trance. When Julia spoke, he was about to walk over to the woman and scoop her in his arms.

"Look at you, Julia. You gained even more weight, you fat bitch."

"And you look even older now if that's possible, so let's call it even," Julia said. "and you leave Bubby alone or so help me-"

"So, help you, what? Julia, you do not want to battle me."

"You guys know each other?" Stu asked now, looking from his crotch for the first time.

"Bruja, go get Cain; he'll know what to do," Booth said, ducking a dick.

"Cain?" Stu said.

"You guys are with Cain?" Bubby asked.

"When this is over, I am going to get you good," Booth told Julia.

"Hey," Bubby said.

"What are you going to do, loser?" Bruja said to Bubby.

"Don't you call him that! And don't speak to Julia, you hear me?" Rex said and took a step forward. Tuco flashed a knife. But he was still busy fighting the airborne horrors.

"I will kill you all!"

"You say anything else against my friends, and I will have to put you over my knee and give you a spanking," Rex said.

"Ha!" Stu laughed.

"It's okay, Rex. C'mon guys, let's get out of here," Bubby said.

"Later, assholes," Rex said.

Bruja turned back to her posse.

"You don't want me to stop this attack?" Bruja asked.

"Si! Si! Make them stop!" Tuco cried.

"No. We don't need Bruja's help," said Booth.

"Yo crazy, ming. Let her help. She knows how to handle *pinga*!"

The buzzing and bumping grew more frantic.

"Shit…they are close. We're about to be bukkaked! Okay! Help us, Bruja!"

"Yeah, help!"

"Stop them!"

"And you boys will let me join you?" Bruja asked.

"Yes! Yes!"

Bruja opened her purse and pulled something out. The cocks backed off. She held her hand high. The dicks screeched and retreated, flying into the western horizon in search of greener pastures and unprotected asses.

"Thank the gods," Booth said.

Then the gaggle of dicks fell to the ground like so many shot birds.

"Thank you," Tuco said.

"I second the motion," said Booth. He'd gone the shade of his ivory horse.

A chorus of screams emanated from the brothel as a group of men came running out. At least twenty of them, clutching their dick-less crotches. As more cocks fell to the ground, the gaggle of johns rushed from the whorehouse, screaming in high voices, and fought over whose dick was whose as they reclaimed their members.

"Hey, that's my cock," a man hollered as an elderly cowboy ran with the younger man's member.

"Unhand that penis!"

"The Malevolent Four," Bruja said. She was looking at one of the wanted posters.

"Wanted, they are," Booth said, gripping his pistol.

"Cash reward," Tuco said.

They faced one another.

"I guess Cain does not trust us to get them," Booth said.

"You think he put these up?"

"Who else. I am going to handle this my way," Booth said, pointing his pistol to the group in the distance and pulling the trigger. The revolver jammed. He peered at Bruja.

"Get your spell off my pistol!"

"Not a chance. Cain said we don't harm them, and we will obey."

"Well then, why don't you cast a spell to bind them, and we take them in?"

"I can't."

"Yeah. Because Julia is a better witch than you give her credit for."

"I hate her."

***

"My spell backfired. Rather than freeing Stu, I released all the, mmm, *thingys* of the other men in the brothel," Julia said.

"You mean to say for each of those flying cocks there's some poor dick-less dude now?" Rex asked.

"I don't know how 'poor' they are, but yes."

"At least we got out of there intact," Stu said.

"Hey, did you hear those guys? They are with Cain," Bubby said.

"Well, if Cain is with those assholes, then we know we can't trust him," Rex said.

They kept walking, Julia looking down at her feet.

"What's wrong?" Bubby asked.

"Me, that's what's wrong. I am going to screw us with my half-baked spells. Every time I think I may finally be getting my turn in this stinking life, reality lets me know I am a loser."

"Don't say that. Back at the inn, you were positive your spell caused trouble. But you didn't do this—it was Cain. Do you realize those others could have killed us if they had not been distracted by those...mmm...those..."

"Flying cocks," Rex said.

"Julia, you have aided us more than you know," Bubby said. Julia rubbed the back of her hand on Bubby's chubby cheek.

"Okay," Stu said, "what now?"

***

They rode in silence for a while.

"So, what spell did you use to get rid of the infernal beasts," Booth asked.

"No spell," Bruja replied.

She pulled out the tampon. The guys freaked out.

"Exactly," she said.

"Bloody tampons. All cocks hate them." Tuco said.

"Genius. Pure genius," said Booth.

"Where exactly did you learn how to shoot?" Tuco asked Booth.

"I was distracted. I was fighting off those *things*, for Christ's sake. I never shot at dicks before."

"You keep telling yourself that."

"I'm going to get them all," Tuco said.

"All but Julia…she's mine," Booth said.

"I'm going to get Bubby," Tuco said.

"Dear, what a violent group we have here," said Booth.

"Problem?" Bruja asked.

"Not at all, my dear. In fact, you're turning me on. I think I may even want to sleep with you in a "slumming it" kind of way."

"You try and sleep with me, and your cock may become detached next. And it won't be a spell. I'll have my little friend here castrate you."

Tuco smiled, licking one of his endless supply of knives.

"Enough," Booth said as he adjusted his fake mustache.

They rode on, Tuco peddling hard to keep pace.

PART III
Haunted Land

CHAPTER SIXTEEN

They stood before the portal to Haunted Land, gob smacked. Most doors leading from Land to Land were lit by the energy of unknown magic (blues, greens, oranges). This entrance, however, appeared before them like so much dark nothingness.

"Give me the book," Julia said. Bubby handed her the *Necronomicon*.

"Are you sure about this? This book is supposed to be powerful," Bubby said.

"I'm not *sure* about anything."

Julia flipped through the book, careful not to tear the hoary pages, and chanted an invocation that sounded to Stu a bit like Latin but was, in fact, a lost language from before the birth of any of the gods still remembered. The door opened and became more solid. They all stood before Haunted Land's entrance.

"It worked," Stu said.

It became blacker as they investigated the portal, opening into a great emptiness. The Four walked closer.

"Thank you, Rex," Bubby said.

Rex didn't answer.

"Thanks for defending us," Julia said.

Rex stopped.

"Look, I only said all that shit because I knew none of you pussies would."

"Don't call me that," Stu said.

"Still, it was good of you," Bubby said.

"Look, you need to man up. I can't defend your drunk ass throughout this whole thing. You may be a chicken-shit, but you're not taking me with you. Got it?"

"Rex-"

"Don't you start, Stu. You can go back home to mommy for all I care."

"What the hell?" Julia asked.

"I'll tell you what the hell. I'm the only one here who has any balls. I'm not carrying a group of losers on my back. A momma's boy, a drunk, and a witch who can't cast a spell to make a cup of coffee without fucking it up. I'm done. And if you don't like it, Julia, you can take a ride on Willy, the one-eyed wonder worm," Rex said, grabbing his crotch, his voice slurring.

"Asshole."

"I must be out of my mind…traveling with you losers," Rex said, laughing humorlessly.

The vortex before them swirled and pulsed.

"Losers? I'm sorry, none of us are TV has-beens! You're not even a has-been. For Christ's sake, *Happy Jack* was a complete flop. Maybe you should go back to '80s Land, where you belong!" Stu said.

"Stu!"

"No fuck him, Bubby. We may be losers, but Rex here is right at home with us and won't face the fact. Seriously, you think you are less of a loser than the rest of us. Then you are not only a loser, but you're delusional, too."

"Stu, you've had a long night and a lot to drink," Bubby said.

"No, let him speak his piece."

"You like treating people like shit. Look at poor Diamond and how-"

"You heard her—him—nothing happened."

"But it almost did. You *thought* it did."

Rex took two steps forward and pushed Stu. Stu went flying and fell on his back, mud splashing a wave into the air. Bubby kneeled to him.

"You mother fucker!" Julia said.

"Never mind. I'm out of here," Rex said, marching away. The swirl into Haunted Land hissed before them.

"Rex, get back here," Bubby said, his voice deep with tears. Rex stopped.

"You're crying," Rex laughed. "Why don't you have another drink."

"Who are you to judge me?"

"What have you ever done that worked, Bubbs? Tell me one thing you were ever successful at other than getting loaded. That's who I am to judge."

"What bullshit," Stu said, getting to his feet.

"Go to hell, Rex," Julia said. But Stu could see Bubby with his face in his hands. He was taking what Rex had said to heart.

"He's right. I'm holding you three back."

"Not true," Julia said.

But Bubby ran through the portal to Haunted Land.

***

Bruja watched as the great Cain listened to them explain the scene at the brothel in complete disbelief. How could a cowboy, a witch, and a serial killer have a tough time with this group of rabble?

"And you were unable to stop them?" Cain asked. His usual cadaverous pallor was growing pink, and his thinning hair stood at all angles.

"Well," Booth said, "the witch with them cast a spell and overwhelmed us."

"Overwhelmed *you two*, not me!" Bruja said.

"But this Julia is not very good, you say?" Cain asked.

"She's a horrible witch-"

"She had pricks flying all over. She's stronger than Bruja here will admit," Booth said.

"Is that so? Interesting," Cain said.

And was that a hint of a smile tugging at Cain's thin lips?

"And she's a cute little thing."

"Oh, please," Bruja said.

"They must be stopped. And I will repeat my wishes—do not hurt them. And you," Cain said, pointing to Booth, "do not touch Julia. Understand?"

Booth grudgingly nodded.

Tuco said nothing. Bruja thought he was unhappy because they were not to hurt the Four. She didn't believe Tuco would obey this rule much longer.

"And the other three with her?" Cain asked.

"A chubby old man, a skinny geek, and some Ralph Macchio-looking mother fucker," Bruja said.

"Who?" Cain asked.

"Did you ever see the Karate K-"

"Never mind. I want them dead," Tuco finally spoke.

"I would like to avoid violence, but this group is getting annoying. I hope they stop being troublesome, or you may very well get your wish."

Cain went to bed (he was getting worn out more quickly than ever), and Tuco, Booth, and Bruja sat at a table in the saloon. A few of Cain's people were scattered here and there. Zack and The Bat drank and alternated between hugging and singing and facing off, often threatening to smash bottles over one another's heads.

"Name your poison," Booth said, positioning himself behind the bar.

***

"We have to go after him," Stu said, holding his bleeding elbow.

"Bullshit," Rex said.

"We have to," Julia said. "You're the reason he went through."

"He's alone in Haunted Land. We can't leave him there alone," Stu said.

"Goddammit, okay. Let's-" Rex said.

A voice from behind them interrupted their decision-making.

"Well, well, well. The Malevolent Four—well, three of you, anyway. You are under arrest."

Julia turned first.

"Oh my god!"

Stu followed Julia's gaze. Three naked men stood behind them, guns trained on them.

"Man, haven't we seen enough dick for one day," Rex said and raised his hands.

***

The clock above the bar was closing in at 2 AM. Bruja had to admit that, for a miniature clown, Tuco could drink. But eventually, his eyes became heavy as his words made less and less sense. Finally, he passed out at the table, hand still clutching his drink. Everyone else had gone to bed, and she and Booth had drunk into the wee hours.

"We will get your friend and those three idiots she's with."

"She's not my friend. Cain wants them, so we will do whatever it takes to get them."

"Wow. You are a sycophant, aren't you?"

"I'm a what?"

"What I am saying, my simple-minded woman, is you sure are a real Cain ass-kiss."

"He's a great man."

"But not as great as you had hoped."

"Why do you say that?"

"Come now, he may have power, but you must admit he's rather unimpressive physically. You can't tell me you want to bed him," Booth said and sipped his devil's whiskey.

"Who said anything about sleeping with him? He's a great man. I never said I wanted to screw him. You have nothing on your mind but sex. And you call me simple-minded?"

"You know, back in Vegan Land, I could bed any woman I wanted," Booth slurred.

"So, you've said. Many times. We are all very impressed."

"I think you should be grateful that I am thinking of sleeping with you."

"Oh? I think you had better go to bed."

"Are you joining me?"

"Not a chance," Bruja said, her speech steadier than his; she drank one for every two Booth had had.

He rose, pulled the clown's hair, lifted his head from the table, and let it go with a hard thump. Bruja winced. Tuco was out cold.

"You know, this is the longest I have ever gone without a woman. I don't plan to wait another hour," he said, his eyes darkening. Bruja attempted to leave, but drunk as he was, Booth was still quick and on her.

"Have you lost your mind? Get the hell off me!"

"You call me a pansy! A dandy! Does this feel like a pansy?" he said, forcing her hand to his crotch. Despite the whiskey, he was rock hard. "I'm going to show you what you get...calling me a dandy," he rasped in her ear and then licked her face with the stink of whiskey and vomit ready to happen. He pinned her to the table. The ridiculous fake mustache falling off his sweating face would have been comical had his intentions not been apparent.

He had her dress up in two seconds, and her panties ripped off in half the time. She tried to think of something— a spell, but the drink had rendered her slow-witted. Then came the metallic *clang* as Booth's belt buckle hit the dusty floor.

And Bruja wished she knew the spell Julia had used to take a man's prick off.

***

The infamous "men in black," who would appear when something peculiar occurred, were called such due to the black suits they were said to wear. However, the men who had arrested them were dressed in black only by way of hats, belts, socks, and shoes. Otherwise, the men were nude, looking like a sad and out-of-shape *Chip n' Dale*'s parody. Two were pale as the bellies of flounders (one skinny who wore square Coke bottle glasses, the other was round like a snowman come to life). The third was a tall, thin black man. His prick hung nearly to his knee.

Rex looked the men over.

"Well, shit, brother! You sure prove the old myth to be true, flanked by these two," Rex said.

"Christ," Julia cried. "Put some clothes on!"

Stu had done articles on the Men in Black several times. While the research proved numerous theories, he'd never found anything to suggest the men being naked.

"The Malevolent Four. We got you," Chubby said.

"The Men in Black, damn! I should have known you guys would show," Stu said.

"We're not malevolent," Julia said.

"Johnson, let's interrogate them, " Glasses said, addressing the black man.

"Johnson, is your name? I love it!" Rex said and laughed.

"Yeah, and?" Johnson asked. He produced a large aerosol can (where he pulled it from, Stu did not care to know) and sprayed the air as if killing a swarm of bees. The Men in Black were immune to whatever was in the can, but they were unconscious instantly.

***

When the drug finally wore off, it was morning, and they woke on military regulation cots in a massive hangar. A flying saucer, silver and sterile, stood in the far corner. The body of a Sasquatch, partly autopsied, was suspended in a giant cube.

The Men in Black attempted to interrogate them all separately. But Julia only giggled and drove them crazy with her backward logic. Stu could not stop crying, and Rex did not say another word. Eventually, they were all questioned together.

"Let's bring their friend here," Johnson said. He tapped a gadget resembling a tablet.

"What, friend?" Stu asked.

Chubby answered: "Mr. Oscar Zoroaster Phadrig Issac Norman Henkle Emmanuel Ambroise Diggs."

Chubby and Glasses wheeled in a cube, like the one the Sasquatch was in, but this one had Diggs imprisoned. The ghost hovered in the tank like a beaten dog in a cage.

"Diggs!" Julia squealed. "You assholes, let him go right now!"

Glasses tried with Rex.

"Mr. Dolan, you're in a lot of trouble."

"Yeah? I got fired for pulling my pudd at work and am now a registered pervert. What do you got on me?"

"Playing with your thingy at work? God, you're gross," Julia said.

"Altering time and space is our charge on you, Mr. Dolan," Glasses said.

"Yeah?"

"Correct, Mr. Dolan," Chubby added.

"And what jury will believe a dildo like me can alter time and space?"

The Men in Black looked at one another, considering what Rex had said. It appeared they believed he had a point. They turned to Stu.

"Stuart Sawyer," Johnson said and looked from a small tablet, "do you know anything about the website *The Unknown Daily*?"

"You know I do. Are *you* the people responsible for all the threats I receive telling me to take my site down?"

"We don't know anything about that."

"Are you guys making all these changes now? Everyone blames Cain. But I think you guys may have done this, too. I may even decide to write about it." Stu said.

"Mr. Sawyer, reality is altered anytime people agree to alter it. Daylights Savings Time, not having the 13th floor in old hotels, changing the definitions of words in the dictionary because enough people use the word out of context. These are all examples of altering reality. These are all examples of the masses agreeing to accept as real that which is not. And anyway, there is no Cain Consequence. It was a weather balloon crash."

"What?" Julia asked.

"That makes no sense," Rex added.

"Yeah, you guys already used that excuse in '47 with Roswell," Stu informed.

"Well, this, too, was simply a weather balloon."

"Huh? A weather balloon can be mistaken for a flying saucer. But this? I think you need a more plausible cover-up."

"You know, Johnson, he's right. The weather balloon thing doesn't work with this one," Chubby said.

"Stu is right. Why are you doing this? We even lived for a few months in a horrible reality where Dr. Phil was president," Julia said.

"We had to deal with that as well, Ms. Faith. Yes, it was horrible."

"Someone has to do something," Stu said, "these changes have gone too far."

"And who are you to judge?" Johnson asked.

"We are people who have lost our lives," Stu said.

"Not so. Everyone has had their lives altered. You guys are the ones who *noticed* it. You are going against Darwin and not adapting," Glasses said, tapping on the cube containing Diggs.

"You knock it off! Diggs is not a fish in an aquarium," Julia said.

"He'll grow accustomed to his new home. To quote a piece of literature: '*a person can get used to anything if given enough time*' — Nicholas Sparks, *The Notebook*," Chubby quoted.

"And you guys think this is all normal? The Lands taking over the Earth is a natural evolution? Sports Land, have you been there? I have—a land where everyone is obsessed with one football team who always wins. And one time, the team lost, and everyone rioted and killed each other because they had no idea how to react to the loss," Julia said.

"She's right," Diggs said. "I was in Doo Wop Land, where everyone had a DA hair-do. They all walk around, snapping their fingers and singing around garbage cans on fire. It was awful."

"I'm more horrified the infamous Men in Black are quoting Nicholas Sparks," Stu said.

"Barclay Cain is back. Are you guys helping him?" Johnson asked.

"Helping him? We're going to stop him," Stu said.

"That's right," Julia said.

"We need to get Bubby back and find Cain, and the Four will take care of the rest," Rex said. It was the first time Rex spoke of them as a group.

"You guys are holding us up," Stu said.

"We have ways of getting information, Mr. Sawyer. We had one hard case, but we broke him by forcing him to watch all the episodes of *Happy Jack* repeatedly. We tickled another man's asshole with a quail feather for seventeen hours before he caved."

"For the record, if you need to torture me, I'll take the asshole feather thing," Rex said.

"What about the Cult of Change?" Julia asked.

"They are all crazy," Johnson said. "We came from-"

"Hey! Never mind all this. We will ask the questions," Chubby said.

"Julia Faith, it says here you've powers. Can you elaborate?" Johnson asked, consulting his tablet.

"Can you guys cover yourselves, please? I can't concentrate with you all naked. It's disgusting."

"We're not ashamed of our bodies," Chubby said.

"That's the problem—you should be," Rex said.

"Please, guys, get dressed."

"I'm afraid it is simply not possible," Glasses said.

"Shit, Johnson, if I were hung like you, I wouldn't cover up either," Rex said, laughing.

Johnson produced another gadget (where was he hiding this stuff?) and turned it on. Two antennae resembling spoons twirled.

"What is that?" Stu asked.

"It's to communicate with spirits," Johnson said.

"This spirit here is your friend, no?"

"Leave Diggs alone; he has nothing to do with this."

The device lit blue, and Diggs became a bit more corporal. He slowly landed on his feet and strolled out of the cube.

"Butt ass naked! Are you kidding me?"

"Mr. Diggs, we have questions for you too."

"You do? Well, I got nothing to say to a bunch of naked mother fuckers."

"We travel through time and space. Clothes hinder us. We must be naked," Johnson said.

"You don't say. Well then…."

Johnson fiddled with his gadget. The antenna moved again, but now the thing lit green. Within a few moments, a form appeared. Before the ghost was even complete, the woman was yelling."

"...Diggs, you son-of-a-bitch!"

Ms. Diggs was back, hand on hip, holding a large wooden cooking spoon. Stu could imagine said spoon going across poor Diggs's ass.

"Oh shit-"

"You promised forever, negro!"

"Ms. Diggs, please; no slurs, if you please," Chubby said.

"Huh? Oh shit, white boy. Where the hell's your dick?"

Chubby pushed in on his belly, and his tiny member protruded ever so slightly.

"Now this brother is swinging," Ms. Diggs said, indicating Johnson.

"Send her back," Diggs said.

"Say what, boy? Where do you keep going? You were supposed to find me in the afterlife."

"I tried, I swear. But-"

"But your black ass. I waited for you in my mama's house in the Kingdom. Your skinny ass never showed."

"Now listen, baby. We were together for damn near forty years. I guess I figured it was a new beginning when we died," Diggs said.

"Oh, yeah? A new beginning without your wife. Is that what your sorry ass means?"

"Diggs, we can send her back. But first, we need your cooperation," Chubby said.

"Don't you dare."

"Where have you been spending the afterlife?" Diggs asked his estranged wife.

"In the apartment?"

"The one on 104th Street?"

"With my mother and sisters."

"Baby, it was bad enough in life. You want me to hang out there in the afterlife?"

"Thant's right. And you won't be running out for cigarettes and taking off, either," she said, hand making a fist on her considerable hip.

"Lord have mercy."

"Never mind all of your foolishness. Now get your bony ass together. You're coming with me."

Diggs and his wife stood together, and Johnson used his device to move them to their after-death home.

"I'll be seeing you guys," Diggs said to his friends.

"Don't count on it," his wife said to them. And then they were gone.

"Goodbye, Diggs!" Julia said.

"What's with the UFO?" Stu asked the Men in Black. "So, it's true. Aliens are here?"

"It's all true," Chubby said. "All the stuff in the magazines, the crazy TV shows. All real."

"Loch Ness Monster?"

"Real, but he moved to the Atlantic in the '70s."

"Bigfoot?"

"Of course," Johnson said. "But they all go to Porn Land in the summer for vacation."

"All true, huh? Is Elvis still alive?" Rex asked.

"Yes. Well no. The King did fake his death in nineteen-seventy-seven, but he died a few years ago."

"All that tabloid stuff is real?" Stu asked.

"All real."

"Oh shit. Does this mean Richard Gere actually put a gerbil up his ass?" Rex asked.

"Rex!" Julia said.

"You know what, I'm out of here," Rex said and rose to leave. All the naked men held their pistols on him. Johnson pointed his gun right in Rex's face.

"I would not do that, Mr. Dolan."

"Wait...that gun," Stu said.

"Don't worry about the gun."

In a quick move, Stu grabbed the gun from the man nearest him and pulled the trigger.

"No!"

BANG! The red flag unfurled.

"You got these from Bubby's warehouse," Stu said.

"Please, don't pull the trigger anymore," Chubby said.

"Yeah, the first time I pulled the trigger, Bigfoot appeared. And then the UFO. Who knows what will happen the next time," Johnson said.

"It was the cursed guns that brought all this here," Chubby said.

"So you guys are not the real Men in Black?"

"Well, no," Johnson admitted.

"Wait, so who the hell are you guys," Julia asked.

"And this bunker?" asked Stu.

"Oh, this bunker did belong to the real Men in Black… I think I said too much," Glasses said.

"You have not said enough, asshole," Rex said and made to grab the man. He took another look at the naked man and thought better.

"We may as well come clean, Johnson," Glasses said.

"Come clean about what?" Julia asked.

"Oh, for cryin' out loud. Just tell 'em," Chubby said.

"We are from Corporate Land. We all worked for the same firm. One day, we went out to lunch, had a few drinks, and ended up in a warehouse of tricks. We pulled the trigger on one of those damned guns and found ourselves here. In this bunker."

"As you said, Mr. Sawyer, the Men in Black *did* investigate. They set up this here, bunker. However, they disappeared. Never to be heard from again," Glasses said.

"We all did well in Corporate Land. But pretending to be the Men in Black is much more fun!" Johnson said.

Rex took a step toward Chubby, fists raised.

"I should knock your teeth in."

"No, please."

"Give me one good reason not to."

"I can tell you where to find Barclay Cain."

While they were on the right track heading to Haunted Land, the man told them what they were looking for was an office building in Haunted Land holding several secrets. This was where the *archives* were. In the end, Rex did not hit the man.

"What do you mean, the archives?" Stu asked.

"I don't know more than that. I only found out from a guy we interrogated years ago. We used the feather on the asshole method to-"

"You know what, guys, enough with the feather-butthole stuff," Julia said.

Stu, Rex, and Julia gathered up and got ready to leave.

"One last question," Stu said, "If you are *not* the Men In Black, and you are *not* traveling through time and space...why are you all naked?"

The three men looked at one another.

"Why not," Chubby said. All the men smiled widely.

"Let's get the hell away from these pervs," Julia said, "and I still wish you guys would put some clothes on."

CHAPTER SEVENTEEN

The cabin stood like a wicked sign pointing to Hell. Though he was exhausted and thirsty (the night's alcohol all dried in his system), Bubby didn't dare go in. This cottage was undoubtedly an evil place. He'd jumped into Haunted Land, hardly thinking, anger and drink, forming his decision without his say-so. He turned around at once, but the way out was gone. So, he'd moved on.

Walking was a chore as the ground here was soft and mossy. The black trees shone with oily condensation, and the air was heavy and musty. Insects Bubby could not identify buzzed, skittered, and flew here and there, creating sounds that caused the skin of his neck and arms to wrinkle.

The aroma of fresh baking stopped him where he stood. Another cabin, with a wildly overgrown botanical garden, stood alone, secretive. The colorful cottage stood in the dark forest like a gingerbread house, something out of an old fairytale, welcoming from the outside but something evil waiting within, he assumed. The door opened, and a diminutive old woman shuffled onto the porch.

"Oh, there you are. I have been expecting you. Do come in."

"Hello. I don't think you're expecting *me*. I'm lost," Bubby said.

"Well, young man, we are all lost, right?"

Bubby had not been called 'young' in many years.

"You live here?"

"Yes, dear. And I hardly leave home. I'm Ms. Essic. Would you like to come in for a cupcake and tea?"

Bubby's stomach grumbled.

"I don't want to be a bother...."

"No bother at all. I'd love the company."

Inside, everything looked like the quintessential cottage. However, where a fireplace should have been, a small TV screen played a yule log. An ancient sword hung above the TV.

"Let me put on some tea."

***

"I've never done drugs before," Brandy Sawyer said to her doppelganger.

"Really? Most of us have experimented in our younger years."

"Okay, so I smoked grass, took a few quaaludes, and tripped on acid once."

"Well, this is most like the acid. But...more. Much. Much. More."

"Oh, God," Brandy said. She drained her drink. "Okay, I'm ready."

"No," Brandy-Two said.

"What's wrong?"

"Oh my God. I am so sorry."

"Sorry about what?"

"I lied to you. This place…this *is* your world," Brandy-Two said, crying.

"I don't understand."

"Was Stuey, *your* Stuey, in a car accident?"

"Yes."

"So was mine. But my Stuey died. I have been jumping into realities looking for one where he survived."

"And you wanted to be with him again?"

"Yes. I'm sorry. I will leave."

"Wait," Brandy said, grabbing her twin's arm.

***

They stood at the entrance to Haunted Land.

"Okay, let's do this," Julia said.

"Wait," Rex said. "Are we sure about this?"

"We have to find Bubby," Julia said. "Who knows how lost he is since those perv weirdos delayed us."

"That's right," Stu added. "Why? Are you scared?"

"Hell no, I ain't a-scared."

"Rex, it's okay if you're nervous. "

"I'm fine. Let's do it."

"One, two, three!" Stu counted, and they jumped.

All but Rex.

***

Unsettling weeping echoed from everywhere in Haunted Land. Julia clutched Stu's arm. In the branches of the black trees where birds should have been perched, diseased, winged babies slept, green and infectious. Stu looked away and spoke to Julia. His voice was distant, muffled.

"Where the hell is Rex?

"Shit. Rex must not have jumped."

"Bastard. He screwed us," Stu said.

"Maybe something happened."

"Yeah, something happened, all right—he chickened out."

"Let's find Bubby."

***

"Well, well, well. Rex Dolan. A man so shifty he could peel an orange in his pocket," a voice in a deep Irish brogue said.

Rex turned to see the tiny man in green. A long red beard….

"Oh my God. You're-"

"Yes, a real-life leprechaun," the creature said, lighting his churchwarden pipe.

"What the fuck. Who are you?"

"The name's Stoops Shillelagh. Can't say it's nice to make your acquaintance, Rex."

"I…."

"Or should I call you Happy Jack? Happy Jack is big as an ape and twice as ugly."

"Don't call me that. I was a kid when I played him. It's not who I am now."

"I'd call you weasel, but I don't want to offend the poor mammals."

"What do you want from me?"

"Look at ye—a face like a slapped ass but only half as fun. Some man you are. Left your friends high and dry."

"No…I was getting ready to jump."

"Horseshit! You wouldn't give your friends the steam off your piss on a winter's day."

"Kiss my ass."

"I'd rather kiss your ass than your face."

"I didn't mean to leave them."

"Maybe they are better off without you. You're not the smartest dame at the dance."

"You little shit."

"You're as thick as pig shit but only half as useful."

"You bastard," Rex said and made to close the gap between them. The leprechaun disappeared and reappeared behind him and gave Rex a good kick in the ass with his heavy buckle shoe.

"Prick!"

"All you live for is to drink, fuck and fight, and you can't do the last two worth a shit. A worthless bastard if ever there was one. Can't look at a lady without thinking like an animal."

"That's not true."

"Spare me. You're as horny as a badger with two mickeys."

"You little turd."

"And dumb to boot. If God himself were to stuff your brain in a bird, the damn thing would fly ass-backward."

"Come here and let me beat your ass."

"If you ever make a baby, I wish your son is born with no asshole."

"A fucking leprechaun. What kind of world is this?" Rex yelled to the sky. "I can't take anymore!"

"Indeed. *A wee bit old to be belivin' in leprechauns, er?*"

"What the hell did you say?"

Stoops disappeared and reappeared behind Rex. As Rex turned around, the leprechaun hit him in the head with his cane. And his world went black.

***

They had been walking for a while, but knowing how long was impossible. Time did not exist in Haunted Land. However, Stu's legs ached, and his bladder was full.

"God, I need to pee," Julia said as if reading his mind.

"There," Stu said, pointing about a block away where a row of houses stood. They made their way over. Once close, they realized all the houses were identical. The address of each home was the same—112 Ocean Avenue.

"What is this?" Stu asked.

Being from New York, Julia knew the house well.

"It's the mash-up Rex and Bubby told us about from the news. It's the *Amityville Horror* house," she said.

The air dipped a few degrees. Mist filled the air. Julia's multi-colored hair was now a wet brown. Something (not a mouse, cat, or possum) ran across Stu's feet and into a sewer too swiftly for him to identify the creature. Its tail, reptilian, and a sick gray-yellow snaked into the grate.

"What was that?" Julia asked.

"I don't even want to know."

There was a *squeak,* and *all* the front doors of the identical homes opened in unison. A gaggle of Joey Buttafuocos exited. The creatures were all dressed in their early '90s best: florid genie pants and a wife-beater tee.

"Oh no…" Stu said as the Buttafuocos (at least a dozen) closed in on them.

"Sweetheart, ditch the geek and come hang out with Joey the Great," they all said, a chorus of dim-witted voices.

The Amityville Horror story was well known. Stu figured he could have handled the swarm of flies, the black goo, and even Jodie, the red-eyed demon pig. But an army of Joey Buttafuocos was nightmare enough for any man (or woman—*especially a woman!*). Stu and Julia ran until they finally came to a house that was not the *Amityville Horror* home. They stood ready to enter but feared what they might find inside. But behind them, the Buttafuocos were closing the void. Stu grasped the doorknob.

***

Rex came to in familiar surroundings. The house was awash with potpourri and something promising for dinner. A dog yipped playfully in the yard. The shelves were crowded with knickknacks and framed photos of vaguely familiar people. At first, he thought he was back home, not in '80s Land, but the home he grew up in—the nostalgia was so compelling. But as he rubbed the back of his head where the leprechaun had whacked him, he realized where he was.

"Son-of-a-bitch!"

The *Happy Jack* house.

"*Happy days are here again!*" his young voice cried from one of the upper rooms, followed by laughter.

The show had been filmed on a sound stage—a three-quarter set made to look like a house on TV. However, he was in a *real* house now—the *Happy Jack* set turned into a true American nightmare.

The banging of pots arose from the kitchen. Rex peeked in to see his TV "parents" preparing dinner. They were not Grace Hanover and Tom Paperd, the actors who played his mother and father, respectively, but instead were his TV parents incarnate. Happy Jack came trotting down the stairs.

"Hello, has-been," Happy Jack said.

"You're not real."

"You've never seen anything so real," the boy said, smiling an unnaturally wide grin.

"What the hell do you want from me?"

Happy Jack peeked into the kitchen to ensure his parents were not listening. His ubiquitous smile finally lowered. Rex remembered having to keep that damn smile permanently plastered to his face back then. Now, the boy's face was a flatline, eyes the color of a drowned corpse.

"You know you don't bring anything but sadness to anyone's life, right?" Happy Jack asked.

"You're not real," Rex repeated.

"Even your parents hate you. They wish you would go away. Every time you call your mother, the poor woman secretly wishes she never had a son. Then, she hates herself for thinking such things. What disharmony you bring to everyone in your miserable life."

Rex readied himself to attack his former self. Then dropped back into the familiar sofa. His face crumpled. The truth has a ring to it; you know it when you hear it. Though this boy was a phantom of the past, he spoke the truth. Rex Dolan knew damn well he had been born into a world with no room for him. He had always known his end would not be grand—loved ones gathered in masse with tales of how he had touched them, enriching their lives. Not even something less wholesome but at least electrifying—a wild life lived well. A legacy of tales filled with drink, woman chasing, and unhealthy habits but leaving a good-looking corpse and volumes worth of stories. Instead, he was to approach this third act alone. Pathetic. A fade-away existence. A miserable, pitiful end.

"It's time to do yourself in. For once, stop being so selfish," Happy Jack said and handed Rex an unmarked orange prescription bottle.

"What is this?"

"Your destiny. You have considered it so many times but, not surprisingly, never had the guts to follow through."

Rex fingered the bottle. Opened the top. Inside was an assortment of pills: round, oval, diamonds. Blues and pinks and greens. Sizeable and minute. Darkness enveloped him like a warm blanket—an old friend. Why the hell not? This was no life. All the despair he'd ever experienced rushed into him at once. Still drunk, he poured the bottle's contents into his damp palm.

"Do it."

Hot tears and cold snot ran from his face and onto his shirt.

"Happy days are here again!"

***

Bubby had had the tea and something to eat, but his eyes were heavy, and Ms. Essic invited him to rest in a spare room. The soft bed had cradled him to sleep at once. He could not be sure how long he had slept, considering it was always night here. He apologized and had more tea with Ms. Essic. Bubby wondered if the old woman was in a loop—perpetually sitting at her table having afternoon tea in Haunted Land.

"Why did you never tell your friends you were once married?" Ms. Essic asked.

"It never came up," Bubby said. "I don't need to tell them exactly how much of a failure I am." He surprised himself, sharing this with the old woman as he sipped the robust, earthy tea.

"Well then, they don't sound like real friends if they would think you a failure."

"Well, it was a marriage that never should have been."

"Poor Bubby."

"I let my friends down. I shouldn't have come here without them."

"They are not your real friends. You think they care about you?"

"Of course they do."

"From what you've told me, they are only here to fix their problems," Ms. Essic said.

"I don't recall telling you about them. Or that I was once married," Bubby said. But he was confused, his head in the clouds.

"You think this *Red*, is it?"

"Rex."

"Rex. You really think this Rex cares about anyone but himself?"

"Oh, he's okay. He's had a tough life."

"And you haven't?"

Bubby lowered his head.

"More tea?"

***

Stu stood with his hand on the handle, the heavy brass knob like ice in his hand.

"Ready?"

"Let's go in," Julia said.

The door held a moment as if locked. But then Stu pushed harder, and they entered the tidy home and found Rex sitting on the sofa like a ghost of his cocky self—his face a crumpled mess. His body was a sack of wet leaves waiting to be tossed into the garbage. He held a fist of pills in one hand and a bottle of something equally lethal-looking in the other. Happy Jack at his side.

"C'mon, do it, Rex," Happy Jack said.

"Rex!"

"Stop!"

"Let him do it," Happy Jack said. He turned his smile to Rex. "God, would you die already."

Stu ran toward the fictitious boy, and the boy ran as if afraid he might touch him and prove he was not real. Julia took a seat next to Rex and put her arm around him. Rex tensed.

"I don't know what happened here, but we need you, Rex."

"No one needs me, Julia. You know that by now; I know it, too."

"We cannot get through this without you."

After a chilling pause, Rex threw the pills across the room and watched them scatter. Stu joined them.

"Thanks for getting rid of him," Rex said. "C'mon, let's get the fuck out of here."

***

When the cottage door opened, Bubby was telling Ms. Essic about his botched stage play, a Jewish version of *Cats*, but spelled *KATZ*.

"Bubby!" Julia said.

Stu, Julia, and Rex entered the cottage. They went to the fireplace to warm themselves. Bubby now noticed the warmth coming from the fire. But before, it had only been a TV playing a video of fire; now, the fire was real. How?

"Welcome," Ms. Essic said. "Sit. I will make more tea."

"I feel your magic. Are you a good witch or a bad witch?" Julia asked the old woman.

"Where have I heard that question before?" Stu said.

"A movie that no longer exists," Rex said.

"I'm not a witch at all, my dear."

"Mmm…. I feel *something.*"

The tea was crude and robust, but Stu enjoyed its warmth. Still, he was uncomfortable here.

"Bubbs," Rex mumbled as he passed Bubby.

"Hey."

"When I was in jail, there was a guy who made tea like this," Rex said, surprising himself. He never told anyone about having been arrested years ago.

"What were you in jail for?"

"None of your business. Something badass—you can count on it."

Ms. Essic only smiled.

"So, you're a witch, my dear?"

"Yes. Well no. I was adopted into a witch family. I learned the life and spells, but…"

"No wonder you can't cast a damn spell," Rex said. But this did not come out like most of Rex's put-downs; all his piss and vinegar lost. Julia figured it had to do with whatever Happy Jack had done to him. She did not need to reply to his comment.

"She's a wonderful witch," Bubby said. "The best."

Julia touched Bubby's face with the back of her hand.

"My mother is dying," Stu said.

"How?" Ms. Essic asked.

"Cancer," Stu said.

"How terrible."

"My parents are both gone," Julia said.

"Consider yourself lucky. My parents stole my TV money. My dad also ruined my credit with gambling debts," Rex said.

"But Rex…you can't compare what happened to you with Julia losing her parents," Bubby said.

"Did your parents steal your life savings? Destroy your credit for life?" Rex asked.

"No. My parents stole my self-esteem, sense of worth, and any chance I had at a meaningful relationship. But they never ruined my credit."

Bubby could not help but notice the old woman's unwavering grin. It was creepy rather than pleasant.

"I want to kill Bruja," Julia said.

"Goddamn, Julia. Look at you!" Rex said.

"So, all, tell me what's on your minds," Ms. Essic said.

"I will tell you what's on my mind. I think these guys are stupid and are going to get me killed," Rex said.

"Yeah? And I think Rex is a selfish prick and didn't even thank Stu and me for saving his life," Julia said.

"You saved his life? What did I miss?" Bubby asked.

"They didn't save shit."

"Yes, we did, and he's too much of a tough guy to admit it. And this tough guy crap is an act. I think Rex is more scared than me," Stu said.

"Bullshit."

"Guys, I think we should leave," Bubby said.

"But this is getting good," Julia said.

"What? Julia, that's not like you," Bubby said. "Guys, something's wrong. We need to leave. She's doing something to us."

"Bubby, are you saying this old colored woman here is influencing us," Rex asked.

"Colored?"

"Her," Rex said, indicating Ms. Essic.

"What?" Julia asked. "Rex, Ms. Essic is white."

"White? Black? Are you all blind? She's a little old Asian woman," Stu said.

They all froze.

"What were you arrested for," Ms. Essic asked Rex.

"JWD."

"Huh?"

"Jerking White Driving. Okay? You happy?" Rex asked.

"God," Julia said.

"What? If that's the worst I have ever done..."

"Guys, we need to *leave*!" Bubby repeated.

A phone rang. They all stopped.

Ms. Essic answered the old-fashioned landline.

"Mr. Goldenblatt, it's for you," she said.

"Me? I don't want it."

Ms. Essic did something, and the phone was now on speaker. However, there was no speaker here. The caller's voice was all around them—a woman's voice.

Bubby spoke: "Hello?

"You loser. I married a loser, " the voice impersonating his ex-wife said.

"Please don't do this."

"Don't what? I married a man who fails at everything. You suck at business."

"Please-"

"You were married?" Julia asked.

"You were shit in bed. I was fucking the guy in the mailroom at work."

"No…."

"And you suck at golf, too."

"You bitch."

"You worthless-"

"You're not real," Bubby said. But the voice was in his head.

"I'm real enough," the voice on the phone taunted. But Bubby observed Ms. Essic's lips moving with the voice.

"You…."

"Me," Ms. Essic said. Then she spoke gibberish, an unknown dialect, words from a people known only in Hell.

"I thought you were a witch. I knew there was magic here. You're not a witch; you're a demon," Julia said.

"Yessss." A serpent's tongue sprang from the old woman's mouth, forked and full of poison.

Ms. Essic jumped in the air and hung there. Large teeth expanded from her diseased gums.

"Shit!"

She floated over to Rex, her overgrown toenails scraping the floorboards, and chomped on his hand with fangs dripping with venom.

"You old bitch!"

A red web spread across Rex's hand. Rex slapped himself with the possessed hand.

"Holy shit, it's like Evil Dead Two," Julia said.

"Like what?" Stu asked.

"Never mind. We need to cut Rex's hand off. Quickly!"

Rex's possessed hand grabbed his hair and slammed his head onto the table.

"Cut it off," Rex begged between blows.

"Oh, God!" Bubby said.

"Stu, grab the sword and cut my hand off!" Rex cried, indicating the weapon on the wall.

Stu grabbed the sword and paused. The red web reached Rex's wrist.

"Cut it off before it spreads!"

"Yeah, cut his fucking hand off," the old woman wailed. Her yellow eyes danced in their sockets.

"I can't," Stu said.

"Ha! He won't be jerking off with that hand anymore," Ms. Essic said.

"I'm right-handed, bitch," Rex said. I'll jerk off in your eye before this is over!"

"I can't," Stu repeated.

 "Cut my hand off, you pussy!"

"'Pussy?" Stu swung the sword. He severed Rex's arm just below the shoulder. The arm fell to the cabin's floor with a meaty thump.

"The fuck, Stu," Rex cried. "The hand Goddamnit. Not my whole arm!"

"You were moving. I'm nervous!"

The Ms. Essic-demon sang in joy, a song from a nightmare. She hovered inches above the floor, gliding like something from a carnival funhouse. Her head lolled to one side. Rex's arm danced on the floor like a newly caught fish on the deck of a boat, active at first but quickly losing steam.

"Let's move," Bubby said.

They all ran to the door, Rex clutching where his arm had been moments ago. They exited the cottage. Outside was pitch and reeked of sulfur and despair.

The Ms. Essic-demon appeared in the doorway, chanting incantations.

"Oh shit!"

Several demons appeared from the darkness. Others sprung from the soggy ground like something from a George Romero movie.

"Everyone, stand close together," Julia said as she rummaged in her purse.

"Christ, Bubby!" Rex said as Bubby bumped against his wound.

"Sorry."

"Dammit, Stu, you fuckin' maimed me!"

Julia produced a jar of salt and made a circle around them. She said a few of her own incantations.

"We cannot leave the sacred circle."

The demons came close but did not enter the circle. The spell was working.

The Ms. Essic-demon left the cottage, the horde of demons parting to allow their master access. She now held a baby to one wrinkled and deflated breast. The idea anything could extract milk from the vestigial appendage was pure madness. She glided over to them. Stu was sure she would grab them, but she stopped short. Her free hand smoothed across the unseen boundary in the air as if they were in a giant fishbowl, and she could not reach through. Her head twitched as she scraped a claw over the air surrounding them. Then the "baby" glared at them. Closer inspection proved it was, in fact, an ancient dwarf.

"Say hello, Mr. Wigglesworth," Essic said.

The thing attempted a smile its biology would not allow. Instead, it licked the pus-green milk from its chin with a long, pointed tongue.

"My God," Stu said.

"Your God is not here, boy," Essic said.

"Shit, Julia, we're stuck here until dawn. Why didn't you make the circle bigger?" Rex asked.

"Rex, stop complaining. At least we are safe," Bubby said. "Thank you, Julia...you saved us."

"Easy for you to say; you still have both arms."

Rex was rapidly getting pale. His wound spilled blood on the grass at an alarming pace. Again, Julia went into the purse. She came out with a bag holding herbs.

"You're rolling a joint now?" Stu asked.

"It's not ganja."

She put a fistful of the herbs on Rex's shoulder and recited a spell.

"What are you doing? Don't fuck me up more than I already am," Rex said.

"I'm trying to help you, asshole. I'm going to grow your arm back."

"Oh boy," Stu said. "This should be interesting."

"Yeah, Stu's right. What if I grow a third leg rather than an arm? Or a second prick!" Rex asked.

"I know what I'm doing."

"I've heard that before," Rex said but did not protest. The demons were chanting along with their leader. But whatever Julia did was keeping them safe for the time being. And Rex's bleeding had all but stopped.

"Shit, it does not hurt so much now," Rex said.

"See?" Bubby said. She knows what she's doing."

"Yeah, Julia, I have to admi-" Rex stopped talking as his voice echoed, two voices rather than one.

"Holy shit!"

There were two Rexes in the circle now.

"Oh no," Bubby said.

Julia grabbed the sword from Stu and cut the left arm off the second Rex. She snatched the arm and, with a new spell, attached it to the real Rex. She chanted again.

"What are you doing now?" Bubby asked.

"Making this fake Rex disappear."

"Wait," Rex said.

"What?"

Before you make him go away, how about a threesome? It will be your only chance to sleep with two of me."

"Asshole."

Despite the situation, Rex smiled.

Julia finished the spell, and the fake Rex vanished. Rex's arm was tingling and slightly clumsy, but he was whole again.

"Holy shit, Julia. It worked. Thanks," Rex said.

"What now?" Bubby asked.

"Now we wait," Julia said. "I always wanted to say that!" She giggled. Exactly *how* long would they have to wait? How long *could* they wait? Then Ms. Essic held out a hand of fire and placed it on the ground.

"Oh shit," Stu said.

***

"HauntedLand?

"Yes. I need you all to go to Haunted Land now. Can you all handle it?" Cain asked.

"Hell yeah," Tuco said.

"Bruja, are you up for this?" Cain asked. The witch had lost all her fire overnight. She had pouted around all day with a lost look in her usually scheming eyes.

"Huh?"

"She'll be fine," Booth said.

"Don't you speak for me!"

"You need not worry; we will stop them this time," Booth said.

"I hope so. The Four have gotten further than they should have," Cain said.

"We'll stop them," Bruja said.

"My dear, are you sure you're okay?"

"I'm fine. Let's go."

***

The fire crept closer; it would not be long before they were engulfed in flames.

"We are going to need to figure something out…and soon," Bubby said.

"Let's hope *you* don't do the thinking," a voice from outside the circle said.

"What? Mom?"

"Ira, look at the mess you got these poor people in. Some friend you are." The illusion was Bubby's mother one moment, his ex-wife the next, morphing over and over upon itself in a bizarre dance.

"Bubby, it's not her. It's Essic. She's shifting. Don't listen," Julia said and took Bubby's hand.

"Damn, Bubbs, did you marry your mother?" Rex asked.

"Pretty much." Bubby closed his eyes.

"Christ, Bubbs, man up," Rex said, flexing. His new arm was weak and numb, but it was working.

"Shut up. Leave Bubby alone," Julia said.

"He's not your friend," the Essic-demon said. "He's only here to stop *Fake Ape* from being made so *Monkey Mom* can be a hit."

"What?"

"Is that true, Bubbs?"

"No! Maybe…I don't know."

"Don't give her your power," Julia said.

The Essic-demon shifted and became a toy—a ventriloquist's dummy, complete in a tiny tuxedo and monocle.

"What the hell is this," Stu asked.

"Oh no…."

"Julia. It's me, Mr. Holmes."

Bubby opened his eyes.

"Who the hell is Mr. Holmes?"

"I'm Julia's friend," The dummy said. "I was the *only* friend she had as a child. She used to talk to me like a real person. So sad."

"Friend. That thing is creepy." Rex said.

"Come out of the circle, and we can return home, Julia. You are not a witch anyway. You can't help them. If they were your friends, you would come with me now and let them fight their battles without an inept witch."

"Bullshit. Julia has saved us more than once," Bubby said.

Rex raised his arm.

"Don't listen to him, Julia. Look at my arm. You saved me," Rex said.

"Go away," Julia said to the apparition. The dummy melted and reappeared as a woman.

"Oh no," Stu said.

"Stu, you can't save me. You can't even help your mother. Look at me?"

His mother was a cadaver—thin, pale, hair all but gone.

"It's not your mother," Bubby said.

The frail and wasted version of his mother looked around, confused.

"Where am I, Stuey? Come out of the circle and help me. What kind of a son are you? You killed your best friend, and now you are killing me."

"Fight the bitch, Stu. She can't hurt us because we are sticking together. She's frightened of us," Julia said.

"Come out of the circle, Stu. Don't be a pussy," the thing said.

"Up your ass!"

When Stu's mother shrunk, they all thought Essic would reappear as Mr. Holmes again. But what appeared was what could only be a leprechaun.

"What the hell is that?" Stu asked.

"Don't ask," Rex said.

"Rex, me boy. Have you done it? Have you managed to get to a timeline where *Happy Jack* was successful? Tell these losers you are only here for greedy reasons," Stoops said.

"Rex?" Stu asked.

"Tis true, boy. Rex here is only looking out for himself. Did you all ever have a doubt? Such a selfish prick he is. Ye can't be dumb enough to trust the likes of him," Stoops said and did a jig on a tree stump.

"That's not true," Bubby said. "Rex is our friend. We trust him. And Julia has saved us over and over."

"Her? She cannot witch her way out of a paper bag," Mr. Holmes said. The flames danced closer.

"Someone tell Mr. Holmes you cannot use 'witch' as a verb," Stu said.

"Stu and Julia saved me from killing myself," Rex said.

"You're all going to die in a way that will even make the demons cringe," Essic said. Mr. Wigglesworth laughed in her arms.

"Don't listen to her, guys," Rex said.

"And he will never find what he pretends to be looking for, isn't that right, Rex? Tell them why?" It was Stoops again.

"What's he talking about?" Julia asked.

"I lied. I never lived in a reality where the damn show was successful. I'm a has-been in all realities," Rex said, all his bravado gone.

"We don't care, Rex. You are one of us. Our friend," Bubby said.

"Bubbs, you don't have to say anything."

"You are our friend, Rex."

"Oh, what a lovely thing. Friends. As if there is such a thing," Stoops said.

"There is," Bubby said, "you're looking at them. We're the Four, ain't that right, Stu?"

"Yes...yes it is."

"What kind of group are you?" Essic asked and laughed.

"A loser," Bubby said.

"A man-child," Stu said.

"The world's most incompetent witch," Julia said.

"A has-been," Rex said.

Julia grabbed Bubby's hand. Bubby caught Stu, who held out his hand for Rex, who hesitated ever so slightly before taking Stu's hand. There was no denying a real power between them. Julia spoke.

"With the power of the Four..." But that was all they could understand. After those six words, Julia's voice became deep, and she spoke in tongues.

The Essic thing began fading.

"It's working," Stu said.

The demon vanished. The other creatures slowly receded into the darkness, their arrogance waning with their master gone.

"Julia, you did it!" Stu hugged her. Bubby enveloped them both in his arms.

"Rex, get in here...group hug."

Rex entered their group embrace. Stu noticed Rex holding back, and then his hug tightened.

"You guys...I-" but a laugh cut off Rex.

"I say, would you look at this," Booth said.

In the flickering of flames, the cowboy stood. He had his hands on the revolvers at his hips, flanked by Tuco on one side and Bruja on the other.

"You..."

"And now, if you let go of one another, we can end all this nonsense. I will take you to Cain," he said.

"Go with you? Are you crazy?" Stu said.

"So, you *are* working with Cain. I should have known." Julia said. "Bruja, is he the great man all you hoped he'd be?"

Bruja's eyes rimmed with tears. Then she stared daggers at her former roommate.

"You shut up—your lips are not worthy to speak his name."

Tuco went for a knife, but Bruja grabbed his arm.

"It won't work. The knives will fly back at you. Julia managed to get *this* spell right," Bruja said. Stu could not help but notice Bruja looked older than she had at the brothel, defeated.

"I knew you were wicked, but this is even beneath you," Julia said.

Bruja looked insubstantial. She was fading. Tuco and Booth followed suit.

"I will need at least one of you to break this circle. Now, who's the weakest? You, sir, if you will let go and step forward, please."

"I am not weak, and I am not letting go," Bubby said.

"Well, I was talking to Rex Dolan, but if you'd like to join us, it would be grand."

"We got you. Everyone, hold tighter!" Rex said.

"Not so fast, Mr. Dolan."

Booth held a small crate. From within came a mewing.

"No…" Rex said.

Booth removed Josh from the crate. The orange tabby was scruffy with fear. The miserable thing whined. Rex went to the edge of the circle.

"You let him go right now, or I will-"

"Now, Mr. Dolan, remove your hands from those of your friends, and I will not snap the creature's neck," Booth said.

"Let him go, you piece of shit."

Rex stood staring right into Booth's eyes, unmoving. Then his shoulders sagged.

"What is this?" Stu asked.

"I'm sorry, guys," Rex said and loosened his grip on the circle.

"Rex, no!" Stu said.

Booth tightened his grip on Josh. The cat moaned, his little face twisted in pain, eyes wide.

"You hurt him, and I promise I will kill you," Rex said. There was none of Rex's usual audacity—this was merely a statement.

"And when have you ever made good on a promise?"

"You can trust me on this one."

And did Stu see if, for only the slightest moment, Booth's overconfident smirk wither? Fear flicker in his beady eyes? But he regained his grandeur swiftly and clenched the cat tighter. Josh whined.

"Mr. Dolan…the next move is yours."

Rex broke the circle.

"Hand him over."

"Rex, no!" Julia said.

"Rex, you can't leave us," Stu said.

"But Josh…"

"Rex, please Julia said."

"You want the beast? Come hither," Booth said.

Cain's cabal regained substance. Rex's hatred for the cowboy came off him like a tangible heat. His concern for the cat was not something Stu could have guessed. Josh's face twisted in pain, his tiny teeth bared, orange fur shocked at all angles. Rex had murder in his eyes. But there was something else in his friend. Rex's concern was patent. He cared so much for this cat. Stu loved Rex at this moment.

"Rex…" Bubby called.

Rex took a step back. Two.

"You're going the wrong way, has-been. I'll twist his little head off," Booth said.

"I'm sorry, Josh," Rex said thickly, returning to the circle. He joined hands with his friends again. Julia resumed her spell. Rex looked at Bubby through his tears.

"Bubbs, it'd serve me right if you laughed at me for crying," Rex said.

Bubby held Rex's hand tighter.

"You, Rex Dolan, are a good man."

Tears came for the first time in many years. No one had ever called him a good man before.

Booth stepped forward, held Josh out, and grasped his tiny head.

"Look away," Bubby said to Rex.

"Oh God," was all Rex could say. But he went to the tip of the circle. He wanted Josh to see him, know he was here.

Seeing Rex, Josh wriggled in Booth's arms and hissed.

"Josh, I'm sorry. Daddy loves you!"

The fire before them grew brighter.

"Son of a bitch!" Booth wailed as Josh clawed his face. He dropped the cat.

"Run, Josh!" Rex said. The cat stood there for a moment, not willing to leave Rex. Bruja walked toward the cat.

"Don't you touch him," Julia told her old roommate.

"Josh, run!"

This time, the cat took off.

"What did you do to Pip?" Rex asked.

"Oh, he's taking a train to nowhere," Bruja laughed.

"Quick, join hands again!"

Before he joined hands again, Rex took a step forward toward Booth.

"Rex, no, get back in the circle," Bubby said.

Rex pointed to the cowboy.

"You and me, partner. We ain't finished, Cowboy—not by longshot. I will see you again. I promise you will die. Now look in my eyes…will I keep this promise?" Rex said. And this time, there was no guessing about it. While Booth's toothy grin never faltered, his eyes changed, lost all their conceit. The cowboy recovered quickly, but the tell was there.

Rex stepped back into the circle and joined hands. Julia resumed the incantation. Booth and his crew began to fade. The flames licked at the bottom of Stu's jeans. Before Cain's people completely disappeared.

"You are dead, poser. I promise."

Stu watched as Booth looked at Bruja, perhaps hoping a witch could protect him from Rex's fury. Bruja looked away.

Julia continued the incantation, and eventually, the cabal outside the circle withered and went black as the fire licked at the feet of the Four.

"Let's go," Stu said.

***

They walked silently for some time, Rex uncharacteristically with nothing to say.

"I'm sorry about your cat," Julia said.

"Yeah…"

"At least he got away; he's alive."

"Yeah, but for how long in this place?" Rex said.

"Something's happening," Bubby said.

"No shit, something's happening. We're in Haunted Land, which is magic and changes reality. There's a little old lady/demon, a leprechaun, and a living ventriloquist's dummy..." Rex said.

"No…he's right. I noticed an energy shift," Stu said.

"Changes are happening again," Bubby said. He turned to see Rex, who now had a mustache.

"Hey, Rex, you look like a porn star," Julia laughed.

"What the hell," Rex said, trying to pull off the mustache, which was still growing under his nose.

Stu found he was wearing a leather jacket, spandex pants, and a KISS shirt. His long hair tickled his face.

"Looks like Stu is an '80s headbanger now," Julia said.

"The Cain Consequence is quickening," Bubby said.

For a moment, Julia was a real plain Jane, looking more like a librarian than her colorful self. Then she was back.

They were not the only things shifting—the landscape was also changing. One moment, they were in a spooky amusement park, a Ferris wheel full of demons observing them, and then they passed a golf course.

"It's my home course," Bubby said. But when they looked, it was the nightmare's amusement park again, all the rides broken and the barkers zombies.

"This is crazy," Stu observed. He was normal again. But Bubby was in a tuxedo, and Julia looked like an off-duty nun, plain and uncolorful again. But as quickly as the changes happened, they all returned to normal.

"This can't be good," Bubby said. "You think the changes are happening all over?"

They kept walking. What else could they do?

***

And…

Pip went round and round in a horrible merry-go-round of an episode of a show he would live in for eternity.

And…

In the woods, the '70s vampire morphed into something less '70s but no more adaptable than his old self. Dressed in 1800s frilly clothes and long blond hair, he looked like a cross between a gay George Washington and a cheap porn parody of the Vampire Lestat.

And…

Tom White (or White Feather) found himself walking the road he strolled to school every day as a kid. As he walked, he kept meeting people from his past—the older woman who took his virginity, the teacher who had introduced him to Norman Mailer and Arthur Miller. He had been the first adult to treat him equally and regard his opinion as valid. The landscape changed with the people of his past. Then he was back in West Land. He tried to turn around on the road, but a man (his first boss from the butcher market he had worked in after school) told him this road only goes in one direction. Spinning around, he could only see a black void before him. He had to return to the Cult of Change and warn everyone their world was being undone.

***

Finally, they stopped morphing. The nightmare visions of a carnival from hell gave way to more normal settings. Stu pointed ahead to a woman standing a few yards in the distance on their path.

"Hello."

"You are the woman from the bar in Pub Land. You're the one who left me the note," Bubby said.

"You're supposed to be dead," Rex said. "Guys, this is Veronica Sinclair."

"Well, I am one of them, yes."

"You're the one who texted me," Julia said.

"You called us here? But why? Why would you want to stop Cain from bringing you back to life?" Stu asked.

"Lies, like so much of Cain's words," Sinclair said.

Stu noticed this version of the actress was different from the one who died in reality. She was older, of course. This Sinclair had lived 25 years longer than her dead 'sister.' She was right. She was a different person.

"What do you mean?" Stu said.

"Cain was never trying to-"

Veronica Sinclair's forehead opened, and her brains exploded in a pink stream, landing in a wet *plop* in the mushy dirt. She took a step forward. Then she stepped back, her left eye drooping grotesquely, before falling into the mound of her grey matter.

Booth stood, revolver smoking about twenty yards away. He'd finally made a shot.

The Four ran.

CHAPTER EIGHTEEN

This insane journey across multiple realities and outside of space and time was a thing of alchemy. So, it made a poetic justice that it ended with something so unremarkable as the sterile office building before them in juxtaposition among the world's most notorious haunted houses. A body of black brackish water surrounded the building. There was, however, a rickety bridge leading to the entrance.

Stu kept expecting Booth to reappear, but the cowboy was nowhere in sight. Bubby had held his chest a moment. He looked better now that he'd caught his breath.

"What the hell is this?" Rex asked, moving to the bridge.

The water bubbled. Then rippled. An enormous, phallic purple and pink polka-dotted serpent rose from the water! Rex stepped back. The creature opened a maw full of razor teeth. Something out of a bad acid trip.

"It stands to reason this is the place Cain wanted to avoid us seeing," Bubby said, pointing to the impossible thing. The creature was beneath the oily water again. Its humps were rolling beneath the surface of the murky river.

"Now, how do we avoid the Lovecraftian creature?" Julia said.

"Huh? You mean the purple, polka-dotted prick monster."

"Yes, Rex, the purple, polka-dotted prick monster."

"Wait," Stu rummaged through his pockets. He unwrapped a few of the Bubby Bars he'd pocketed. He tossed them into the water. For a moment, nothing happened. Then the creature chased the bars.

"Sweet! Excellent job, Stu," Julia said and clapped.

"Quick, while it's eating."

They ran across the bridge to the front door.

They entered the building. The place resembled a medical building—clean and ordinary. To Stu, this did not appear to be a magical place. However, if he'd learned anything in the past week, it was to not judge anything on its appearance. They checked the office's many doors. Julia opened one door to find eyeballs floating around. Their pupils (hazel, brown, blue, gray) stared at her. They flew to and fro, their optic nerves trailing behind like squirrel tails. One bumped into her arm, cold and sticky. She slammed the door shut.

"Gross."

Bubby stood before the door he'd opened. He was looking into an eight-foot aquarium, yet no glass separated him and the sea. However, not a drop of water entered the hall. Fish of all sizes and colors swam. He touched the wall of water. His finger was wet until he removed it from the room, where it became dry again. When a green shark passed, he slammed the door and joined the rest.

Stu and Rex opened the only door to anything normal. They all crowded into the small room resembling a dad's den from the '70s, all dark paneling and bulky furniture.

"Wow, this looks like it's from your day, Bubbs," Rex said.

"It's like a time capsule from the nineteen-seventies," Bubby said.

"Well, considering how time and space work here, this room might actually *be in* the '70s somewhere," Stu said.

"What a strange thought," Julia said. Stranger still was this idea was likely the case.

"Oh boy, a VCR!" Bubby said.

"A what?" Stu and Julia said together.

"You owe me a beer, Stu," Julia laughed.

"It's how we recorded video before smartphones."

"Forget the VCR. Look at the TV it's connected to," Julia said.

The TV was bulky and looked more like a classic furniture piece than a TV.

Rex pointed to a photo on the dark paneled wall.

"It's Cain and Veronica Sinclair."

Sinclair was stunning in the photo. Cain had a full head of hair, only hinting at his widow's peak today. He also sported a mustache and wore horn-rimmed glasses— looking more like someone from a band on the Ed Sullivan show than an occultist.

"This must be Cain's room."

"What is all this?" Stu asked.

Bubby opened a large cabinet and found a cache of papers and two VHS tapes.

"Bingo."

"One tape says 'CAIN,'" Julia said. She grabbed the tapes.

"Oh shit," Stu said. He was rummaging through a second cabinet.

"What?" Rex asked and came to Stu's side, looking in the cabinet.

"Oh boys…check it out," he said, removing a pistol.

"A gun," Bubby said.

"Yeah, a *real* gun," Rex said.

"Maybe we should leave the pistol alone," Bubby said. But Rex was already trying to match the pistol to one of the many ammo boxes the cabinet held.

Bubby grabbed the tape labeled 'CAIN.' He and Rex then spent the next few minutes powering up the TV and VHS deck and getting the video in the machine. Finally, a picture appeared on the TV. The video and audio went in and out for a moment, but eventually, the video stabilized.

Cain appeared on the TV, a little older than he was in the photo but clearly from many years ago. He sat in this very room, which had not changed since the recording.

> *"I am sitting in my archive room, in Haunted Land. When I began working on The Great Secession, I decided to see if I could control the changes. And, of course, change the world. You see, around the end of the new millennium's second decade, people could no longer get along with anyone with a different opinion. It started with politics—as it often does—but quickly degenerated from there. I first separated the two major political parties as they had grown so intolerant of each other the two groups could no longer live together without becoming violent. Things were fine for a time, but the two halves split into several others due to religious beliefs. Next, they split more over how tax money should be spent. Before long, there were Lands based on sexual preferences, musical tastes, and smokers and non-smokers. The world has been convinced this was all a side-effect of my trying to bring Veronica back. This is false. That wretched*

*woman was nothing but a thorn in my side—
she even had me disown my daughter. My true
goal was always an attempt to create the Lands
to save humanity from itself.*"

Bubby paused the tape.

"Holy shit," Julia said, "Cain wasn't trying to bring Veronica Sinclair back at all! That's what she was trying to tell us before Booth killed her. The Lands are not a side effect. He was trying to stop all the violence. This changes things."

"It doesn't change shit," Stu said. "He's still modifying our realities and has no right to do it."

"But Cain is not the bad guy we thought he was."

"Are you kidding? He may not be as self-seeking as we thought, but this is still not his world to alter as he sees fit," Bubby said.

"We are here to stop Cain. Nothing has changed," Rex said.

"I don't get it. Stu, you want to help your mother. I wanted to get away from a world I never fit in with. Bubby, you wanted to see if you could make your businesses successful. Rex, why did you come here if you were lying and *Happy Jack* was not successful in another reality?" Julia asked.

Rex stepped forward.

"Because this shit is wrong. And for once in my miserable fucking life, I am going to do the right thing."

Stu held the other tape titled 'MIB.'

"This must be the Men in Black," he said, swapping tapes in the VCR.

"If it's the naked guys, I am not watching," Julia said.

"Remember, the *real* Men in Black were once here," Rex said.

The video began, and mercifully, the man on the TV was clothed. He did look like a prototypical man in black—a black suit and tie, white shirt, short, cropped hair, and dark glasses.

"I'm number 12. Our investigation into Barclay *Cain finally revealed several findings. One thing: there were no records of Cain until about the 1990s. However, many have postulated he goes by a few pseudonyms. Others stated Cain was either a myth or a combination of several people.*

There are no records of Cain's education or work history. After arriving at the Lands, we found this place was a vortex. We used all the science at our disposal to understand and conclude, as Arthur Conan Doyle said in Sherlock Holmes, *'Once* you eliminate the impossible, whatever remains, no matter how improbable, must be the truth.' *This is indeed a magic place.*

We came here to stop the Cult of Change. However, they are indeed clueless...

In magic circles, it's prophesied a group will form to stop Cain. Here, the magic texts differ slightly on how this group will come to be. Some books call the group 'Tetrad,' yet others call it 'Quatern' *or* Four. *This group will include a Selected. The Selected will be a clairvoyant, a sorceress, or a witch."*

"Four. Us!" Stu said. "The Selected, it's what the woman in the Thursday Inn said. One of us is The Selected."

The tape ended here.

"Julia. It's you." Bubby said.

"It can't be…"

"Yes, it can. You are our savior, Julia," Bubby said. "I think if we all trust our intuition, we have known it all along."

"It's you, Julia," Rex said.

"I'm not even a real witch."

"Julia, Remember when Bruja had me under her spell? I found something out," Bubby said.

"Huh? What are you saying?"

"Julia, there's something I need to tell you," Bubby said.

***

"Wait."

"Why? I lied to you. I'm going back to my reality," Brandy-Two said.

"No, you're not."

"I don't understand."

"Are you sick?" Brandy asked.

"Sick? No. Why?"

"Well, I am."

"What are you talking about?"

"We are still going to switch. You are staying here, and I will go to your reality."

"But why? Stu's dead in my world."

"I'm dying. Don't say anything, please. You will be here with Stuey. It all makes sense."

"But-"

"No buts."

"Are you sure?"

"I'm sure. Now, what do we do?"

***

"Cain's my father?!"

"I'm sorry. I should have told you sooner but could not find the right time. It's why Bruja was so distraught when she found out. When I came home that day when she and I were…together," Bubby said.

"Wow," Stu said.

"Shit, Julia, you *are* The Selected," Rex said.

Julia thought about the door that had appeared in her room the night before she left with Bubby to come here. It seemed a lifetime ago and had happened to a different woman. She recalled how she had escaped the encounter in the Port-a-Potty. How all of her "failed" spells ended up working for their good, as Bubby had so often told her.

"Guys, this is too much pressure. This isn't a movie. This information will not make me powerful all of a sudden."

"That's right. You've had the power all along," Bubby reminded her.

"That's right. You have always been The Selected— now you know it," Stu said.

"But-"

Look at my arm," Rex said, rolling his sleeve. "My arm was gone. You brought it back. Does that sound like someone without power? Could someone incompetent have done this?"

There was a loud *crash* outside.

"So now what?" Stu asked.

"This whole thing goes too deep. Maybe we should escape and get out of here," Julia said.

"I don't know about you guys, but I know I can't return to my old life now," Rex said.

"He's right. Too much has changed. We are going to have to fight," Bubby said.

There was an explosion, and the building shook. The sound of wood shattering. Plaster dust rained from the ceiling.

"Guys, I think we need to get out of here," Stu said.

***

Brandy-Two packed a pipe with a sickly pale-yellow substance.

"Are you sure about this," she asked.

She was sure. Brandy had four months to live—six if all the stars aligned. She would go to the world where Stu had died and allow Brandy-Two to be Stu's mother in this reality.

"Yes."

They smoked.

Brandy was thrown into another reality as she exhaled the third hit. She held her twin's hand, but when the world stopped spinning, the hand she held was green. A woman resembling the Wicked Witch of the West (she remembered *The Wizard of Oz*) looked back at her.

"Where have you been? Welcome back."

"What is this?"

"Where do you want to go?" asked the Wicked Witch. At first, Brandy did not understand. But then she looked into multiple windows, scenes from her life. She was at a desk in her first job in New Jersey at nineteen years old. Another showed her dancing at her best friend's wedding. In yet another, she was in her school play in the third grade, her parents in the first row, her mother tearing up. She realized she could get off this ride at another point in her life. The temptation was enormous. But she pointed when she came upon Brandy-Two's reality—the one littered with photos of a dead Stu. And the world spun again. She focused on the framed pictures of Stu—a morbid memorial. When the world stopped swirling, she made a considerable drink—no ice cubes.

At peace, knowing she had done the right thing, Brandy lay on the sofa and covered herself with her favorite blanket. Her pain pills, which she had put in her pocket, had thankfully made the trip, and she gave God thanks for this. Then she dumped them all into her fist and washed them down with whiskey. She waited to see what happened after this life was over.

***

The room shifted, and they were momentarily back in Bubby's warehouse, but the transference continued. They flashed into the bar, the Amityville house, and then things stopped in Porn Land. An earthquake was taking place alongside the reality glitches. A gaggle of naked men ran past, their erections bobbing frantically. Two women with breasts larger than nature had ever allowed followed.

"God, *this* is where we end up!" Julia said.

Luckily, the shift resumed, and they returned to the archives room. Something whizzed past Stu's ear, and he watched as a knife went into the wall where his head had been a second before, vibrating with a cartoon *boing*.

"Look out, Stu!" Julia said as Tuco threw another knife. This one nicked Stu's ear, but he escaped severe harm again. But he knew a third knife was bound to find its mark.

In the movies, loading and firing a gun was a skill every person possessed, but Stu noticed Rex struggling to load the pistol they'd found. The drawer held bullets of all sizes. Bullets silver and brass. Bullets fat and thin. But no shells fitting the damn gun. Rex stuffed the pistol and all the bullets into his jeans and hurried with the others.

The building was being unmade, brick by brick. As Stu crossed the bridge, he paused, unable to look away as the creature finished chewing one of Cain's people. The Bubby Bars had not left it sated, apparently. He was disappointed it was not Tuco the monster swallowed.

As the creature was finishing its meal, they crossed the bridge. A good thing, as the bridge exploded only seconds after they reached the other side. Considering the fishy gore that rained upon them immediately following the blast, two things were clear: someone had detonated an explosive, and the serpent was a casualty of the detonation.

"Freeze," Booth said as he turned the corner. He'd finally made his cowboy movie entrance. He had his revolver pointed at Julia.

"I wouldn't do that," Rex said, pointing the pistol he'd found at Booth.

Though Rex's pocket was heavy with the bullets he'd found in the archive room, he'd yet to find one to fit the pistol. Stu knew he was bluffing and prayed Booth did not consider this.

"How about I put one right between your eyes, cowboy," Rex said.

"How do you know it won't be my bullet that finds you?"

"I've seen you shoot."

Bruja let out a laugh. Booth shot her a look. But the exchange made Rex look away, and Booth disappeared behind a corner. The land was changing again, morphing beneath their feet. Water flowed from nowhere and everywhere, spouting from trees and the ground. The stars in the sky lacked verisimilitude, like the dayglow stickers Stu's mother had put on his ceiling when he was a boy. The ruse was caving.

A thin and unmoving man in the distance watched the scene.

"Cain," Stu said. But the man disappeared.

They moved across the landscape, the ground shifting beneath them like something from a carnival. In the distance, they could see Bruja and Tuco join Booth. There were also others with the cowboy, witch, and clown.

"Well, I guess this is it. The time to fight is now," Bubby said.

Stu put his arm around the rest.

"I love you guys. We are the Four."

"The Four."

"The Four."

"The Four," Rex said. "You guys are my family now. Let's fuckin' do this."

CHAPTER NINETEEN

Booth fired shooting wildly. One of his bullets found a tree, removing a strip of bark in a clean line. Another of his rounds ricocheted off a massive rock in the ground, causing sparks in the dusk. As bad a shot as the man was, Stu knew he'd hit one of them shortly. He was thinking of what to do next when Rex acted.

"Right here, dick-bag," Rex said and ran *toward* Booth. "C'mon, cowboy, see if you can take me out!"

"Rex!" Julia said. "He's going to get himself killed."

Knives flew. The first two found the ground. The third caught Bubby in the leg.

"Bubby!"

"I'm fine," Bubby said. "Hey, clown! That didn't hurt!" Bubby said and limped in another direction, taking Tuco's attention away from Stu and Julia. Outnumbered as they were, they were holding their own. But how long could they last?

***

Rex fumbled through his pockets for a bullet to fit the pistol. A twig snapped, and he looked to see Booth closing in, revolver trained on him. Rex raised his empty gun.

"Well, looks like a Mexican stand-off."

"I'm not worried, considering how you shoot," Rex said.

"That may be. But I have a hunch that pistol of yours is empty."

"Is that a chance you're ready to take?"

For a moment, Booth appeared unsure. Then he cocked his revolver.

"Yes, it is."

Rex was ready to take a lethal dose of unknown pills not too long ago. Now, he thought of how little he'd accomplished in his forty-plus years. He wanted time. Time to change. Time to make amends. Time to live. But if his life were to end here, now, he'd end it fighting with the only friends he'd ever had in his life.

***

Bruja cringed as Cain used his magic to disappear and reappear, observing the battle but not helping—the fucking coward. Cain had undeniably known what Booth had done to her (through his vision, he knew everything that went on with his people) and never said a word. She tried to track Cain but lost him as the man vanished again. Then she noticed Booth closing in on Rex. Bruja grabbed a pipe from the building's rubble.

***

A shot rang off a tree, nearly finding Booth. Bishop stood there with an ancient musket in his gangly hand, Mr. Giggles, the monkey, perched on his back with a slingshot.

The monkey put a nut in the slingshot and hit Booth in the face below the eye.

"Son-of-a-bitch!" Booth said and ran, blood trickling where Mr. Giggles's nut had hit him.

"You were right, asshole," Rex said, raising his pistol. "It's not loaded."

The rest of the Cult of Change scattered, joining the battle.

"Hell yeah!" Rex said, seeing the Cult join the war.

"Cain! Cain, we need help," Booth yelled. But his fearless leader was absent.

"He does not care about you, jerk," Julia said from the brush where she hid, "That's Barclay Cain for you...he used you all."

Bullets, arrows, knives, and stones flew as reality continued "flickering" in and out to different Lands. It always stuck on Porn Land a moment or two longer than any other. Even the apocalypse was obsessed with pornography.

***

Stu was delighted to see the Cult of Change members fighting alongside them. A half-man-half-bull rammed into The Bat, sending the round man flying and hitting a half-buried tombstone with a sickly crunch. His brother Zack screamed.

Even Steven fired a rifle and hit one of Cain's people right between the eyes. He then looked at Stu and managed to say, "Oh, shit," he said, realizing his error as a bullet found him in the exact location.

Bishop was punching Zack in the stomach. All the while, his little monkey beat the man on the head with the handle of his slingshot. Zack became smaller with each blow of the stick until he was little enough for Bishop to grind into the mud under one chunky boot.

We may get out of this alive, Stu Sawyer thought.

***

Julia stopped all the panic rising in her and chanted an incantation. From her vantage point, she could see Booth in the distance and created a curse, rendering the cowboy's feet heavy and clumsy. Julia watched Bruja in the distance. Her old roommate clutched a weapon of some kind. Then Bruja disappeared behind a bush. A vast naked man with bronze skin ran through the middle of everything, like a golden version of *The Incredible Hulk*. It appeared to Julia the man belonged to neither side of this war nor had any skin in who were loser and victor. There is no clear objective other than to get his hands on Barclay Cain.

"Cain! Cain, I'll find you. I'll get you!" the man said, disappearing into the distance.

***

Rex noticed Booth was struggling with his feet and took this opportunity to recheck his bullets.

Nothing.

In the distance, he could see Bubby ducking knives, limping his way *toward* Tuco.

What the hell are you doing, Bubbs? Rex thought. *You're heading in the wrong direction! You're going to get yourself killed!*

The little clown was firing madly at Bubby, ignoring anything else happening around him, dead set on killing a man who had never hurt a soul in his life.

Hang in there, Bubbs, my friend. I'm coming, Rex thought.

Booth was shooting again; he'd freed his feet a bit. Rex ducked and ran to another spot to see if he could get to Bubby.

***

Julia stopped chanting and opened her eyes to find Booth right before her.

"And now, little girl, it's payback time," he said. He held his revolver on her with his right hand and undid his belt with the left. Even in the middle of the battle, the sick fuck had one thing on his mind.

"You bastard."

"Hold still. Even I cannot miss you from here," Booth smiled. "Get ready-"

"You're not touching her, asshole!" someone said.

Booth's head made a sickly hollow THUNK! And Julia assumed Bruja struck the man with everything she had. Indeed, she could see the pipe still vibrating in Bruja's hands. Morbidly, Booth was the last to know what had happened. He opened and closed his mouth a few times, about to make one of his wise-ass comments, but then halted, his mouth still moving but no sound coming. Then blood washed over his face, first in a trickle, then in a wave. He fell, first to his knees and then flat on his beautiful face. Julia was reasonably sure the blow did not kill him. But he sure as hell was never going to be the same smug son-of-a-bitch ever again.

Julia looked at Bruja.

"Go!" Bruja said.

Julia ran. Screams came from all directions. She ran until she came upon Tuco and his never-ending supply of daggers. Fire exploded in her right leg. A small knife stuck out of her thigh. Another scarcely missed her. She regarded the man, who was sure to be her executioner. Then she spotted Bubby rushing Tuco.

"Bubby, no!"

***

Bubby checked his pockets for anything he could use as a weapon but came up empty. A pint of whiskey fell and shattered on a half-buried scarlet stone. His hand discovered something in his coat. He pulled the old dollar bill on a fishing line gag from his jacket. Bubby said a quick prayer and rushed the clown.

***

Stu found Rex behind part of the building that had yet to come down entirely.

"Julia is still alive."

"And Bubbs," Rex asked.

"I can't find him."

"Cain's hiding, the little shit."

"What now?"

"Now, Stu, my boy, we go and finish this shit."

"How? We have no weapons."

Rex grabbed the back of Stu's head and brought their foreheads together.

"With balls, Stu. We finish this with nothing but our balls."

***

Tuco got about half a dozen knives into Bubby, but the older man hardly even slowed! Tuco doubled his efforts, throwing so many blades in the next few seconds his little arm was on fire. But Bubby had managed to get behind him and had something around his neck. He would have thought the guy would have had no energy left—he'd be dead shortly from the blood loss alone. But Tuco was being strangled with a toy...one of the man's fucking toys! He was losing his grip on conscienceless and quickly. There were stars, then lightning, then only blackness.

Dead by one of Bubby's fucking toys.

***

"Bubbs!" Rex said, running toward his friend. He passed Booth lying face down in the mud. The rest of Cain's people were running away or dead. Bubby had an obscene number of knives in his belly, chest, and neck, as well as one through his cheek and one buried to the hilt in his right eye. A horrible amount of blood poured from him.

"Hang in there, Bubbs. I'll get you out of this."

"I'm not getting out of this one, Rex."

"Don't say that, Bubbs. You're getting home and can re-open Bubby's Boutique Gags."

Had this been a movie, Bubby would have said some wise words, given the answer to all the world's problems, or made a miraculous recovery. But life wasn't a movie where characters all at once found the words where none had ever been and a lifetime of horrible luck turned around instantly in a neatly written script.

Bubby's good eye was blurring around the edges. His mind was traveling. He was five years old and pushed against the fence of his old schoolyard by AJ Moran. He was eleven and listening to his parents argue about money. He was fourteen and telling his middle-school guidance counselor, Ms. Carter, he was in love with her. The counselor had shown great care and explained he did not know from love at his age, and in a year at most, he'd laugh about having ever made such a declaration. She had said he would not remember his feelings at all. A year later, Ms. Carter had been correct.

He was sixteen and on his first date and touching hands with a girl for the first time. He was eating in his favorite Italian place with his future ex-wife. He was light now—no more pain.

"I'm dead...."

"No, you're not," Rex said.

"I fought back, Rex...did you see it? I got him," Bubby said, gripping Rex's hand with blood that was already sticky rather than slick.

"You sure as hell did, Bubbs. You saved Julia; you saved us all."

Stu and Julia appeared behind him. Julia covered her mouth, crying soundlessly. Stu looked into Bubby's remaining eye but knew Bubby no longer saw them.

Bubby stopped breathing.

"Rex, we have to go," Stu said.

"Okay, let's get Bubbs moving, and we can get out of here."

"Rex-"

"Bubbs! 'C'mon Bubbs!"

"Rex, he's gone. We need to move," Julia said.

"Stu, get his feet, and I will get his shoulders. Then, let's get Bubbs to a doctor."

"Rex, please," Julia said.

"Julia, can you do something?" Rex turned to look at her, a forlorn hope in his eyes.

"I'm sorry."

"You grew my arm back, for Christ's sake!"

"I can't bring the dead back. Bubby's gone, Rex."

Julia knelt, ran her hand across Bubby's salt and pepper stubbled jowls, and sobbed.

Rex held Bubby's jacket.

"I will never forget you, Bubby," Stu said thickly.

"Stu, zip it. Okay…Bubbs, wake up!"

Stu and Julia lifted Rex. It was like moving a sack of rice.

"Why Bubbs?" Rex said. He stood and pulled the pistol from his pants, searching for someone to shoot, but the skirmish was over.

"Rex, give me the pistol," Stu said, even though he was pretty sure Rex had never found bullets to fit the damn thing. To his surprise, Rex handed him the pistol with a trembling hand.

They lifted Rex. Rex took a last look at the body of the man he wished he'd treated better. Finally, they walked.

Bishop was kneeling before the body of his yellow monkey, Mr. Giggles, sobbing.

"I'm so sorry," Julia said to the giant man.

There was a sound from behind a bush.

Meow.

Josh poked his orange head out.

"Oh my God," Julia said.

Rex ran to the cat, scooped him in his arms, and whispered behind the cat's ear.

"My little boy. My baby. Daddy's got you. I love you so damn much."

Poor Josh was soaked in Rex's tears within seconds, looking like a drowned kitten.

Julia's breath caught, and she covered her mouth. She did not know this Rex. Stu hugged her, and they cried together while Rex cooed in Josh's tiny ear.

"Sorry 'bout your friend. He was a good man," Bishop said.

"He was the best," Rex said.

"Thank you," Julia said as White Feather came limping over.

"You okay," Stu asked.

"I'm fine. Won't be running a marathon, but I have not run one of those in..." he looked sideways, and his mouth moved as he silently did the math, "...in *never*!" White Feather laughed.

Other members of the Cult of Change came over to join them. Most were injured.

The Four (three now, but they would always be the Four) bid their goodbyes to the remaining members of the Cult of Change and headed out of Haunted Land. The name was funny now. Like midnight's shadows were amusing in the morning where six hours earlier, one was convinced he was terrorized by something from beyond.

Stu averted his eyes from the few bodies scattered here and there.

"Wait," Rex said.

Rex stopped at the body of Booth.

"In the movies, they always move on without checking if the villain is dead," Rex said.

He flipped Booth over. Sure enough, the man was breathing. His eyes did not see anything, however. Nor was he able to find his voice. Still, Rex placed a hand over Booth's mouth and nose until the man died. Rex kissed Josh's head and walked on.

Josh purred loudly enough that Stu could hear him from a few feet away. Soon, they were back in West Land. However, the place had become undone. Parts of saloons and stables stood like the wreckage of a bomb. Other areas resembled the set of a play in mid-construction.

Bruja sat on the porch of a general store, weeping, looking far off at a dead dream only she could see. She glanced at the sound of their footfalls. Julia regarded her old roommate with something like pity and said: "Thank you."

Bruja hardly noticed her. Despite herself, Julia found herself asking:

"Do you want to come with us?"

"I don't think so."

"What will you do?"

"If West Land is not over, I will see if I can work in the brothel," Bruja said.

"You don't have to do that."

"I think I do."

"I don't think the Lands are going to survive."

"Then I am going with it."

They continued through West Land, and Stu thought he could almost imagine an Ennio Morricone score playing. The world around them continued to shift. One moment, they looked at dirt roads, covered wagons, and saloons; the next, they were on a city street.

"You think you've won? No one has won," Cain said from a saloon step. His remaining people surrounded him. Mainly the elderly who were not involved in the battle.

"You're a fuckin' coward, Cain," Rex said. Josh hissed at the man.

"Your people are gone," Julia said.

"Your world is crumbling. The Cain Consequence is dying," Stu said.

"You understand nothing," Cain said.

"You convinced yourself you were doing it for the good of humankind."

"I was."

"Maybe you told yourself that. But, you know what I think—I think you did it to see if it would work," Rex said.

"It *will* work the next time."

"There is no next time. It's over, father. You're done."

"So, you know," Cain said.

"Yes. And I am ashamed to have come from you," Julia said.

"I did this for you. For all of you!" Cain said. "Do you not remember what the world was like before the Lands? Are you old enough to remember? Politics? People fighting about anything and everything? Riots? Families tearing themselves apart due to who their members voted for. This would have worked. Should have worked."

"You don't know what the fuck you're talking about. You're nuts," Rex said. "A real class-A coward. Look around you. Your people are gone. Your Lands are about gone. It's over."

"It will never be over as long as I breathe."

"And if I kill you?" Stu asked.

"I can't die. I'm too important."

"Important? To whom?" Julia said.

"To everyone! I give everyone a chance! After all, what is a man but an aggerate of his choices? Like your drunk friend who perished at the knives. In my world, he could have a chance to be something more than a serial loser."

"You piece of shit. Don't you talk about Bubbs. You are not half the man he was," Rex said.

"Mr. Dolan, I'm *not* the villain in this story," Cain said.

"Well, you sure as hell are not the hero," Stu said.

The few people around Cain slinked away, leaving the great occultist frail and alone.

"I'm not a monster or a killer. I did not kill anyone. I only eliminated *versions* of some. A speck of dust in an infinite universe."

There was more "flickering," and the old West was all but gone now.

"You're finished!" Stu said.

"You guys can help me," Cain said, his eyes coming ever so slightly alive. The saloon steps were gone; he stood near a dumpster on a littered street.

West Land and reality continued fighting to take control. Then they were in Cooperate Land, the enormous-headed Wall Street monsters dying in the streets. A hundred other lands flicked in and out, a radio in a moving car failing to key in on one station.

Stu held Cain at gunpoint with the pistol he'd taken from Rex only moments ago.

"I'm going to kill you."

"Stu, don't," Julia said.

"You still don't get it. Being dead or alive is the same thing. Can't you see this by now?"

Bruja had crept behind them.

"I got him," she said to them.

Cain held out his arms and chanted something toward Bruja. Bruja did the same. A duel of magic. However, the witch had no chance against Cain.

And then there was a beastly growl as the man who was once called Sampson grabbed Cain from behind in his bulging bronze arms. Cain attempted to turn his spell on Sampson, but it took only a second for the enormous man-monster to snap the great occultist's neck. Dead at the hands of the man Cain had left in an insane world to die alone.

They ran.

The Lands came apart quickly now that its architect was dead. They ducked and made their way out—at least it *looked* like they were out, but it was hard to tell. Then, the world went fuzzy. Then only blackness.

CHAPTER TWENTY

D r. Duben smiled and took a sip of his Diet Coke. Stu had been seeing Dr. David Duben since the incident. While Duben was not overly concerned at first, once Stu confided in him that he had woken one day to an altered life, which led him on a fantastic journey to a place called the Lands—this *was* cause for concern.

He'd noticed this disturbing trend among several of his patients. Many of them had false memories. Some were innocuous enough, like remembering movies differently than they were. Others, like Stu Sawyer, had memories of a life that had never existed. Being both a neurologist and a psychiatrist, Duben was an expert in how false memories worked. These people remembered these non-existent events as clearly as reality.

Over the last six months, Stu had come a long way. He no longer believed in his delusion.

"Stu, you are doing well. Today is the last time I will have you explain your break-down fantasy to me," Duben said.

"I created a fantasy world due to my never feeling at home in the world around me, compounded with not accepting my survival in the crash where my only friend died. Oh, it didn't help that I was also confusing my subconscious with everything I read, wrote, and researched about unknown phenomena for my site."

"Very good. Go on."

"I created characters who, when you think about it, could never exist—Julia, a witch. Rex, a child star turned sociopath. Bubby Goldenblatt, who owned a gag business of cursed items...it's embarrassing to even talk about it now."

"Well, this tells me exactly how far you have come."

"Imagine a world of Lands? I don't even know how I could have even invented this crap," Stu said.

"Well, as I have said, this delusion was your subconscious compartmentalizing the various aspects of your psychological makeup. Can you tell me about this?"

"Rex was my unrealized alpha male. Bubby represented the part of me fearing failure. Julia represented innocence, and the magic life should hold. No wonder her last name was Faith."

"Very good."

Duben stood to say goodbye. They shook hands.

"Stu, I think we can begin to meet as needed. I believe you are ready."

***

He had enjoyed many years of total irresponsibility, but now was the time to grow up and put his mother's mind at ease. Back home, Stu explained everything to his mother. Her sickness was even gone. There remained no trace of the cancer, which months ago the doctors had predicted would claim her life shortly. The doctors called it a miracle, and while Stu thought his mother would have been ecstatic over this remarkable recovery, she appeared rather unimpressed—as if the whole cancer thing had never been real. However, she was different in a way he could not put his finger on. She had doted on him more than usual for a while before then fell back into their typical ways.

"I don't have to see Dr. Duben every day anymore."

"That's great, Stuey!"

"I'm going to head downstairs and get to bed early."

"Love you."

"I love you, too, mom."

Stu checked his site and found no new developments. He had stopped authoring articles about unknown phenomena since working full-time; truthfully, he was no longer interested. He knew the truth now.

Dr. Duben had cut him free today, and this was good. He was working these days and saving money. Soon, he'd have a place of his own. Living in New Jersey was not too bad and was infinitely better than living in Church Land. His mother, of course, did not remember Church Land—no one did. No one remembered any of the Lands.

Duben had bought his bullshit. While Stu did not like lying, he thought it best to let his mother believe he was finally done with all the Cain Consequence stuff; she was happier with his pretending everything he'd experienced had been in his mind.

What Now? He wanted to find Rex and Julia.

Stu powered off his computer and put on the TV. He was watching an entertainment show when a story about *Monkey Mom* caught his attention. The cartoon was slated to be a huge budget Hollywood movie. But, of course, the show was now created by someone other than Ira "Bubby" Goldenblatt, as he had never existed here. The live-action film was set to star Leonardo DiCaprio and Jennifer Aniston. *What an injustice*, Stu thought.

***

Stu sat on the bench and watched Rex Dolan leave work. Rex worked as a forklift operator in a warehouse and even appeared relatively happy. However, he'd been following Rex for a while and found this was not *his* Rex. He'd put himself in Rex's field of vision a few times, but there was no recognition whatsoever. One time last month, Rex had confronted him.

"What is this shit? Are you following me? What are you, a fanboy of *Happy Jack*? Is that what this is about? Leave me alone, okay, kid."

Stu knew this was a different Rex. He hoped Rex, *his* Rex, would come back to this reality and notice him one day.

He did the same with Julia, and it only took a few days before she recognized him.

"Stu? Oh my God, Stu!" Julia had said and clapped her hands before grabbing him into a hug.

The two of them followed Rex until one day, Rex came out of work, looked at them, and ran toward them. He was back! They had first asked about his friend, Pip. Rex explained while Pip, unfortunately, remembered everything—he was unharmed. When they asked about Josh, the cat, Rex assaulted them with an endless sea of photos on his phone. Josh eating. Josh watching TV. Josh sleeping.

"What now," Rex asked, looking away from his cat photos.

"I don't know. Keep on the lookout for changes. Anything strange. Be ready to fight," Julia said.

"I'm in," Rex said. "Let's do it for Bubby."

A Place that was once New Jersey, then Church Land, and is New Jersey again

He hadn't seen anything like it in his twenty years of practice. So many people had false memories, but nothing as vivid and fleshed out as Stu Sawyer's fantasy. He could not shake the sensation there was something to Stu's delusion.

It had been a long day. Doctor David Duben looked forward to getting home, eating dinner, and getting to bed early. The traffic was terrible, but he listened to an audiobook and got lost in its story on the drive home. Anyway, joy filled him. Stu Sawyer would be okay. This is why he originally got into his field. Seeing the lights come on with a patient was reassuring. It had been a good day.

However, some of his patients could not let go of the delusion that reality had changed. So many of them were perfectly normal in every other way. It was maddening. The detail in some of their stories was uncanny. Like Stu Sawyer's tale of The Great Secession, a world divided and subdivided due to society becoming so intolerant of others save those with their exact same beliefs—it was ridiculous. But still, wasn't the world heading in that direction? He shook the thought from his mind. Of course, the world was becoming intolerant, which is why Stu's fantasy made sense to him—why Stu had created it in the first place.

He pulled into the driveway and got out of his sedan. It grew dark earlier than ever, as if time was moving faster. *Could* time be moving more rapidly? When David Duben was in grade school, they counted seconds by chanting *one Mississippi, two Mississippi*....at an average pace. One of his patients (someone who was convinced time *was* moving faster now than in the past) had Duben count like this, and when he got to thirty Mississippi, the stopwatch app on his phone was closing in on a full minute! How? It was a mistake. He counted more slowly than he had as a kid. That had to be it.

Inside, he ran for the bathroom and then kissed his wife. She'd already put the baby to bed. That made three nights in a row Duben had not seen his kid other than when sleeping. He would have to reduce his hours.

He looked at the photo of him and his wife at a friend's wedding on the living room wall. He was wearing a red tie. But he'd never owned a red tie. He was sure of it.

He shoved the plate his wife, Donna, saved for him into the oven and went upstairs to kiss the baby before eating as he'd done so often of late.

He came out of the baby's room as if walking on the surface of another planet.

"My God, you look like you've seen a ghost. Are you okay?" Donna asked, her smile falling.

"Uh…I'm tired. Overworked."

"Did you kiss David Jr. goodnight?"

"Yes."

"Coming to bed after you eat?"

"Yes, my love."

"See you in bed, doctor," she said, touching his face.

He wanted to tell her. He wanted to scream. But Dr. David Duben did not have the heart to tell his wife they had always had a daughter and never a son until this very moment.

About the Author

Sal Cangemi is the author of several successful books for both adult and younger audiences. His work has been described as horror, speculative, satire, and comedy. A New York native, Sal is working hard on his next novel. You can visit him online at www.salcangemi.com

OTHER HELLBOUND BOOKS
www.hellboundbooks.com

The Demon, the Dumbwaiter, and the Douchebag

Kyle Jarvis is hiding. He has moved into Le Trou Du Cul, a pleasant suburban apartment complex, to hide from those he has wronged. But the well-hidden complex is not as quiet as he had hoped. And there are the odd neighbors. A reclusive old actress, a man who listens to Christmas music year-round, and the Horn Family - the patriarch of which has found a way to travel back in time to his 1980's hay-day - are fighting a demon!

The forest surrounding the complex is ready to engulf the building. Unknown animals are appearing on the grounds - including a family of Sasquatch and a Nessie-like serpent in the small man-made lake. A ghost is haunting one apartment while another shrinking. And a demon, the (almost) evil SLYMIND BRAINTWIST, is the cause of it all.

When the Horn Family's son, the trouble-making Timmy, disappears, the tenants must ban together and form an alliance with Jarvis as their unlikely leader, in hopes of returning the boy home. It is up to Jarvis and Summer, a neo-hippy, to lead the way. Summer has enlisted the help of the flamboyant clairvoyant, Anton Snow, to fight the battle.

An absurdist allegory about conforming, lost dreams, and regret, overflowing with horror and humor, The Demon, the Dumbwaiter and the Douchebag is a hilarious social satire that will have its reader cringing and laughing in equal measure.

Colleen

"Sexy, intriguing, terrifying - Colleen has it all! " - James H. Longmore, author of *Tenebrion.*

Lacey, a goth introvert with sketchy people skills, befriends Colleen, a dazzlingly beautiful ghost, during a solo Ouija board session. At last, her loneliness comes to an end.

An eclectic pairing indeed, but they form an odd-but-satisfying and far-from-platonic friendship.

When Lacey begins work as a stripper, she and Colleen find themselves with a conspiratorial mystery to solve in the strip club.

Unfortunately, Lacey's newfound supernatural lover has a secret... or two and isn't what she seems to be at all.

Colleen is not a ghost at all, but a succubus with an unfortunate habit of killing people.

Accidentally.

It's not long before the mounting number of deaths occurring around Lacey draws the attention of a tenacious homicide detective...

Can Colleen uncover the shady happenings at the club and keep her beloved Lacey out of jail?

I am Joe's Unwanted Penis

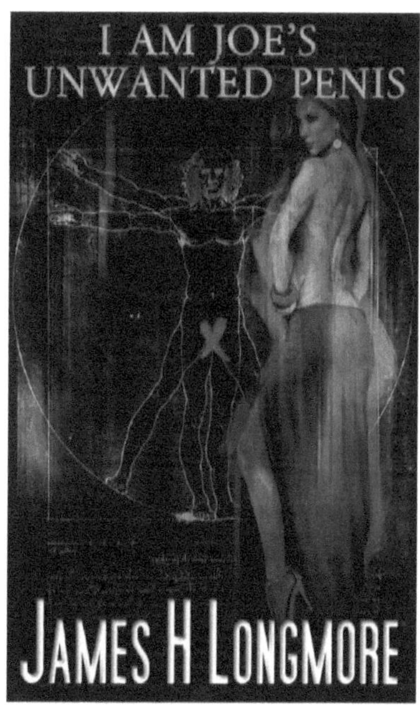

A darkly comedic tribute to the much-loved Reader's Digest series *'I am Joe's…(insert body part here)'* and a bizarre parody of the Bruce Jenner story, *I Am Joe's Unwanted Penis* is told from the point of view of a penis discarded as a man is surgically transformed into a woman.

Upon learning if his high-profile previous owner's regret at having made the transformation, the penis embarks upon a perilous journey for them to be reunited - aided and abetted by a motley, wonderfully personable, and engaging selection of other discarded body parts.

In parts grotesque, laugh-out-loud funny, and undeniably poignant, in others, *I Am Joe's Unwanted Penis* is a buddy-story absolutely like no other!

The Gentleman's Choice

"Caught in a whirlwind of adverse publicity following a viewer's death, the streaming show, The Gentleman's Choice becomes the target for a sadistic killer – and it's up to PI Vanessa Young to put a stop to it before more young women are murdered."

A sleazy internet dating show blamed for a viewer's death, a host with a dark, secret past, and a killer with a sadistic grudge…

Someone is kidnapping and murdering previous contestants from the popular streaming show *The Gentleman's Choice* – a strictly-for-adults hybrid of *The Bachelor* and *Love Island*. Private Investigator, Vanessa Young, is hired by a victim's family to infiltrate the show as a contestant to expose and capture the killer.

Vanessa and the show's charismatic star, Cole Gianni, begin to fall romantically for each other, until Vanessa's plan goes terribly awry when they're drugged and taken to a remote location to take part in their captor's own brutal, ultimately fatal, version of *The Gentleman's Choice*.

The Horror Writer

"The most definitive guide into the trials and tribulations of being a horror writer since Stephen King's 'On Writing.'"

We have assembled some of the very best in the business from whom you can learn so much about the craft of horror writing: Bram Stoker Award© winners, bestselling authors, a President of the Horror Writers' Association, and myriad contemporary horror authors of distinction.

The Horror Writer covers how to connect with your market and carve out a sustainable niche in the independent horror genre, how to tackle the writer's ever-lurking nemesis of productivity, writing good horror stories with powerful, effective scenes, realistic, flowing dialogue and relatable characters without resorting to clichéd jump scares and well-worn gimmicks. Also covered is the delicate subject of handling rejection with good grace, and how to use those inevitable "not quite the right fit for us at this time" letters as an opportunity to hone your craft.

Plus... perceptive interviews to provide an intimate peek into the psyche of the horror author and the challenges they work through to bring their nefarious ideas to the page.

And, as if that – and so much more – was not enough, we have for your delectation Ramsey Campbell's beautifully insightful analysis of the tales of HP Lovecraft.

Featuring:
Ramsey Campbell, John Palisano, Chad Lutzke, Lisa Morton, Kenneth W. Cain, Kevin J. Kennedy, Monique Snyman, Scott Nicholson, Lucy A. Snyder, Richard Thomas, Gene O'Neill, Jess Landry, Luke Walker, Stephanie M. Wytovich, Marie O'Regan, Armand Rosamilia, Kevin Lucia, Ben Eads, Kelli Owen, Jasper Bark, and Bret McCormick.
And interviews with: Steve Rasnic Tem, Stephen Graham Jones, David Owain Hughes, Tim Waggoner, and Mort Castle.

**A HellBound Books Publishing LLC
Publication**

http://www.hellboundbooks.com/

Printed in the United States of America

9 781953 905895